VIKING
Mystery
☠
Suspense

The Face
on the Wall

A HOMER KELLY MYSTERY

ALSO BY JANE LANGTON

Dead as a Dodo

The Shortest Day

Divine Inspiration

God in Concord

The Dante Game

Murder at the Gardner

Good and Dead

Emily Dickinson Is Dead

Natural Enemy

The Memorial Hall Murder

Dark Nantucket Noon

The Transcendental Murder

T h e

Face

o n   t h e

Wall

A HOMER KELLY MYSTERY

Illustrations by the Author

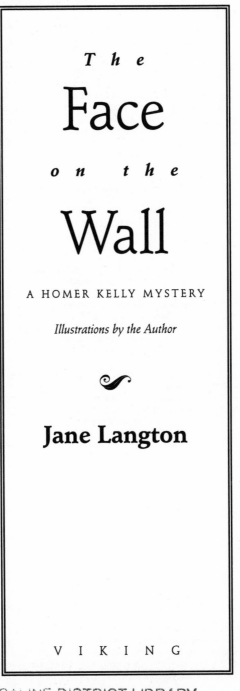

Jane Langton

V I K I N G

VIKING
Published by the Penguin Group
Penguin Putnam Inc., 375 Hudson Street,
New York, New York 10014, U.S.A.
Penguin Books Ltd, 27 Wrights Lane, London W8 5TZ, England
Penguin Books Australia Ltd, Ringwood, Victoria, Australia
Penguin Books Canada Ltd, 10 Alcorn Avenue,
Toronto, Ontario, Canada M4V 3B2
Penguin Books (N.Z.) Ltd, 182–190 Wairau Road,
Auckland 10, New Zealand

Penguin Books Ltd, Registered Offices:
Harmondsworth, Middlesex, England

First published in 1998 by Viking Penguin,
a member of Penguin Putnam Inc.

1   3   5   7   9   10   8   6   4   2

Grateful acknowledgment is made for permission to reprint selections from
The Complete Grimm's Fairy Tales by Jakob Ludwig Karl and Wilhelm Karl
Grimm. Copyright © 1944 by Pantheon Books, Inc., and renewed 1972 by
Random House, Inc. Reprinted by permission of Pantheon Books, a division
of Random House, Inc.

Publisher's Note
This is a work of fiction. Names, characters, places, and incidents either are
the product of the author's imagination or are used fictitiously, and any
resemblance to actual persons, living or dead, events, or locales is entirely
coincidental.

LIBRARY OF CONGRESS CATALOGING-IN-PUBLICATION DATA
Langton, Jane.
The face on the wall / Jane Langton.
p.   cm.
"A Homer Kelly mystery."
ISBN 0-670-87674-7
1. Kelly, Homer (Fictitious character)—Fiction.   I. Title.
PS3562.A515F3   1998
813'.54—dc21   98-2832

This book is printed on acid-free paper.
(∞)

Printed in the United States of America
Set in Stempel Schneidler • Designed by Ann Gold

The Face
on the Wall

A HOMER KELLY MYSTERY

Prologue

The child fell. He fell past Aesop, and the hare and the tortoise. He fell past the Homeric bard and the ship of Odysseus, past Lewis Carroll and Scheherazade, past Hans Christian Andersen, Long John Silver, and the raft of Huckleberry Finn and Jim on the Mississippi River. He fell past Edward Lear, and the Owl and the Pussy-cat in their beautiful pea-green boat.

The child fell past the tales and the tellers of tales, all those who make bearable the sorrows of the world.

Part One

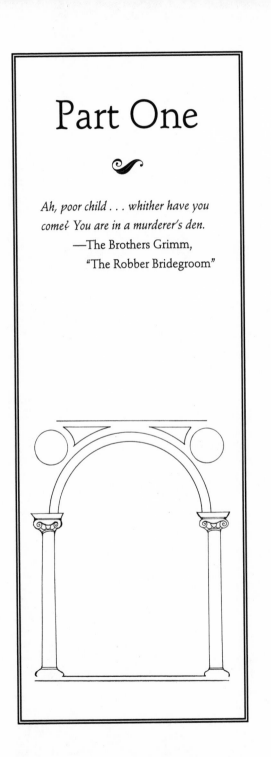

*Ah, poor child . . . whither have you
come? You are in a murderer's den.*
—The Brothers Grimm,
"The Robber Bridegroom"

Chapter 1

❧

*Once upon a time a poor fisherman caught a magic fish. "Throw me
back, good fisherman," cried the fish, "and I will grant anything you
desire."*

*At once the fisherman threw him back in the water, saying, "Thank
you, Lord Fish, I want nothing."*

*But when he went home and told the story to his wife, she said,
"You fool! Why should we live in this miserable hovel? Go back! Ask
the fish for a palace!"*

Wishes are tricky things. In folktales, when they are fulfilled, when every greedy request has been supplied, they often turn sour. The old storytellers understood very well that granted wishes were in defiance of the natural order.

And yet Annie's seemed safe enough. She had earned her dream. She had worked for it, she had paid for it herself. It did not depend on any other human being in the whole world. Her wish was for a house. Not an entire new house, because she already had a house. What Annie wanted was a new wing on the east end of her house, to replace the tumbledown shed.

❧

"My God," said Homer Kelly, slowing down his car on Baker Bridge Road and staring across the field, "Annie said it would be big. It's big."

"Wow." Mary stared at the house too, as a car behind them blatted its horn.

Homer pulled over and parked beside the stone wall. "Big

doesn't come cheap. She must have her mouth right under the faucet."

"Well, her picture books are selling very well. *Jack and the Beanstalk* made her fortune."

They sat in the car and gazed at the clean new wood of Annie's house. Across the cornfield, through the bare branches of the November trees, they could see the small figures of carpenters climbing ladders and kneeling on the roof.

Mary Kelly's interest in Annie's house was not merely passing curiosity. Anna Elizabeth Swann was her niece, the daughter of her sister Gwen. Mary had watched the girl grow up, and then she had stood by Annie during her teenage nuttiness, her insane marriage and awful divorce. Annie's mother and father were often away in India or Pakistan or Nepal, supervising the planting of fruit trees for miscellaneous maharajahs and state agricultural schools, leaving Mary to act as a substitute parent in one crisis after another. Now, at last, Annie's troubles seemed to be over. It was a relief to enjoy her success.

What Homer and Mary could not foresee, as they stared across the field at the rising rafters and listened to the thunk of the nailing machines, was the misery that was about to descend on Annie's house, and the notoriety to follow.

If they could have forecast all these things in a crystal ball they might have seen themselves inside the enchanted glass along with Annie—because her long-suffering Uncle Homer was about to be drawn in again. Several times already in Annie's checkered career he had lent a hand, first in disentangling her from that bastard Grainger Swann, second when she was arraigned for possession of cocaine, third when she was picked up for drunk driving.

Poor old Homer. Once again his past life was about to catch up with him, those distant days before he had started teaching, the old days of his youth, when he had been a lieutenant detective in the Office of the District Attorney of Middlesex County. Since then, by some weird fate or astral influence, Homer had made a habit of stumbling over one dead body after another. Again and again he had been forced to set aside scholarship for the pursuit of psychopaths all over the state of Massachusetts, and in places as far-flung as Florence and Oxford.

"Well, she's a funny girl," said Homer. "Headstrong. Likes to get her own way."

"Well, of course she does. So do I. So do you." Mary watched the first clapboards going up on the east wall of the new wing, and thought about her niece. Annie was a big-boned tall woman with ample breasts, a slightly hooked nose, and a mass of chestnut hair spraying out from a clasp at the back of her head. She looked more like an allegorical figure on a pediment—Peace, or Justice, or Bountiful Nature—than anyone's cuddly little friend. And yet for a piece of monumental statuary she was surprisingly excitable and apt to go off half-cocked. "You know, Homer," said Mary, "she's my niece, not yours, but it's amazing the way she's so much like you."

"Really?" Homer smirked. "You mean brilliant and good-looking? A breaker of hearts?"

"No, no, that's not what I mean at all. She's big and noisy, rash and impulsive. And obsessive. She gets an idea in her head and won't let it go. She's like a dog with a stick. That's Annie. That's you. There's a truly remarkable resemblance."

"Well, gee, thanks a lot."

"Of course, you don't have anything like Annie's artistic talent. She gets that straight from her great-grandmother. Oh, Homer, you should have seen my grandmother's cakes. Five layers high with confectionary swans and castles and three-masted ships, all in spun sugar. She was amazing."

Homer gave one more glance across the field as he turned the key in the ignition. "You know, that's a hell of a big house."

"Well, she's just going to live in the new wing. She's already rented the old part to a family named Gast. Nice people, she says, with a couple of little kids."

"Well, good, maybe the rent will pay her taxes."

As they drove away Mary caught a last glimpse of the bright new boards heaped on the ground beside Annie's house, until they were hidden by the trees around the conservation field. Then she saw only the tractor that was turning under the remaining stalks of corn, and a couple of crows flapping low over the ground, looking for morsels turned up by the plow.

Chapter 2

ᕫ

There were three ravens sat in a tree,
Down adown, hey down, hey down. . . .

Old English song

There were crows too around another house, twelve miles away, in the village of Southtown. Months had gone by. It was March, not November, a warm melting day with puddles in the ruts of the driveway.

When Pearl's brother got out of his car and moved toward her front porch, four or five of the crows were settling in the trees, harshly cawing, as though they had flown up all at once and were just coming back down. There was no other sound but a faraway cheeping like squeaking wheels, the chatter of birds on the rusty towers of Fred Small's sand-and-gravel company, over there to the south, beyond the farthest reach of Pearl's land. The birds were stopping to rest on their way north, fluttering from the gravel-sorting hoppers to the crushers and back, taking possession of the abandoned quarry.

When Joe entered the house he sensed at once that something was wrong. There was a shivering in his skin, the vibration of a noise still battering the walls. With his heart in his mouth he raced up the stairs and threw open the bedroom door upon a scene of carnage.

They were both bleeding. Small held his left arm high over his head, doctoring himself with a scarf, tugging at one end with his teeth. There was no way of doctoring Pearl. She lay folded up on the floor, face down in her own blood.

Joe fell to his knees beside her, and put his hand in the bushy tangle of her yellow hair. "Pearl," he said, "oh, Pearl." Then he rolled her head to one side and cried out, because there was nothing left of her face but a bloody hole.

Springing to his feet, he threw himself at Small. But Pearl's husband had finished knotting the scarf around his arm. His right hand held a revolver. Joe recognized it as the little Ruger he had bought for Pearl from a good-natured goon in an East Boston bar. He stopped short and backed up, his throat bursting with sobs.

"I thought you'd turn up," whispered Small. "It was your idea, right? Give her a gun, she'll kill me while I'm asleep? That's what women do, you're asleep in bed, they blow you away. Well, you should have done your own dirty work." Small's eyes were large and shiny, gleaming with miniature reflections of the bright panes of the window. "Because she made a mess of it. She stood beside the bed sniveling and crying, so I woke up, and then she couldn't handle the fucking firearm, and she shot wild. So I grabbed it and defended myself. What else could I do? And guess what?" Small's expression changed. He grinned and brandished the firearm. "She signed that piece of paper. Did you know that? She signed it."

"She didn't. She couldn't have. You're lying."

Frederick Small's wild whispering stopped. On the highway a truck went by, then another. Small lowered his wounded arm and steadied the gun. A spasm jerked in his face, and he fired.

The crash sent the crows up again from the trees, flapping their dark wings and frantically cawing.

❧

> *The one of them said to his mate,*
> *"Where shall we our breakfast take?*
> *With a down, derry, derry, derry down, down.*

Chapter 3

❧

Once more the fisherman rowed out into the sea. Leaning over the side of his boat, he cried, "Oh, my Lord Fish! I am sorry, but my wife wants a palace."

At once the fish rose from the water and said, "Go home, my friend. She has her palace."

❧

The new house was finished, and it was perfect, because Annie had designed it all by herself. For months she had worked on plans and elevations. It had been a year since she had made a single drawing for a new picture book, but that could wait. *Jack and the Beanstalk* had made her a lot of money, and the royalties from *The Owl and the Pussy-cat* were still pouring in. The new addition to her house had been expensive, but Annie was still a wealthy woman. Wisely, she had consulted her old boyfriend Burgess, that swashbuckling freelance investment broker who knew all there was to know about the stock market. She had followed his advice, and now she was set for life.

Of course, her new house wasn't really a house, it was just a wing attached to the old farmhouse she had bought from her brother John and his wife two years ago. But the new part was complete in itself. Annie had transferred all her furniture, emptying the house for the tenants who were moving in tomorrow. There were five compartments in the new wing: an enormous room with a kitchen at one end and four additional small spaces—a bedroom, a laundry, a bathroom, and a hall.

Money, how wonderful it was! Last summer Annie had indulged herself in Caucasian rugs, straw-seated chairs, a long table with massive feet like cannonballs, and a plaster bust of Hermes from some Victorian parlor. It wasn't greed on her part, surely you couldn't call it greed? After all that labor, surely she deserved a little self-indulgence? It had taken her ten weeks to complete the picture of the beanstalk, with all the birds and animals hiding among the leaves, and she had spent two months on the speaking harp and the rich border around it, entwined with weasels and stoats. If her books sold well, if Curtis Publishing kept right on sending her large checks, and if she gave big chunks of the money to various good causes, why should anyone blame her? Why couldn't she wish for the world's most wonderful room, and design it herself and live in it happily for the rest of her life?

Actually, it wasn't quite true that Annie had designed the house all by herself. In the end she had hired an architect to make working drawings. It had not been a happy connection. The architect had been wary of do-it-yourself designers. He had looked suspiciously at Annie's paper model, eager to show this woman she didn't have a clue. "Look here, you haven't got any windows on the north side. That's a big expanse of blank wall."

"That's just want I want, a blank wall."

"But look at it! Believe me, you'll be sorry if you don't break it up somehow."

"I won't be sorry. Don't touch it."

The contractor had been full of suggestions too. "How about I put a couple of windows on the north side? Thirty-five feet without a window is like a big blank. I mean, look at it. It's nothing."

"Nothing?" Annie laughed. "Well, fine. Nothing is just right."

There came a week when the plasterers gathered up their buckets and drop cloths and went away. The backhoe shoveled dirt around the new foundation, the kid from the nursery seeded it, and the flossy garden designer directed the laying of the stone walk. At last Annie stood at her kitchen counter and paid off the contractor with a stroke of the pen.

She was alone. The furniture huddled in the middle of the floor.

No, she was not alone. A small child ran across the newly seeded lawn in front of the windows. A woman screamed, "Eddy, come back here."

The woman was tomorrow's new tenant, Roberta Gast. Annie went outside and said hello.

"Oh, I'm terribly sorry," said Roberta. Reaching for the boy, she jerked him back off the lawn. "This is Eddy. He's eight years old. He's been away at school, but he'll be living at home from now on, going to a special school in Concord."

One glance at Eddy made it plain what sort of special school it would be. His face was not like his father's or his mother's. It was as though he came from a different gene pool, that family of look-alike children born with Down's syndrome.

"Glad to meet you, Eddy," said Annie, smiling at him.

He looked back at her shyly, and said hello. His voice was thick, as though his tongue couldn't wrap itself around the word.

"We came to measure the rooms," said Roberta. "Come on, Eddy, dear, let's go back to the car."

Roberta's husband, Bob, appeared at the front door of the old house, a slight man with a high balding forehead. As the metal tape measure in his hand rushed into its container it lashed up and cut his hand. He laughed and said good morning and sucked his finger.

Coming out of the house beside him was a pretty little girl. Roberta introduced her. "Annie, I don't think you've met our daughter, Charlene."

"The champion swimmer?" Annie grinned at Charlene.

"That's right," said her father proudly. "Charlene's got a whole shelf of trophies and blue ribbons."

"Well, congratulations, Charlene."

Charlene ignored Annie. She stared at her brother and said, "I'm not going to babysit."

"I know, dear," said her mother. She tugged at Eddy. "Come *on,* Edward."

The Gast family retreated, the boy Eddy trailing behind, looking back over his shoulder at Annie.

She waved to him, then went back inside and forgot him. At the kitchen counter she opened her new cupboards and made herself a sandwich.

Then Annie turned around and looked at her long blank wall.

Chapter 4

❧

There was to be a picture on Annie's wall, stretching from one end to the other, thirty-five feet long. Annie had never painted a wall before. It didn't matter. She would figure out how to do it.

She had worked on the sketch for months while the foundation was poured, the walls were raised and roofed over, the inside was plastered, and the tile floor laid. Now that the house was complete at last, the plan for the framework of her painting was finished too. She had blocked it out in measured squares on a long piece of paper. There was to be an architectural fantasy on the wall, a painted gallery with five round arches resting on six painted columns.

Early in the morning after Annie's first night in the new house, her Aunt Mary Kelly came over to help her lay it out. "Thirty-five feet divided by five is seven feet," she said, looking up at the long expanse of blank plaster. "Is that right? Seven feet between centers? Good. Here goes." Mary stretched her tape along the wainscot and made a pencil mark.

Annie spread sheets of newspaper over her library table and set out her jars of paint. There were dozens of them. Cheerfully, her heart beating with excitement, she picked them up one by one and arranged them on the newspaper. There were seven shades of red, six of blue, eight different greens, and two dozen soft colors without names, dun purplish browns and olive-grays.

When Mary finished marking off seven-foot intervals and came back to the table, her attention was caught at once by a scrap of newspaper stuck to the bottom of one of the jars of paint. It was a torn fragment with a dim photograph. She picked up the jar, peeled off the piece of newsprint, and looked at the picture. "Don't I know this woman?"

Annie looked too, and read the line of print under the photograph. "Her name's Pearl Small. She seems to have disappeared."

Mary slapped the scrap of newspaper down on the table. "Pearl Small! Of course I know her. She was a student of mine. It was a seminar, a graduate seminar. Nobody called her Pearl, they called her Princess, because of her long yellow hair. It was a joke. She was Princess Pearl." Mary's glasses were on a string around her neck. She put them on and bent over the fragment of newspaper.

Annie snorted. "She doesn't look like a princess to me."

"Oh, but she is. Last time I saw her she was still as lovely as ever, except—" Mary peered at the newsprint and read the broken sentences aloud.

> *S. PEARL SMALL*
> *VANISHED*
> *uliar circumstances.*
> *are allegations of*
> *omestic violence.*
> *wice-widowed*
> *ederick Small*
> *es not answer*
> *hone calls.*
> *umored that*
> *large parcel*

There was no more. The rest of the page was gone.

"Except what?" said Annie.

"Except for the bruise on her cheek and a black eye. Oh my God, poor Princess! The bruises must have been his doing. Look, that's what it says right here. 'Allegations of domestic violence.'"

Annie didn't believe it. "She was a battered wife? From *Harvard?*"

"Well, why not? Annie, when was this? Where's the rest of the paper?"

Annie fumbled with the sheets of newspaper under her jars of paint. "These are all from the *Boston Globe*. That one must be from another paper. The type is different."

"Have you got the rest of it around somewhere?"

"No. I cleared everything out when I moved. All the old newspapers went to the dump. Except these. I wrapped dishes in these."

Mary looked again at the pink dots that were the printed face of Pearl Small. "Poor Princess, I wonder what could have happened? Tell you what." Mary snatched up her coat. "I'm going to show this to Homer. Maybe he can do something."

Annie laughed. "Oh, poor Uncle Homer. I'll bet he's got enough to do. Every time I see him he looks more harassed. So long, Aunt Mary."

She stood in the doorway and watched Mary Kelly zoom away down the drive. Then she went back inside and gazed up at the emptiness of her wall. For a moment she thought about the battered wife, the princess with long golden hair. Maybe she was like the wife of that wicked monster Bluebeard, who killed wife after wife and stored their bodies in a forbidden room. Was Princess Pearl another victim? Was she stowed away in a dark chamber with the bloated remains of his earlier wives, that long succession of slaughtered women?

Annie dragged a ladder to the far end of the room and told herself she had folktales on her mind. "Bluebeard" was just another story to put on her wall, along with "Snow White" and "Sleeping Beauty" and "Cinderella" and "Little Red Riding Hood." There were evil creatures in all those stories—wicked queens, wicked ogres, wicked fairies, wicked stepmothers, ravening wolves. Their common wickedness was dark and mythological, but surely it mimicked real life, in which ravening wolves abounded. Annie picked up her straightedge, put a pencil in her teeth, and got to work.

By midmorning she had achieved the outline of the arcade. Six penciled columns rose on the wall, their center lines seven feet apart, their capitals still only a few ruled scrawls. Standing on a ladder with thumbtack, pencil and string, she traced five half-circles between them. Then, swiftly, she ran a line high on the wall between the columns, all the way across. It was the sea horizon.

At last, standing back, she looked up at her morning's work. Her fingers were trembling. She had imagined it so many times, she had sketched it so often on paper, hardly daring to think there would one day be a real succession of round arches marching across a thirty-five-foot stretch of wall. Now the two-dimensional surface fell away, revealing a deep space beyond the room, a kind of porch or gallery opening on a mock outdoors. The penciled lines were so light, no one else would notice them, but to Annie the essential framework was there. The wall had become a not-wall. It was framed in solid elements and poised in open air.

There was a knock at the door. Simultaneously her new telephone rang. Annie froze, then picked up the phone, said, "Just a minute," and went to the door.

It was a stranger, a guy in a baseball cap. He was juggling three pebbles, tossing them up, catching them neatly, his eyes darting after them, not looking at Annie.

She stared at him, too surprised to speak.

"I was just wondering," he said, pocketing the pebbles, "if you'd like somebody to paint your window frames."

"My window frames?" Annie couldn't think. "Excuse me, there's someone on the phone. Wait a minute."

"Annie?" said the powerful voice on the line.

In spite of herself Annie felt a lurch of joy. "Jack?"

"Annie, look, I've got to talk to you."

Her old grievances came flooding back. Jack was one of her post-divorce boyfriends. He had walked out on her three years ago to move in with a girl named Gloria. She couldn't forgive him. Warily, with her eyes on the stranger at the door, she said, "What is there to talk about?" The stranger had turned away. His jacket said WATERTOWN BRAKE AND MUFFLER.

"A thousand things. God." Jack grunted with disgust. "Look, I'll be out on Friday, okay?"

Say no. Hold out against him. "Well, okay," said Annie.

She hung up and went back to the stranger. "Look," she told him, "I'm not going to bother with the window frames now. Too many other things to do first."

"Well, all right." Smiling, he turned away. The pebbles reappeared. Annie could see them rising and falling above his head as he ambled down the walk, heading for the odd-looking vehicle parked in the driveway, a pickup truck with a wooden structure mounted on the back, a sort of gypsy caravan. A stovepipe stuck out of the roof.

Impulsively she called after him, "How much would you charge?"

A couple of bananas appeared from nowhere and soared into the air. He named a reasonable price.

Annie laughed loudly and made up her mind. "Well, I don't see why not. When do you want to start?"

"Right now, if you've got the primer. The wood has to be primed first."

"Well, I could go out and buy some." Annie looked uncertainly at her car.

"I'll wait." He pulled a paper bag out of his pocket. "I'll eat my lunch down the hill."

"Fine." Annie went back inside, closed the door, and hurried into her bedroom. She combed her hair and pulled a jacket over her shirt and jeans. Then she went around the house locking doors against the juggling stranger.

As she got into her car she could see him down the hill, sitting on the grass, which must still be damp from the gentle spring rain of yesterday. He was facing away from the house, eating his lunch.

He was a traveling mountebank. Who could tell what he might magic away, if he managed to get inside? The new stainless-steel sink, the beautiful new stove, the CD player?

With a flick of his clever fingers he might even—it was idiotic, but Annie couldn't help glancing back over her shoulder at the north side of her house—he might even destroy her precious wall.

❧

And so the prince was hired as the Imperial Swineherd.

Hans Christian Andersen, "The Swineherd"

Chapter 5

❧

"Know then, my husband," answered she, *"we will lead them away, quite early in the morning, into the thickest part of the wood, and there make a fire, and give them each a little piece of bread. . . ."*

The Brothers Grimm, "Hansel and Gretel"

It was moving day for the Gasts. Bob and Roberta scurried around their Cambridge apartment, labeling cardboard boxes, ordering Charlene and Eddy to pack up their toys. "For heaven's sake, Charlene," said her mother, "your poor dolls. Be more careful. They cost a fortune. Why don't you wrap them in tissue paper?"

Charlene tumbled another flouncy doll on top of the others in the box. "These aren't any good anyway," she said, looking sullenly at her mother. "I wish I had a princess doll."

"Oh, Charlene," said Roberta, "I've told you over and over again. Those dolls are just too expensive."

"Alice has one, and she's really, really poor. Her mother's a cleaning lady."

"Well, good for Alice." Roberta plucked off the wall the antique mirror she had inherited from her mother. The surface was age-flecked and spotted. *Oh, God, there were spidery wrinkles on her upper lip.* She set the mirror down on the bed and snapped at Eddy, "Why don't you throw out those old broken crayons?" But when he made protesting noises, she threw up her hands. "Well, okay, I don't care. Keep them. What about the drawings? You don't want to keep all those old drawings, do you, Eddy?"

Eddy burst into tears and gathered them to his chest.

22

Roberta shouted at him to shut up. Her husband looked up and said mildly, "Oh, for heaven's sake, Roberta."

✑

Robert Gast was a talented and clever man. He had been a *summa* at Princeton, majoring in philosophy. He had written a prizewinning dissertation on the metaphysics of ethics. His mother had wanted to know what philosophy was *for.* "Honestly, Bobby, what can you do with it? Why don't you study something practical from now on?"

And then she had financed two years at business school, where Bob did indeed learn useful lessons, like how to set up in business for himself. The result was his own company, Gast Estate Management, specializing in the development of large pieces of open land. Bob's ideals as a land developer were high, having their source in the concept of the universe as a spiritual kingdom (Leibniz) or a city of God (St. Augustine). His method was simple. You put most of the land into conservation, but at the same time you guaranteed the owners a fair return by selling off a few expensive house lots around the edges.

So far Bob's commercial endeavors had not produced a city of God, but someday he fully intended to follow through on his noble plan. For now, the problem was finding the right sort of real estate in the first place—finding it, and then persuading the owners to work exclusively with Gast Estate Management. Just give him time. He was negotiating a promising deal right now.

Bob's marriage had been another good move. Roberta was a brilliant and beautiful woman, almost a junior partner in the famous Boston law firm of Pouch, Heaviside and Sprocket. Within a year of their marriage they had been blessed with the birth of Charlene, that perfect child, who was now the prettiest and smartest kid in her fifth-grade class and a champion swimmer, headed for the Junior Olympics.

There was only one fly in the ointment, and that was their second child.

They had met other parents of Down's-syndrome kids who seemed to take it in stride, but the Gasts had been crushed from the beginning.

Roberta found it especially hard. Most of Eddy's care fell to her, because her hired nannies kept resigning. And his special schooling was hideously expensive. The greater part of Roberta's salary at Pouch, Heaviside and Spocket went for Eddy's care. The rest went to Weston Country Day, Charlene's private school.

"If only we didn't have to pay for Edward," complained Roberta, "think how we could live. I told you what the doctor said. There's no reason he won't survive into old age. We'll be stuck with him all our lives."

Bob looked soberly at his wife. He too was deeply regretful, hopelessly angry at fate, and dangerously apt to fly off the handle at his eight-year-old son. But in one withered chamber of his heart he felt a fatherly concern. "Well, he's kind of a sweet little kid, don't you think? He can't help being different."

"That's easy for you to say—you don't have to take care of him half the time. Oh, Bob, I can't stand it. Do you know what he did yesterday? Remember, I had to take him to work with me because I couldn't get a sitter? He wet his pants right there in front of Dirk Sprocket."

"My God."

The conversation was nothing new. They had repeated it in different ways a thousand times.

❧

". . . then we will go to our work, and leave them alone, so they will not find the way home again, and we shall be freed from them."

The Brothers Grimm, "Hansel and Gretel"

Chapter 6

❧

"I fear thee, ancient Mariner!
I fear thy skinny hand!
And thou art long, and lank, and brown,
As is the ribbed sea-sand."
> Coleridge,
> "The Rime of the Ancient Mariner"

He had an odd name, Flimnap O'Dougherty. "Flimnap?" said Annie. "Where have I heard that name before?"

"It's Icelandic," explained Flimnap, grinning at her. "There are Flimnaps all over the place in Reykjavík."

Did Irish-Icelandic people have big noses and lank brown hair? It didn't matter. Whatever Flimnap's origins, he seemed to know what he was doing. Working indoors, Annie could hear small thuds from outside as he moved his ladder, clicks and creaks as he opened and closed the windows. Mostly there was no noise at all. It was oddly exhilarating to work on her wall while Flimnap looked in from outside.

It turned out that he could do anything he set his hand to. When a truck arrived and tipped a load of cow manure down beside the vegetable garden, Annie called a halt to the priming of the window frames and sent Flimnap down the hill to dig it in.

The manure was supposed to be well rotted, but it wasn't. It was fresh and green and reeking. Would he object to a dirty job? For a moment Annie watched him drive his spade into the heap. He showed no reluctance. He was attacking it with a will, heaving up sloppy spadefuls, dumping them on last year's weedy dirt, forking them in.

Then Annie forgot about Flimnap and thought about Jack, who was coming out today. What would she say to him? She didn't know.

And then she forgot about Jack too, and bent her head to look at the books lying open on the table.

They were collections of folktales and nursery rhymes and picture stories for children. *Babar the King* lay on top of *The Arabian Nights*. The cherry nose of *Asterix the Gaul* glowed from a dog-eared paperback. And there were beautiful new books by Annie's fellow illustrators—the dazzling wild colors of Miguel Delgado's *Big Book of Clowns*, the clever simplicities of Jemima Field's ABC, the thick round bodies and crazy perspectives of *Gulliver's Travels* by Joseph Noakes, the spidery interlocking details of Margaret Chen's *Yellow River Folk Tales*.

The books were her obsession. Since childhood, when she had sat beside her father on the sofa among a listening mass of siblings, she had stared at the pictures in the books while he read the stories aloud. She had fallen into the pictures, lived in them, loved them. Loved them too much, because one day bad girl Annie had scribbled all over the precious stories and the wonderful pictures, wanting to write them and draw them herself, and she had been spanked. Even now she couldn't just look at the books and turn the pages and look again. She had to scribble on them in a new way, she had to *use* them somehow.

One way was to distill them into her own picture books, to make new editions of *Jack and the Beanstalk* and *The Owl and the Pussy-cat*. They were compendiums of everything her eyes had wondered at—the thorny trees of Rackham, the purple seas of Wyeth, the bewitched line drawings of Bilibin and Shepard, Blegvad and Williams.

The other way of using the old stories was to put them on her wall. Annie sat at the newspaper-covered table and made greedy lists. She crossed out *Treasure Island* and *The Enchanted Castle*, then put them back and added more.

When a car drove up outside, she thought, *Jack!* and ran to the door.

But it wasn't Jack. There were two cars in the driveway and a giant moving van. Of course, it was her new tenants. They were moving in.

"Welcome," said Annie politely, as Robert Gast climbed out of a big Ford Bronco and grinned at her. Roberta Gast came forward too, emerging from a bright-blue Mazda convertible with daughter Charlene and the little boy named Eddy.

Flimnap O'Dougherty appeared suddenly, coming up from the vegetable garden, his manure pitching all done. Annie introduced him to the Gasts—mother, father, Eddy, and Charlene.

Flimnap nodded courteously and Bob said, "How do you do?" and shook his hand.

Charlene wrinkled her nose and said, "Pee-yoo, you stink."

Her father was shocked. "Charlene!"

"It's all right," said Flimnap. "She's right. It's cow manure." He paused, then said, "I stink, therefore I am."

Annie burst out laughing. Bob Gast laughed too. Roberta didn't get it.

O'Dougherty vanished. Annie too made herself scarce. Sharing a house was going to call for tact, even though their two sets of living quarters were separated by an insulated wall and a workshop. The Gasts should be able to come and go without interference. So should she. It wouldn't be difficult. Her front door was on the north, theirs on the south.

Afterward, when the moving vans lumbered down the driveway, Annie wondered about the Gasts' two cars. When the realtor had brought them to look at the house they had been driving an aged Chevy. She had been charmed by their simplicity, their enthusiasm, their apparent poverty, and at the realtor's suggestion she had cut the rent in half.

Where was the old Chevy now, with its pitted chromium and missing hubcaps, its cracked windshield and dented side?

Then Annie forgot about the Gasts and climbed her shaky
ladder with a jar of thin ocher paint in one hand. Clinging to
the ladder with toes and shins, she leaned forward and began
washing color on the wall, relieving the awful whiteness of the
bare plaster. The ladder wobbled. Soon the background color
was done and she scrambled down, picked up a narrow brush
and climbed up again. Carefully, with her hand moving surely
and slowly, she began tracing the hull of a vessel over the light
pencil marks beneath the ocher paint. *With beating heart Ulysses
spreads his sails.* Quickly the craft took shape, floating on the
horizon, which in this part of the wall was the Adriatic Sea. Farther to the right it would become the Mississippi River, and
then Lake Windemere, and the coast of Coromandel.

There was a noise behind her. Looking over her shoulder,
Annie saw Flimnap working on the latch of the French door.
"Kind of loose," he said, holding up a screwdriver.

"Well, good," said Annie, smiling, turning back to the wall.
She had known Flimnap for less than two days, but already she
could see two distinct sides to his character. On the one hand
he was skillful with tools and handy with a paintbrush, on the
other there was a gossamer insubstantiality about him, a sort of
comic playfulness. Beside the solidity of Robert Gast he seemed
a flimsier order of being. He was clever, anybody could see that,
and yet oddly dyslexic at the same time. Yesterday, when she
had asked him to design a simple cupboard, he had not been
able to handle a pencil.

Annie came down from the ladder and found him examining
the sketches lying on the table. One was her drawing of an old
Greek bard. He was supposed to be telling the story of
Odysseus. His mouth was open, his arms were flung out, his
whiskers were wild.

"Santa Claus emerging from the bath?" said Flimnap, and
Annie laughed. She watched as he turned to look up at the wall
and sweep his pale eyes across it from left to right, taking in the

five-part arcade and the ship on the horizon and her pencil sketch of Aesop with the tortoise lumbering along at his feet and the hare sleeping under a bush.

Flimnap made no comment. Instead he pointed at the far end of the wall. "Who's that supposed to be?"

"What?" Annie looked. On the pure white plaster there were two small green blotches superimposed on an orange blob.

It looked like a face. "It's nothing," said Annie, "just some sort of stain. Mildew or something."

"I'll take care of it." Flimnap went out to his truck and came back with a can of shellac.

Annie watched him coat the stain with a few strokes of his brush. She wanted to ask what he thought of her great project. Surely he could see how marvelous it was going to be? But Flimnap O'Dougherty said nothing at all. Annie told herself she was not disappointed. He was one of those people without any interest in artistic things. Well, that was okay. Half the world was like that.

But the truth was, she could have used a little praise.

Chapter 7

❧

One of the stars fell, making a long fiery trail across the sky. "Now
someone is dying," said the little girl, for her old dead grandmother . . .
had told her that when a star falls, a soul goes up to God.

Hans Christian Andersen, "The Little Match Girl"

Homer Kelly had been Mary's husband for a long time. He
was a big man with a coarse gray beard and a rough head
of hair like the thick fur of a dog. His impulsive enthusiasms
had often led him into absurdities in the past, but half a lifetime
with a sensible wife had mellowed him a little. So had his experience with violent criminals. At one time or another Homer
had been half drowned, knocked senseless, threatened with
edge tools, firearms, oncoming trucks, burning buildings, and
explosive devices. Did danger build character? Who could tell?
In middle age Homer Kelly was a more rational and sympa-
thetic human being than he had been in his youth. One thing,
however, was still an unchanging part of his makeup. Fortunately (or perhaps unfortunately), his chromosomes still
sported a mutant gene prompting unpredictable behavior, occasional silliness, and sometimes—rarely, erratically—a stroke of
genius.

Today Homer's genius was out to lunch. "You must be out of
your mind," he said, staring at the dim photograph of Mary's
former student, the missing princess with the long golden hair.
"She just walked out on her husband, I'll bet, that's all. High
time, if he's been beating her up. What's this about a parcel? 'It
is rumored that a large parcel'—of what? A leg of lamb? A side
of beef?"

"No, no, Homer. It's only the British who use the word 'par-cel' like that. In this country it means a piece of land."

Homer held the scrap of newspaper to the light. "Look, if this isn't the *Boston Globe* it must be one of those sensationalist rags they sell in supermarkets. You can't believe a word they say. The editors, they sit around smoking cigars and making up headlines about aliens seducing rock stars. They're fairy stories."

"But Pearl is real. She's not a fairy story. And something's happened to her." Mary fixed Homer with a fierce blue eye. "Look, Homer, you're not doing anything in particular right now except teaching a couple of graduate seminars and a fresh-man course and writing a couple of books. Couldn't you just take the time to find out where she lives? I mean, where she disappeared from?"

"I'm not doing anything in particular!" Homer groaned and thrust his hands into his hair. "That's a joke, right? My light schedule? Which also includes, I might add, counseling inmates in the Concord prison once a week."

"Good heavens, Homer, when did that happen?"

"This morning. They called me up." Homer grinned at his wife. "What about you? You're free as air. Why don't you look into your old pal's disappearance yourself? She's your friend, not mine. You're not doing one single thing beyond running the extension school and writing a history of women poets through the ages and grading a few hundred freshman papers and cook-ing a thousand meals."

"Oh, Homer, that's not all. I've just been appointed Historian in Residence at a private school, Weston Country Day. I'll be teaching fifth-graders about history."

"My God, how did that happen?"

"They wrote me a letter. I was flattered. They said Judge Aufsesser's daughter is in the class. I guess I was attracted by his fame."

"Judge Aufsesser won't be in your class, you nitwit, just his daughter."

"I know, but maybe he'll come to parents' night or something." Mary grinned foolishly.

Homer sighed. "The truth is, we're both doing too much. Neither of us has time to look for missing princesses with golden hair. Anyway, she's probably been turned into a frog by now. It's a job for a magician, not a couple of overworked scholars." He glanced again at the picture of Pearl Small. "This isn't from the *Boston Globe*, but the *Globe* might have run a story at the same time. Why don't you call them? See if they have any record of her so-called disappearance. If they ever did a story on her, it would be in their file. Tell them to look under Frog."

❧

Mary tried. She called the *Globe*. After a couple of misdirected tries she was connected to a librarian in the archives department.

"Nope," said the librarian, staring at her monitor and scrolling through the alphabet. "The name Pearl Small has never appeared in the *Boston Globe*."

"Try Frog," murmured Mary, disappointed. "Try Princess. No, no, that's fine. Well, thank you very much."

Mary put down the phone. She had an appointment with the heads of all the departments in the Harvard Extension School, and if she didn't get going, she'd be late. She ran down the porch steps, jumped into her car, revved the engine, and charged up the hill.

Homer had been right. The lurid story about the disappearance of Pearl Small had the melodramatic flair of the headlines in the supermarket rags, those sleazy periodicals that rejoiced in the torrid affairs, the aborted pregnancies, and the drunken brawls of film stars, sports stars, TV stars, hunks, and sex kittens. How did one get in touch with those editorial boards?

The woods fled past, the dirt track gave way to a paved road. Mary told herself to stop at the supermarket on the way home—for oranges, broccoli, a roasting chicken, and a copy of every flamboyant journal in the store.

Chapter 8

❧

*"Why," said he, "greed is the best, for if it were otherwise . . . I should
never be jogging along through the world with six servants behind me."*
Howard Pyle, "The Wonder Clock"

Jack was a bigger presence than Annie remembered. He had
gained weight, but he was still horribly good-looking. He
had the kind of striking face that tells across a room.

Annie let him gather her in a fond embrace. He tried to kiss
her in the old way, but she had enough dignity to turn her head
away. "No, Jack, don't."

He let her go, and looked up at the house. "So this is your
castle? Little Annie made it with her widdoo paintbwush, all by
her widdoo self?"

"Oh, shut up, Jack."

He was impressed, she could see that. Indoors he gaped
around at her library, staring up at the windows, the high
shelves of books. For an instant his cocksureness was shaken
when he caught sight of the painted columns on her wall, but at
once he dismissed them as Annie's sort of thing, and sank into a
chair. "Your dream house, is that it? Some dream. Must have
cost you a bundle." He turned and stared at her. "You're famous. Best-selling kiddie books. I saw you on TV."

She shrugged. "You want a beer? I made sandwiches."

They sat at her table, and Jack poured out his resentment
against his now ex-girlfriend, Gloria. "God, her high-flown no-
bility. Homelessness, Christ, she kept bringing people in off the
street."

"Well, good for her," murmured Annie.

"Oh, Jesus."

"Are you still an art director?" she said, changing the subject, although as a rejected lover she couldn't help rejoicing in the downfall of Gloria. "Where is it? Oh, I remember. It's that big publishing house in Charlestown."

"Art director, God." Jack drained his beer, heaved himself up from the chair, walked heavily to the refrigerator, and helped himself to another bottle. "Whole department closed down. Bunch of shitheads anyhow. Matter of fact, I'm doing something else now. Insurance. I'm with Paul Revere."

"No kidding? Well, congratulations."

Jack sat down with his beer and looked at her slyly. It was at once apparent why he was there. "How's *your* portfolio, by the way? Have you got a policy for personal injury? Suppose somebody slips and falls on that big stone in front of your door, they could take everything, every cent. And listen, Annie, how much fire insurance have you got on this place? Oh my God, is that all? Jesus, Annie."

Partly because she was persuaded by his dire predictions and partly to get rid of him, Annie signed up for a huge personal-injury policy and a hefty increase in fire insurance.

She stood up, hoping he would take the hint and go away. Jack got to his feet, but instead of leaving he threw his arms around her in their old movie embrace. It was a private joke. He bent her backward and bowed over her like Rudolph Valentino.

"No, Jack," she said, pushing him back and struggling to stand up.

"Annie, Annie, I made a mistake." He clutched her. "I was a fool. Come back to me, Annie. I want you, I need you."

"No, no." But she was weakening. Triumphantly Jack heaved her off the floor. Her big feet dangled. She swore, "Oh, goddamnit, Jack," but her fingers stopped pushing at him and her head lolled back. The doorbell rang.

The spell was broken. Annie burst out of Jack's arms and ran to the door. "Shit," said Jack.

It was Flimnap O'Dougherty. His cheery face looked at Annie, not seeming to notice the glowering presence of Jack behind her. "Sorry, I forgot my wrench. It's in the bathroom."

"Well, come on in," said Annie, trying to catch her breath.

He glided past her, dodged into the bathroom, and came out again, flourishing the wrench. "Thanks," he said, and was gone.

"Okay, Jack," said Annie, "out with you. Come on. I mean it."

Jack's voice deepened. "You don't mean it, Annie. You know you don't." He came closer and reached out.

She backed away. "No, Jack, stop."

The doorbell rang again. Once more it was O'Dougherty, apologizing. "I forgot to tell you I can't come Monday after all. But I could come tomorrow afternoon, how about that?"

Annie laughed. If Jack was Rudolph Valentino, Flimnap was Stan Laurel, the earnest simpleton. "Fine. Bring along your derby hat."

"What?"

"Never mind. I'll see you tomorrow."

She closed the door, but when she opened it again for Jack, O'Dougherty was still there in the driveway, tinkering with his truck.

Jack hurled himself into his car and drove violently forward, narrowly missing O'Dougherty, who skipped out of the way. Jack's horn blared, and he lunged down the driveway.

Flimnap too was leaving. He slapped down the hood of his truck, climbed into the cab, nodded mildly at Annie, and drove away.

She went indoors to the bathroom and looked at herself in the mirror. Her hair was frowsy, her eyes were wild.

Had there been a wrench in here this morning? No, surely

not, or she would have noticed it. The wrench was an excuse to come back. Flimnap had brought it in just now, and then pretended to find it.

Unless of course it was an enchanted wrench. Flimnap the prestidigitator had simply plucked it out of the air.

Chapter 9

❧

Fred Small had been out on the road again, searching for Pearl's brother, because Pearl's goddamned brother had tripped him up that day and then plunged down the stairs and cleared out. Where the hell was he? God, he had to be someplace. The man was dangerous, he was a loose cannon.

It was the first day of spring. For the last week Fred had been looking for the son of a bitch, but so far without success.

In the meantime, there was something else he had to do, and this time it was no problem, except that right now his hands were shaking. Small sat at a table in his bedroom, bowed over a piece of paper. Sunlight poured through the window and lay on the bed like a cloth. Looking up, he could see in the distance the towers of his failed sand-and-gravel company, and he frowned. Then he reminded himself that before long the towers would be obscured by twenty or thirty large and impressive houses. At this moment he could almost see them looming up here and there along the Pig Road, ghostly shapes outlined in air. Soon they would actually occupy the land, lining the curving drive that had been laid out on paper so cleverly by his friend the developer, maximizing the number of lots.

Small looked down again at the curlicues and scrawls on his piece of paper. They still weren't right. He couldn't seem to get the hang of it, that big generous upright hand with its looped l's and tightly closed a's. Pearl's signature should not look cramped. It should seem quick and unstudied. Absently he watched the jerky movement of his pen, thinking at the same time about the two irons he had in the fire. "Irons in the fire," it was a blacksmith's term. When the irons glowed red, the smith took them out of the fire and hammered them into shape.

40

The first of Small's irons was heating up, the second was growing cold.

Iron number one was the development of Pearl's land. Now that her stubborn resistance was no longer a factor he could at last get started. Pearl had inherited the place from her uncle the pig farmer—the house and ninety-nine acres of land.

No, watch it, the slant still isn't quite right. Small took a firmer grip on his pen.

He had tried to make her see it as a bonanza, prime real estate, ripe for intelligent development. Especially with Meadowlark Estates going up next door, setting a high tone for a neighborhood that had once been a rural slum, with third-rate malls and sleazy discount stores and pig farms like her Uncle Charley's. But poor old misguided Pearl, she'd insisted on seeing her ninety-nine acres as some sort of natural paradise, a haven for wildlife. Small's pen trembled as he remembered the look on Pearl's face when she reached down and touched the soil under her feet, compacted by the hooves of a thousand pigs.

Come on, Fred, be careful, don't let the letters run downhill.

She had talked wildly about the trees she was planting, pines and birches, mountain laurel and hemlocks. Pheasants would find cover in her shrubbery, Pearl said. Rabbits and foxes and deer would hide in her woodland. She had shown him the red-tailed hawk perched on the very top of the tallest of his gravel-sorting towers. "Someday," she had said dreamily, "that hawk's descendants will perch in my white-oak trees." *Goddamnit, Pearl! Why couldn't you see the opportunity? Why couldn't you get it through your thick head?*

But she didn't see. No matter what he said to her, no matter what he *did* to her—and he'd done plenty—no matter how many times he showed her the developer's figures, she still didn't get it, she just sulked and turned her head away. She was *stupid,* that was the trouble.

Well, it was no longer a problem. Pearl was out of the picture. He could go right ahead. Any day now he'd pull that red-hot iron out of the fire and strike it a mighty blow.

Unfortunately, the second iron was rapidly growing cold. His sand-and-gravel company was on its last legs. It had already been in trouble on the day he ran into Pearl for the first time. There she had been on the other side of his chain-link fence, a pretty girl with yellow wisps of hair peeking out from under her kerchief. She had been planting trees along the southern edge of her property—a lovely girl with yellow hair and ninety-nine acres of land!

Pearl had wanted to know at once how long the conveyor belts and sorting bins and rusty towers were going to remain right there beside her *wilderness,* her *wildlife refuge,* her *bird sanctuary.*

"Oh, not long at all," he had told her, enchanted by her fairy-tale prettiness. "I'm selling out. It's all coming down, everything, even the asphalt plant."

The truth was, Fred Small had no choice. He merely leased the land on which his sorting towers stood, with their crushers for six-inch boulders, their hoppers for pea-sized and half-inch gravel, their screening decks and belt-driven conveyors. The owner of the land wanted to sell. And anyway the site was exhausted. The ground had been scraped clean of sandy topsoil. Sooner or later Fred would have to dismantle all the rigs and move them to New Hampshire, even the asphalt plant, which had at last begun to break even.

It would cost millions. All the more reason to carry through with the development of the old pig farm! Couldn't Pearl see that? Then, for an instant, Small's hand stopped its exercise in penmanship on the paper in front of him. He remembered something he had read a thousand years ago, a story about sailors turned into swine. Maybe all the pigs in Southtown had been human once. Now the poor creatures were long gone, turned into sides of bacon and a thousand miles of sausage.

Before long their old stomping ground would be turned into house lots, exclusive pieces of real estate. No ghostly pigs would ever snuffle around those stately homes.

⤥

> *Instant her circling wand the Goddess waves,*
> *To hogs transforms 'em, and the Sty receives.*
> *No more was seen the human form divine,*
> *Head, face and members bristle into swine . . .*
>
> Homer, *The Odyssey*

Chapter 10

❧

She reached a slimy place where large fat sea-snails were crawling about; and . . . a house built of the bones of human beings. . . .
Hans Christian Andersen, "The Little Mermaid"

O nly one of the supermarket scandal sheets was published in Boston, *The Candid Courier*. On the cover in enormous black type were the words SHARON SHUCKS SHEIK. The typeface on the inside pages was the same as that on the scrap of newsprint Mary had found on Annie's table, the fragment about Pearl Small, who had disappeared.

Mary flipped the pages and found a tiny masthead on the back of page one, which confessed to an office on Washington Street.

That was easy. If she left within the hour she could park at Alewife, take the T to Park Street, walk a block or two, talk to the crummy people, and be back home by lunchtime.

❧

Washington was a street in transition. The department stores had moved out of town to the suburban malls, to be replaced by high-rise office buildings, little boutiques, and junky souvenir shops. Farther along the street, to the south, the old red-light district had insinuated itself back again after being cleaned up yet one more time.

The office of the *Courier* was halfway between north and south, on the second floor, above a joke-goods store, in an old brick building. Mary paused on the sidewalk to look in the window at hilarious items like plastic dog turds and artificial vomit, and rubber masks of skulls and the living dead. One was especially villainous, a ghastly monster with its left eye hanging down its cheek.

Upstairs the sign on the door was discreet and businesslike, as though the *Courier* were a respectable suburban weekly, reporting on church suppers and high-school sporting events. Mary was not fooled. Inside she would find a receptionist who looked like a whore and a bunch of sleazy thugs with three-day growths of beard.

To her surprise there was only one occupant of the small room, a pink wholesome-looking young man in a trench coat that was a miracle of grommets, buckles, straps and flaps, leaning back in an old-fashioned office armchair. There were no girlie calendars on the wall, only a map of the world studded with pins in bright colors.

"Good morning," said the young man, springing to his feet, looking at her eagerly. "Can I help you in any way?"

Mary held up her copy of the *Courier*. "There was a piece in your paper recently about a woman who disappeared, Pearl Small. She was a friend of mine. I'm trying to find out more about it."

The young man sank back into his chair. "Oh, God, I thought you were from the *Globe*. I'm expecting a response from *The Boston Globe*." He gestured with a languid thumb at a file cabinet beside the window. "I don't know any Pearl Small. Big stars, that's all we keep on file."

"Well, have you got a collection of back issues? If I could go through them, I'll bet I could find it."

He gestured at a heap on the corner of his desk, and picked up the phone.

"Thanks." Mary began leafing through the pile, while the editor of *The Candid Courier* dialed a number and began talking quickly. His voice was soft, but she couldn't help overhearing. "Personnel Department? Oh, good morning. My name's Jackson,

George Jackson. I think you've recently received an application from me? I'm an experienced investigative reporter, but I'd like to add to my application that I'd be willing to accept a position as stringer in London or Paris, or, say, Barcelona. Of course I'm very busy, but I could take time off for an interview, if you—"

There was a pause. Mary could hear a polite voice fending him off.

"Well, I must say." For a moment the eager young man seemed incapable of saying anything. Then he spoke up in a tone of grave indignation. "Well, then, I guess your loss is somebody else's gain. I'll have to try *The New York Times*." Clashing down the phone, he stared angrily at Mary. "You've got to know somebody. Today it's all buddy-buddy, you know what I mean?"

"Right," murmured Mary, flipping through the stack of recent issues of the scandal sheet, skimming the headlines—

FELICIA FIGHTS FLAB

WORLD'S HAPPIEST COUPLE?
GUESS AGAIN!

SIZZLING FLING ENDS IN RAPE CHARGE

MURDER VICTIM?
WHERE IS BATTERED WIFE?

Mary slapped the page. "Here it is. Thank you. I'll just make a few notes."

The editor-in-chief, who was also the entire staff of *The Candid Courier*, was not interested in Mary's discovery. He jumped up and began moving the colored pins around on his map of the world. The pin for Bosnia went to the Gobi Desert, the one for South Africa to Tierra del Fuego, the pin for Jerusalem to Kamchatka. *Jab, jab, jab.*

Mary read the part of the article that had been missing from the scrap on Annie's table.

> . . . It is rumored that
> real estate is involved, a large parcel
> of land upon which Frederick Small
> intends to build a gold-plated housing
> development of million-dollar homes.
> The deal awaits the signature of the
> missing Mrs. Small.

"Mr. Jackson," said Mary, "where did you get this story?"

"What?" He turned away from the map and looked vaguely at the folded page Mary held under his nose. "God, I don't know. Somebody phoned it in. I've got these people out there"—he waved his arm at Washington Street, and, out of sight beyond the girlie theater across the way, the rest of the world, beginning with Boston Common and the Charles River—"they send in stuff."

"I see. Well, thank you." Mary went out and closed the door gently, feeling sorry for George Jackson. The poor kid had aspirations for higher things. He wanted to interview heads of state. He wanted to race down a bomb-cratered road in an armored Jeep. Instead, he was here in Boston, on Washington Street above a joke-goods store, mired in shameless voyeurism and subpornographic trash, neck-deep in shucked sheiks and sizzling flings. Poor wretch.

Mary glanced in the window of the joke-goods store on her way out. The gruesome drooping eye of the monster ogled her. Its ghastliness was exactly what she had expected to find upstairs in the office of the *Courier*. And perhaps she really had. Perhaps that pink-cheeked would-be foreign correspondent was actually a monster in the flesh.

She turned away, shuddering. It was beginning to rain. On the way home the heavens opened. Lightning flashed. Mary had to pull the car to the side of the road, because the windshield wipers couldn't handle the water sheeting down the glass.

Chapter 11

❧

Brave soldier, here is danger!
Brave soldier, here is death!
Hans Christian Andersen,
"The Steadfast Tin Soldier"

"I'm afraid," said Eddy. His hair was drenched. Rivulets of water poured down his cheeks. He struggled after his father up the difficult ascent behind the house. It was a long walk in the downpour to the top of Pine Hill.

"It's just a little rain." Bob Gast had to shout to be heard above the thunder, which rumbled and crashed like lumber falling downstairs. The lightning was simultaneous. "We've come out to watch. I really want you to see this, Eddy." There was a sharp splintering noise behind them, and Bob Gast jumped. Turning, he saw a split tree fall slowly, crashing through other trees, snapping the trunk of a big white pine.

Eddy cowered against his father. He had to be dragged up the steep side of the underground reservoir at the top of the hill.

"Here we are. Now we can see everything, Eddy. See? We can see *everything* from up here." Gast gripped his son's hand and braced himself on the battered grass, while the trees below them lashed to and fro, their branches snapping and crashing heavily to the forest floor.

He did not look down at his terrified son. Clearing his throat, he shouted the words he had been rehearsing in his head. "Okay, Eddy, now I want you to go over there and bring me my knife. I lost it right over there. See it over there, lying on the ground? Just go over there and get it for me, okay, Eddy? Just go get it and bring it here."

Eddy gaped up at his father. Gast had to give him a little shove. "Now, Eddy, you've got to be brave. Go ahead."

Eddy started forward toward the clearing at the crest of the hill. Around it the lightning struck down in a ring, once, twice, thrice. Soon it was a perpetual circle of white fire. Running on his short legs, Eddy stopped in the center and gazed around, turning to see it all, his small figure dwarfed by the broad landscape and the surrounding forest of storm-tossed trees. Thunder fell out of the sky and lightning danced in a ring of searing white light. Eddy was enchanted. He was no longer afraid. He could see that the thunder and lightning meant him no harm.

"Eddy," shouted his father. He was crying. "Eddy, come back."

The lightning dimmed and moved away. The thunder grumbled softly. The rain diminished and stopped. Slowly Eddy trotted back out of the ring of fire, his mind alight. Water streamed from his wet hair, it poured down his cheeks and ran into his open mouth. It tasted of tears and the pure water of heaven.

☙

Next day Eddy knocked on the south door of Annie's house. Flimnap, who had been staining Annie's cabinets, let him in. He greeted Eddy cheerfully and helped him take off his jacket.

Annie turned away from painting Scheherazade on the first division of her wall and greeted him warmly. "Well, hello there, Eddy."

Eddy said nothing. He stared up at the wall, gazing at the big figure of Aesop and the little ship on the horizon, and in the foreground the hare and the tortoise. He was suddenly excited. "Whassat?" he said, pointing at the wall.

Annie explained. She told him about the race between the hare and the tortoise, and about the ship full of men who were trying to get home after winning a war. It was not enough. He wanted to know about the boy with the sword. "Whassat? Whassat?"

Annie was pleased. Here at last was someone who appreciated her wall. She sat down beside Eddy on the sofa and told him about the sword that was stuck in a rock until the future king of England came along and pulled it out. He wanted more. She showed him her own picture book of *Jack and the Beanstalk*, and he was charmed. "Whassat?" he said, putting his finger on the speaking harp. "Whassat?" He stared wide-eyed at the giant, towering over Jack, and Annie growled, "Fee, fi, fo, fum!"

"Fee, fi, fo, fum!" echoed Flimnap, grinning at Eddy.

"Fee, fi, fo, fum!" shouted Eddy.

Flimnap was finished with Annie's cabinets, and he went away. But Annie went on and on. She couldn't stop. There was so much to tell Eddy, so much to show him—all of Hans Christian Andersen and Edward Lear and Beatrix Potter and Babar and Dr. Seuss. The boy was hungry for stories. But then Annie looked at her watch and called a halt. No more today. She had to get back to work.

She tried a diversion. "Here, Eddy, why don't you draw too?" She made a place for him at her table with sheets of drawing paper and a collection of colored pens. "Look, aren't they pretty? Red and blue, and, see here, silver and gold."

At once he grasped the pens and, without hesitation, began to draw. Annie watched him bend his small bullet head over the paper and pick up the silver pen. He seemed content.

For the next two hours she sketched the story of Scheherazade, and forgot about Eddy. When she finally came down the ladder, stiff and sore, he was still working on the same piece of paper.

She looked at it in surprise. "Why, Eddy, that's really good. Where did you learn to draw like that?" It was a portrait of yesterday's storm, with silvery spears of rain and golden shafts of lightning.

"For you," said Eddy, thrusting it at her.

"Oh, thank you," said Annie, really meaning it. After Eddy went home she tacked it up on the kitchen wall, where it shimmered and glowed.

When Flimnap came in, he admired it too. "My God," he said, "did you do that?"

"I wish I had. It's Eddy's. Isn't it wonderful?"

After that Eddy came every day. No one came with him. No one came to get him. There was no sign of his parents, or of his sister Charlene.

"Whassat?" he wanted to know. "Whassat, Annie, whassat?" One day he was the first to notice a blotch on the far right end of the wall. "Hey," he said, "lookit, whassat?"

Annie looked. On the blank white plaster beneath the fifth arched opening of her painted gallery there was another orange stain, with two greenish blobs like cartoon eyes, surrounded by a smear of sulphur yellow.

"It's a stain," said Annie doubtfully. "It's just a stain." But she was alarmed. Would her whole wall be spoiled by damp and mildew? Where was Flimnap? Once again he would know what to do.

By this time Flimnap was a fixture at Annie's house. He slept in the gypsy caravan mounted on the back of his truck, and he took his meals there too, using whatever cooking apparatus was connected to the stovepipe that stuck out of the roof.

Annie was grateful for his readiness to turn his hand to anything. *Do this,* she said, *do that,* and he did it. What if she were to say, *Kiss me, Flimnap!* Would he obey like a good servant? Sometimes Annie imagined it, but she wasn't about to try. Nevertheless, she couldn't help noticing the nimble grace of Flimnap's lanky body and the deftness of his narrow hands. What, she wondered, did he think of Annie Swann? Most of the time he was respectful and amusing, but a little remote. Perhaps he liked pretty cuties who sat with their legs crossed

coyly, not big busty women who laughed loudly and sat with their legs wide apart and their feet planted firmly on the floor.

So it was probably just kindness, the way he took such care of her safety. Her ladder, he said, was shaky. He would make a scaffolding with a platform on top and wheels underneath, so she could roll the whole thing easily from left to right.

"But won't it be unsteady?" said Annie. "Won't it roll out from under me?"

"No, no. There'll be locks on the wheels." On the next sunny morning, he set up a rented table saw and drill press on the lawn, along with a pile of four-by-fours from the lumberyard and a set of wheels. The saw screamed, the drill press buzzed and whined. Then Flimnap took the pieces indoors and bolted them together, attaching the wheels and fastening the ladder to a rail so she could move it from side to side.

"Show me how the brakes work," said Annie.

"You just flip down these tabs," he said. "See? It won't budge. And then, when you want to move it, you flip them up again."

Annie flipped the wheel tabs up and trundled the scaffolding sideways. "That's great," she said, beaming at him. "It rolls like anything."

From then on her work was much more comfortable. Sitting on the edge of the platform, she was at just the right height to work on the middle level of the wall. For the top there was a clever second platform near the ceiling, twelve feet above the floor.

Now, when she showed Flimnap the second appearance of an ugly blotch on her wall, he was not dismayed. "I'll use sealer this time," he said. And within the hour the stain was gone.

Chapter 12

❧

"So, Homer, you've got to talk to the police in Southtown. That's where Pearl lived. Find out if her husband's still there. His name's Small, Frederick Small. See if there are any charges against him. You know, like wife-battering. Find out who called *The Candid Courier* with information about Pearl."

"Oh, no," groaned Homer, "you're not back on that princess stuff again?" He made a pathetic face and waved a hand at the top of his desk. "Look at this!" A tippy pile of bluebooks landed on the floor with a slam.

"Oh, Homer, it's all right. I'm just saying do it when you have time. Just whenever you have time."

"Time! Why don't *you* talk to the police department in Southtown? Go over there yourself and have a cozy chat." Homer rolled his eyes at the ceiling and whirled around in his chair, knocking the rest of the bluebooks to the floor.

"Me? Oh, Homer, I can't do anything this week, nothing at all. And right now I've got to get over there to Weston Country Day and teach some kind of history to all those little girls in the fifth grade. What an idiot I was to agree to be a so-called Historian in Residence! How could I have been such a fool?"

Homer looked at her balefully. "Because you're sweet on Judge Aufsesser."

"Oh, Homer, don't be ridiculous."

❧

When Mary walked into the private girls' school called Weston Country Day, she was greeted by the nervous headmistress, who shot up from her desk, clasped her hand, and propelled her down the hall to the fifth grade that was to be her headquarters.

55

"Mrs. Rutledge's class is so talented," said the headmistress. "Charlene Gast is a champion swimmer, and Judge Aufsesser's daughter is in the class, and many of the others have very influential parents. Of course they are all a little high-strung, naturally, like thoroughbred racehorses. Perhaps you could be a steadying influence?"

"I'll do my best. Did you say Charlene Gast?"

"Yes, do you know her? Such a brilliant child!"

"No, I don't really know her. My niece does."

"Right this way. We're all so pleased you'll be teaching about the Greeks. It fits right in with our theme for the year."

"The Greeks! Oh, well, all right. The Greeks it is."

They walked into Mrs. Rutledge's homeroom without knocking, and Mary was at once confronted by eighteen pairs of eyes. Eighteen sets of parents were paying twelve thousand dollars a year so that their ten-year-old daughters could be exposed to teachers like Mrs. Rutledge and protected from the imperfections of the public school system.

Mary grinned cheerfully as she was introduced, and most of the little girls smiled back. Which one was Judge Aufsesser's daughter? They looked like good kids.

Mary wasn't so sure about the teacher, who seemed damp with insecurity. She was given to speaking in italics. "The class is so *excited!* We could hardly *wait.* Right, class?"

There was a pause—obviously the class was uninformed. Mary plunged in, saying how much she would enjoy telling them about the Greeks. (She would have to bone up in a hurry.)

"Shall we introduce ourselves to Mrs. Kelly?" said Mrs. Rutledge. "We'll start at the back. Cissie, will you begin?"

The little fat girl whispered her name. "Speak up, Cissie," said Mrs. Rutledge sharply.

"Cissie Aufsesser," murmured the little fat girl, looking down at her lap.

Beverly Eckstein, Carrie Maxwell, Becca Smith, Julie Ingledinger, Amelia Patterson, the names went on and on. They ended with a pretty child in the first row. "Charlene Gast," said Charlene.

"Charlene is a champion swimmer," said Mrs. Rutledge proudly, smiling at her.

"Well, good for you, Charlene," said Mary.

❧

Charlene was indeed a champion swimmer. Her bedroom in the house her parents rented from Annie Swann was a museum of medals and plastic trophies. She practiced obsessively, swimming laps for hours every day in the pool in the club her parents belonged to in Lexington. For Charlene the daily practice wasn't a chore, it was a joy. Like most people who are good at something, she loved it with all her heart. Water was Charlene's element. Last week she had beaten all the other young female swimmers from swimming clubs all over New England in the hundred-meter backstroke. Everyone knew she was headed for the Junior Olympics.

She always won. Well, not always. Last year she had lost one event, and it had been so shattering that nine-year-old Charlene had vowed never to lose again. Since then her record had been perfect. Losing was out of the question. Prizes fell into her hands, medals were hung around her neck. And it wasn't just swimming trophies, it was other things as well. Getting what she wanted had become a habit. After all, she and she alone was *Charlene Gast.*

If her father, that ex-student of philosophy, had been paying attention, he would have identified his daughter's mind-set as a case of solipsism, the belief that the self is the only reality. Charlene was a living, breathing solipsist. All other creatures in the world existed merely to serve her needs.

On the day Mary Kelly walked into Mrs. Rutledge's homeroom for the first time, Charlene was keeping a sharp eye on

Alice Mooney. Alice owned something Charlene wanted, a princess doll. It was really *dumb* that Charlene couldn't have one of her own, just because her stupid parents kept saying no.

It was indeed a beautiful doll. Alice Mooney loved it. Her mother wasn't a cleaning lady, as Charlene had told her parents, she was a dietitian at the Concord-Carlisle High School, but she could not normally pay $69.95 for a doll. "This is your only present, Alice," she told her daughter as she handed her the big box on the morning of her birthday.

"Oh, oh," breathed Alice, tearing at the tissue paper. "Oh, thank you, thank you. I don't want anything else, not ever."

She shouldn't have taken the doll to school. That was her mistake. All the other girls in Mrs. Rutledge's fifth grade envied her. They fingered the bouffant dress and touched the sparkling crown and stroked the silky hair. They watched as Alice tenderly removed the pretty little plastic slippers and put them on again.

"Now, Alice," said Mrs. Rutledge, "put away your doll. After recess, class, I'll want your math homework. I hope you all worked hard. Report cards go out to your parents next week."

There was a scraping of metal chair legs on the floor, an orderly parade out the door, then an eager rush for the playground.

Mrs. Rutledge was not on call that day for playground duty. Gratefully she beckoned to Mary Kelly, and together they headed for the coffee machine in the teachers' room.

Behind them, the classroom was no longer empty. Alice Mooney had crept back indoors. Holding her doll, she moved cautiously to the desk belonging to Julie Ingledinger. Julie was the best math student in the class. Her homework lay on top of her desk, ready to be turned in. Softly Alice put down her doll and picked up the piece of yellow paper.

"I see you," said Charlene, appearing out of nowhere.

Alice's hand jerked away from Julie's paper. She stared in horror at Charlene.

"I'll tell," said Charlene.

"No, no," whined Alice. "Oh, Charlene, please don't tell."

"Your doll," said Charlene. "I want your doll."

"My doll?" Alice's face flushed. Her frightened eyes opened wider. She picked up her doll and hugged it to her chest. "My princess doll? Oh, no! Oh, no, no! Oh, please, Charlene!"

"Well, then, I'll tell." Charlene turned as Mr. Orth walked into the room, looking for Mrs. Rutledge. "Oh, Mr. Orth!"

Alice caught her arm, weeping. "Okay, it's okay."

Mr. Orth looked at them. "What is it, Charlene?"

Charlene grinned at him. "Nothing, Mr. Orth. Never mind. It's okay."

"Well, all right. Oh, Charlene, congratulations on winning that swimming meet last week. We're all so proud of you. Now it's on to the state level, is that right?"

"That's right, Mr. Orth."

He was gone. Alice stroked her doll's nylon hair and straightened her pretty crown, then handed her over to Charlene. Tears ran down her cheeks.

Charlene hid the doll in her schoolbag. But at home she showed it proudly to her mother.

"Why, Charlene," said Roberta, "where did you get that lovely doll?"

"Alice gave it to me. She has oodles of dolls."

"Why, what a generous gift!"

Alice's mother wasn't so easily bamboozled. "Alice, dear," she said, "where's your princess doll? I've got a scrap of velvet left over from your dress. We'll make her a royal cloak."

"Oh," said Alice, her voice hollow. "I left her at school."

Next day she claimed to have forgotten again. The day after that she started to cry, and said she had lost it.

"Oh, Alice, how could you?"

Mrs. Mooney called the school. At once an announcement about the lost doll was made over the school intercom. Alice sat dumb and suffering, while everyone in the class turned to stare. Mary Kelly pitied the poor kid, she looked so desolate.

The doll was never found.

ℳ

"Lord Fish," cried the fisherman, gazing over the side of the boat, "I'm afraid my wife has another request."

The great fish appeared at once, and looked up mildly at the fisherman. "What is it now?"

The fisherman was ashamed. "She is old and ugly, Lord Fish. She wants to be young again."

A cloud drifted across the sun and cast a shadow over the sea. "It is done," said the fish, sinking beneath the waves.

Chapter 13

❧

Then she took up Hansel with her rough hand, and shut him up in a little cage with a lattice-door, and although he screamed loudly it was of no use. The Brothers Grimm, "Hansel and Gretel"

There was a thump of feet on the porch steps. The door slammed. Mary was back. "So?" said Homer. "How did it go?"

She tore off her coat and dumped it on a chair. "Oh, I don't know. They're nice kids."

"Was the great Judge Aufsesser there in all his judicial glory to meet his daughter's new teacher?"

"Oh, Homer, of course not."

Homer snickered. "What's his daughter like?"

"Very shy, I think. The star of the class is Charlene Gast. You know, from the family renting Annie's house."

Homer swarmed together all the graded bluebooks and shaped them into a cube. He looked up at Mary gravely. "What do you know about that Flimnap character? I get the impression he's there all the time. Is Annie getting involved again? I thought she'd sworn off men. I should think that last episode with Jack Whatshisname would have taught her a lesson. And Whoseywhatsis before that, Burgess, the hotshot stockbroker."

"Homer, you haven't even met Flimnap. He's just a handyman around the place."

"Maybe he's handy in the wrong way," hinted Homer darkly.

Mary changed the subject. She looked at Homer and said sweetly, "Oh, good, you're finished with all those bluebooks.

Now maybe you've got time to see that police chief in Southtown."

Homer was indignant. In a ridiculous falsetto he parodied his wife. *"Hurry up, now, Homer. You've got to rescue a princess, find an enchanted frog, fall down a rabbit hole, and drive fifty miles down 128 to bawl out the chief of police."*

"Oh, Homer—"

"Well, never mind," said Homer gruffly, getting up from his chair. "I already called him. He sounds like a jerk, but I'm supposed to go down there tomorrow. Today, for Christ's sake— how did I get into this?—I've got to talk to those kids in the Concord prison."

"Oh, Homer, darling, thank you!" Mary threw her arms around him, and murmured into the shoulder of his coat, "Poor Princess, I know something terrible has happened to her. We've just got to track her down."

🙘

Being admitted to M.C.I. Concord was a lengthy affair. Homer had been through it all before, but he'd forgotten some of the details. You had to register in the lobby and wait at the heavy door while new inmates in chains arrived under guard.

At last the big door ground heavily to one side to let Homer into the locked space called the trap. Under the supervision of a guard he had to take off his shoes, his jacket, his belt, his wristwatch, and empty his pockets before walking through a metal detector.

"Hey," he said, "I don't remember all this. Did you always make people take all this stuff off?"

"You're lucky you're not a woman," said the officer, handing back his jacket. "Sometimes they got a wired bra, sets off the beeper."

Released from the trap, Homer walked past the isolation block and the chapel, then marched through J Building and into

H, where the corridor was full of inmates waiting to enter the canteen. The library was locked, but when he knocked on the door the librarian opened it and said, "Your class is expecting you."

Homer was interested to see that the place looked like a normal library, with walls of cheerful-looking books, a blocked-off corner for the librarian, and sunshine falling through high windows. The room was empty. Homer looked left and right. "Where are they?"

"The law library's up there." The librarian pointed to a second level at one side. There they were, looking down at Homer through a wire grille. He followed the librarian up the stairs and waited while she unlocked the door. Once he was inside she nodded goodbye, locked the door again, and went back downstairs.

There were six of them sitting around a table, inmates in blue shirts looking up at him warily. Homer said, "Good morning," and sat down. Then he beamed around the table, trying to put them at their ease. "Why don't we start by introducing ourselves? My name's Homer. I teach American literature, but I've got a law degree, so if I don't know the answers to your questions, I should be able to find out." He nodded at the good-looking kid with the earring. "You want to start?"

"My name's Fergie." The kid leaned forward, his blue prison shirt bunched up around his shoulders. "Repeat offender, I got this parole violation. What I want to know is, how much of my hard-earned good time will they take away?"

"Good time?"

"Like I rake leaves, repair vehicles, get paid shit. They take off two and a half days a month from my sentence. Now they're gonna put some of it back. It's like I never did no work."

Homer didn't know how much good time Fergie would lose. He said he'd find out.

Gordie spoke up boldly. "Suppose, like, somebody has a lot

of cash nobody knows about, do they have to, like, pay taxes on it?"

I don't want to hear about it, Homer wanted to say. "All income must be declared," he said, knowing he sounded stuffy. "With confirmation from the source. Confirmation might be—uh—sort of difficult, if the income was improper or illegal in some way." *In other words, don't bring it up at all, you dumb kid.*

"Shit," said Gordie softly.

"My name's Hank," said the thickset boy with red hair. "I just got in this place last week. I got money problems too. There's this guy owes me money. Only now I'm here he thinks he don't have to pay me." Hank's voice trembled with his sense of grievance. "See, while I was on the outside, he hired me to do something for him, so I did, only at that particular time I was out on bail, and then I got sentenced and they dumped me in here, so now this guy don't want to pay me."

"Do you have the agreement in writing?" said Homer.

"Nah, it was like, you know, a verbal agreement."

"Well, maybe you could try suing him in small-claims court. I could help with that."

"Nah, nah, I don't wanta bring it up in court. Jesus!"

"I see," said Homer, who didn't see. "Let me think about it."

"I'm Jimmy," said the broad-shouldered young African-American, "and my wife, we're getting a divorce, only she thinks I don't need no money in prison, she can just take everything."

"Everything?"

"Right. I got this neighbor, he tells me she's gonna take off with the car, the entertainment center, the twenty-eight-cubic-foot fridge, the king-size bed, the living-room suite. I bet she's forging my name on checks. She done that before."

Homer made a note. "Well, that's no problem. We can do something about that."

"Ferris, my name's Ferris," said the kid with the harelip.

"They give me a lousy public defender, like he really messed up, I didn't do nothing, I'm innocent, but he wasn't no help."

This too was fairly straightforward. "Well, the first thing would be an examination of the court records. I'd have to see if anything improper was said or done. I doubt incompetence on the part of your counsel is enough to call for a retrial. Have you got a transcript? No? I'll see if I can get one."

"My case is rather complex," said the fat middle-aged man with thick glasses. "Barkley Pendleton Haywall's my name, and I've been reading the literature." He nodded at the law books lining the walls. "There are several very interesting precedents to my case, all tending to the view that it has been mishandled. The first was the *Commonwealth of Massachusetts* versus *Hemelman*, in 1976, in which the judge concluded—"

There were impatient shufflings of feet under the table. Hank, Fergie, Gordie, and Ferris all grimaced as Barkley went on talking. His sentence was for child molestation. His fellow inmates were not repelled by theft, drug dealing, assault, rape, or even murder, but they were disgusted by Barkley's crime. He was a skinner, the lowest of the low. They looked at him with loathing, and edged their chairs away.

Barkley didn't seem to notice. He was completely wrapped up in the ramifications of the seven other cases in which the molested children had been older or younger, and more submissive or more combative. There was also the important question of whether they had actually been penetrated or merely handled.

"Jesus," whispered Gordie, nudging Ferris. "Yuck," said Ferris. "Christ," muttered Hank, shuddering. "Gawd," said Fergie, making a noise like vomiting.

Chapter 14

❧

Then the mother took the little boy and chopped him in pieces, put him into the pan and made him into black-puddings.

The Brothers Grimm, "The Juniper Tree"

Annie drifted out of her bedroom just before sunrise, while the house was still wrapped in dusk. The chairs and tables were still there, and the white keys of the piano. After the long night of unconsciousness and dreams she was happy to see that her perfect house existed still. It had not been blown away in some mighty readjustment of the world. Her painted wall was still there too, flowing through the room like a river.

Annie picked up her chalk and waded into the river up to her knees. By the time she had finished sketching the outlines of Hans Christian Andersen, complete with his tall top hat, it was ten o'clock. She stopped and came down the ladder and leaned against the kitchen counter to have breakfast. With her coffee cup in her hand, she turned around to gloat at her wall.

At once she saw the stain, a new unwanted addition to her procession of majestic figures.

This time it was not an accident, not an accumulation of mildew and damp. It was a face, a blank face surrounded by an aureole of yellow hair. Drips of red paint streamed down from the face like drops of blood.

Annie's happiness turned to dread. What the hell was going on? Someone was invading her wall, encroaching on her enchanted territory. While she was sleeping someone had come in silently and used her own brushes and her own jars of paint.

She recognized the chrome yellow, the alizarin crimson. But when she climbed the scaffolding to look at her jars and her can of brushes they looked the same as always. Was one of the brushes wet? No, all of them were clean and dry.

Annie climbed down the ladder again and walked back to the place where the new face had appeared, thinking about her artistic friends. Last week she had invited a lot of them to a housewarming party. They had all seen her wall. Any one of them could have played this trick on her. Of course they couldn't all draw as cleverly as this. Perry Chestnut was a potter, Minnie Peck a sculptor, and Henrietta Willsey a minimalist poet. Wallace Feather specialized in whole-body casts, Henry Coombs constructed big things he called installations, and Trudy Tuck made fancy candles she insisted were works of art. And yet—

"Oh, no, my God." It was Flimnap, staring up at the new face. He had come in silently, carrying a garden fork.

Annie didn't have to tell him what to do. He got to work at once, unlocking the wheels of the scaffolding, rolling it along the wall, locking the wheels again, and climbing up to eliminate the blank white face, the mop of yellow hair, the drops of blood.

Annie watched. Flimnap's hands were wonderful in action, those hands that could juggle balls and bananas and pebbles so deftly and paint window frames so neatly. His long fingers moved as if they had brains of their own. They gripped and lifted and carried, adjusted and tested. She imagined them touching her hair and cradling her face.

"It was you, wasn't it, Flimnap?" she said dreamily. "You put it there. You painted that face yourself."

He glanced at her from the high plank, then came down the ladder. "Look." He picked up a piece of chalk and scrawled something on the newspaper covering the table, a clumsy pair of circles with two ears and a tail. It was a child's drawing of a cat. "That's the best I can do," said Flimnap, and, smiling at her, he put down the chalk and climbed up the ladder again.

He couldn't draw, and yet he seemed to know about children's picture books. Not hers, but Miguel Delgado's crazy clowns and Antonio Amici's dazzling colors, and one day she saw him leafing through Joseph Noakes's *Gulliver's Travels*.

Annie was surprised and pleased. "He's great, don't you think?"

Flimnap closed the book and said, "I hear he's dead."

"Dead!" Annie was shocked. "Oh, no! Who told you that?"

"I read it somewhere."

"Oh, I'm really sorry." Annie stared at Flimnap, feeling a sharp sense of loss. "What a shame! I love his impossible staircases that go around and around, and that picture of Gulliver tied down by his hair, with every strand casting a shadow. Oh, I can't believe it."

"Well, I guess it's true."

This morning, when he finished blotting out the bleeding face with its yellow hair, Flimnap picked up the garden fork again, tossed it over his head, caught it behind his back, waved it at her, and went back outside.

Annie watched him descend the hill in loping strides. Then she went into her bedroom and looked at herself in the mirror over her dresser.

The thing was, never to be wistful again. Never to yearn after somebody, never to be pathetic. Not after all those gruesome mistakes in the past, getting married to Grainger Swann, and then falling stupidly in love with that screwball Burgess, and then with jut-jawed Jack, only to be dumped not once but twice. Never again would she be abject. The hell with Flimnap's wonderful, nimble, extraordinary hands.

The mirror was whimsical, as usual. Three or four days a week she looked all right, as though a good fairy were in charge of the mirror. But then an uglifying witch elbowed the fairy aside. The state of Annie's looks was completely random. She was beautiful sometimes—really!—homely at other times, and most of the time only so-so.

Today she was so-so.

On the other side of the wall that divided the old and new parts of the house, Roberta Gast too was looking in the mirror, the beautiful Chippendale mirror she had inherited from her mother. She had hung it in the living room, where the light was just right, flattering her, doing away with the awful wrinkles she had seen on her face on moving day. Now, in the morning light, it gave back the image of a handsome, clever-looking woman. Smiling, Roberta walked away from the mirror and looked out the window.

Was the car there? Yes, Bob had left it on the brow of the hill, at the very edge of the sloping lawn, just as he had promised.

Eddy was playing outside, stumbling slowly over the grass, following a meandering parade of ants. All the ants were carrying tiny green pieces of leaves.

Roberta did not see the ants. She put her face against the screen and called to Eddy, "Look, Eddy, there's the old car. Wouldn't you like to play in the car? Look, one of the doors is open. Why don't you play in it for a while? You can pretend to be driving a car, a real car."

✎

Annie was back at work, mixing paint, trying to get the right depth of black for Andersen's tall hat, when she heard the squeal from outdoors and Flimnap's shout. Running to the window, she saw him race across the hillside, trying to intercept the car that was plunging toward him in free fall.

Annie threw open the screen door and ran after him, screaming, "Stop, stop! Let it go!" But he wasn't stopping, he was galloping along beside the car, throwing open the door, heaving himself inside. The car skidded as he wrenched at the steering wheel, but instead of slowing down it plunged faster and faster, heading for the thick forest of oak trees at the bottom of the hill. While Annie stumbled after it, shrieking, there was an awful grinding as the driver's door burst off its hinges and the left side of the car crunched and scraped past one tree, narrowly missed another, and came to a stop in a wild arching thicket of buckthorn and honeysuckle.

Sobbing, Annie floundered through the thicket and grasped the shuddering frame of the door. Flimnap looked up at her, his face white, his hands shaking on the wheel. There was a whimpering bundle on the seat beside him. It was young Eddy Gast.

"Oh my God, Flimnap," whispered Annie.

And then Roberta Gast was there, opening the door on the other side, extracting Eddy. "He loves to play in the car," she said, her voice trembling. She turned away and started up the hill, carrying Eddy, whose frightened face looked back at Annie over his mother's shoulder.

Flimnap got out. Shakily he turned away from Annie and looked at the car. "Where the hell did it come from?"

"I don't know, but I've seen it before."

The car that had plunged down the hill carrying little Eddy Gast was not his father's Bronco or his mother's Mazda. It was the old Chevy in which Robert and Roberta Gast had appeared in Annie's life for the very first time.

Chapter 15

❧

"Then get thee gone, and a murrain seize thee!" cried the Sheriff . . .
"I have a good part of a mind to have thee beaten for thine insolence!"
Howard Pyle,
Merry Adventures of Robin Hood

The police and fire departments in Southtown were housed in a big flat-roofed brick building. Most of it belonged to the fire department. Huge red engines filled the driveway, their chromium fittings glittering in the sun.

Homer found the entrance marked POLICE and walked in. The white-haired officer on the other side of the counter looked up from his computer screen and said, "May I help you?"

"Chief McNutt?"

The officer shook his head and stood up. "Sergeant Kennebunk. You're Homer Kelly?" He smiled and glanced at his watch. "The chief's expecting you. You're right on time." He stretched out his hand. "Glad to meet you. You're pretty famous around here."

"For bungling and general mismanagement?" But Homer was flattered. Grinning, he shook Kennebunk's hand and glanced down the hall. "Is the chief here?"

"I'll get him." Kennebunk disappeared.

Homer looked at the pictures on the wall. They were all alike, photographs of a tubby man in a tight uniform standing beside one famous person after another—Ronald Reagan, Tip O'Neill, Ted Kennedy, Ross Perot. One showed him smirking beside a gorgeous woman who might be Madonna, or perhaps some other shapely female.

Kennebunk came back, looking embarrassed. "He'll be a minute or two."

"Well, maybe you can help me, Sergeant. I'm looking for a man named Small who lives in Southtown. I understand Mrs. Small has disappeared. She was a student of my wife's."

"Yes, I know Small." Kennebunk spoke hesitantly. "He runs a sand-and-gravel company, or used to. I hear he's in real estate now. He lives way out on the Pig Road. I mean Songsparrow. It's Songsparrow Road now. All the old pig farms are being turned into housing developments. Meadowlark, Songsparrow, there's a whole lot of new ones out that way."

"They're trying to forget the malodorous past, is that it?" Homer leaned his elbows on the counter and leaned closer to Sergeant Kennebunk. "Do you know if there's any truth in the rumor that Small beat his wife? Mary read it in one of those supermarket scandal sheets. What do you think? Was he the kind of creep who knocks his wife around just for the hell of it?"

Kennebunk glanced warily down the hall. "Well, maybe. Sometimes she had bruises on her face. I felt sorry for her, but there was nothing we could do unless she lodged a complaint."

"And now she's disappeared. Do you think she ran away?"

"Perhaps, but, then again, I wouldn't put it past Small—" Kennebunk stopped in mid-sentence. "I guess you'd better wait and talk to the chief." He sat back down and stared at his monitor, making it clear that he would answer no more questions.

The chief of the Southtown Police Department kept Homer waiting for twenty minutes. When he bustled down the hall at last, Homer stood up to greet him, but Chief McNutt didn't look in his direction. He barked an order at Sergeant Kennebunk: "You're due at the mall in ten minutes. What the hell are you doing here?"

"Tomorrow, sir," said Kennebunk patiently. "That's tomorrow. Griscom's there today."

Chief McNutt had lost face. "Well, then, get those invoices

out pronto, and I mean right now." Turning, he glowered at Homer.

Homer was charmed. Chief McNutt was that rare bird on the face of the earth, a genuine son of a bitch. There was nothing Homer enjoyed more than a good hate. He beamed at the chief and explained his errand.

At once McNutt shook his head. He did not offer Homer a chair, or invite him into his office. This was obviously a matter to be swept out the door. "Your *wife* thinks Fred Small was a wife-beater?"

It was clear that the testimony of wives was unreliable. "It was in the paper," explained Homer, "the rumor that Mrs. Small was a battered wife."

"My God," said Chief McNutt, "it's all the rage today, weepy women claiming they've been mistreated by their husbands. It's like a virus, one female gets hysterical and the infection spreads and pretty soon they're all screaming they've been beat up. Christ! It's worse than sexual harassment." McNutt reached across the counter, snatched up a folder from Kennebunk's desk, and held it under Homer's nose. "This here's all rape cases. *So-called* rape cases. Oh, yeah, maybe one or two's legitimate. Boys get liquored up, grab the nearest piece of flesh. The rest, well, you know those women, they invite it. Look at the way they dress, with those real tight skirts and low-cut necklines showing their tits. I wouldn't mind having a go myself." The chief slapped the folder down on the counter and laughed loudly.

Homer's good humor vanished. He could clearly see the burly chief wrestling some poor woman into the back seat of a car. "But in this case, I think—"

"Forget it." The chief turned and walked away, firing a final shot. "Fred Small is a law-abiding citizen of this town. His wife, the story is, she's got a boyfriend. There's some guy, used to hang around. Take my word for it. She's gone off with some gigolo."

Homer gaped at McNutt's retreating back, and called after him, "Well, thank you very much."

There was silence. Then Sergeant Kennebunk stood up and said softly, "I'm going off-duty now. How about meeting me at Jacky's? Doughnut place, just down the road."

"You bet," said Homer. Outdoors, he sucked in deep drafts of air uncontaminated by the lewd breath of the chief of the Southtown Police Department, and climbed into his car.

Jacky's stood in a sea of asphalt, sandwiched between a gas station and a mattress outlet. A gigantic plastic doughnut wobbled on the roof in the wind from passing cars. Inside, the place was fragrant with good smells wafting from coffee machines and kettles of simmering fat. Homer ordered coffee and a plate of sugary doughnuts and sat down with Kennebunk. The two men loomed over the plastic table nose to nose. Homer picked up a doughnut and ate it hungrily, spilling powdered sugar all over his coat.

Brushing it off his necktie, he said, "Why aren't you the chief of the Southtown Police Department instead of that creep?"

Kennebunk burst out laughing. He had a hearty laugh. It was obviously a release from the groveling tension of life as a traffic cop under Rollo McNutt. Heads turned at other tables. Homer grinned. Then Kennebunk stopped laughing. "His father's town manager. His uncle's on the board of selectmen. His brother—"

"Oh, right, I get the picture." Impulsively Homer said, "Look, why don't we work on this together? You and me? And nail that Bluebeard Small?"

"Bluebeard?"

"Oh, it's my niece Annie. She's obsessed with folktales. Bluebeard murdered one wife after another. There was this locked room full of corpses."

"You think Small's like that?" Kennebunk looked at Homer soberly. "You think Pearl Small didn't go away, he killed her?"

"And maybe six or seven wives before her." Homer was carried away. He waved his doughnut at Kennebunk. "Princess, they called her Princess. She's got this long golden hair."

"Princess, oh, right." Kennebunk's rugged face softened. "Her hair is yellow as straw. She's like the princess in the tower, the one with her long golden hair hanging out the window. She always reminds me of that."

"What, another fantasist in our midst?" Homer beamed at Kennebunk. "You're as bad as Annie. Listen, do you have any idea who told *The Candid Courier* she was missing? Somebody must have given them all that stuff about Pearl's disappearance."

Under his thick white hair Kennebunk's ruddy face grew redder still. "It was me, I'm afraid. McNutt wasn't doing anything about it and he refused to let me look into it. Small's his old drinking pal and lodge buddy. So I thought a little publicity wouldn't do any harm. I tried the *Globe* and the *Lowell Sun*, but they didn't seem interested. So I worked my way down to the *Courier*."

"I see," said Homer. "Well, good for you. At least it got my wife all excited."

"There's something else that's sort of strange," said Kennebunk. "After Pearl disappeared, Small showed up with his arm in a sling."

"Oh? How did it happen, did he say?"

"I asked him, when I stopped at his house to ask about Pearl."

"Well, how did you know she was missing?"

"My wife's her boss at the Southtown Public Library. When Pearl didn't show up for work, Dot was worried. She suspected for a long time that Pearl was being knocked around. One day she asked her point-blank why she didn't leave her husband, and Pearl said she couldn't leave her trees."

"Her what? Her trees?"

"That old pig farm. Pearl was trying to improve it, planting trees."

"I see. So what about Small? You asked him about his wife?"

"Right. He was mad as hell. Said it was none of my business. If a man's wife chooses to go off for a while, it's no business of the police, that's what he said. And then of course Small called McNutt, and McNutt bawled me out."

"You poor bastard. Well, what about the sling on his arm?"

"He said he fell downstairs. He'd been drinking, he said, and he fell downstairs. I'd like to think Pearl knocked him down, but she was pretty small and fragile."

"What about a doctor? Did he go to an emergency room or anything?"

"Apparently not. I checked with the hospital. I mean, my wife kept after me. My wife—"

"You don't have to tell me about wives." Homer laughed. "She should get together with Mary Kelly, they're two of a kind." He stood up. "How about another doughnut?"

"Oh, no thanks," said Kennebunk. "My wife's got me on a diet." He took an appointment book out of his pocket, wrote down Homer's phone number, and promised to keep in touch.

Left alone in Jacky's, Homer ordered two more doughnuts and ate them slowly. They were a mistake. When he waddled outdoors and climbed into his car, the four deep-fat-fried morsels sat like a dead weight in the bottom of his stomach.

Chapter 16

❧

Weave a circle round him thrice,
And close your eyes in holy dread,
For he on honey-dew hath fed,
And drunk the milk of Paradise.

Coleridge, "Kubla Khan"

As soon as Annie walked into the house with her bag of groceries, she heard a strange noise, a rhythmic humming. She dumped the bag on the counter and turned around.

There was a whirl of color on the floor in front of the window. It was a spinning top. It droned and hopped and spun as though it would never slow down.

"Flimnap?" called Annie. At once there was another sound, a loud engine-driven noise, the lawn mower. Flimnap was outside, cutting the grass for the first time.

Mesmerized, Annie watched the top until it wallowed to a stop and lay on its side. Then she picked it up and looked at it. It was an ordinary old-fashioned wooden top. Her brother John had owned one just like it a long time ago.

Later on, when Flimnap came in from mowing the entire front lawn, Annie showed him the top. "This is yours?"

"Perhaps." Flimnap took it, pulled a string out of his pocket, wound it carefully around the top, and flung it on the floor. Again the top whizzed and sang.

Annie laughed and began putting away her groceries, comparing the prosaic contents of her kitchen shelves with the sprightly presence of Flimnap O'Dougherty. Flimnap didn't belong in the world of paper bags and canned tomatoes and cartons of milk. He was a refugee from her wall, an escapee, a participant in its astonishing events. He belonged up there in that gallery, along with Aesop and Beatrix Potter and Hans Christian Andersen. Their enchanted plaster was the air he breathed.

Someone knocked on the glass of the French door. "Hello there, Eddy," said Flimnap, opening it, letting him in.

"Oh, Eddy," said Annie. "I'm sorry, but I can't read to you today. I have to go to Cambridge."

"It's all right," said Flimnap. "I'll be here for a while. Come on, Eddy, look at this." Once again, while Annie hurried the rest of her groceries into the refrigerator and slammed her cupboard doors, Flimnap spun the top.

Eddy wanted to try it. Flimnap wound the string for him, but when Eddy threw it down, the top fell on its side and rattled across the floor. Annie hurried into her bedroom and changed her clothes. When she came back, Flimnap was juggling plastic plates. "One, two, three—whoops!" The fourth plate bounced on the floor. "I can never manage four," said Flimnap, grinning at Eddy. He tried again, while Eddy laughed and clapped his hands.

Annie spent half the day in Harvard Square, taking a holiday from her painted wall. She met Minnie Peck for lunch. Min made huge metal sculptures from car parts, bedsprings, and old washing machines. Annie was envious of Min's cosmopolitan life. She was always popping off to New York for a gallery opening or a play. She knew everybody in the contemporary art scene. Today at lunch she told Annie about a party for some illustrator, Miguel Somebody.

"Miguel Delgado?"

"That's right. He does those crazy clowns, right? And elephants? Green and purple elephants?"

"Oh, yes, that's right. What's he like?"

"Oh, really good-looking, sexy. Long black hair, and he's got these burning eyes."

"Oh, Min, did anybody mention Noakes? Joseph Noakes? I've heard a rumor that he's dead."

"Oh, no, he was there. He's not dead."

"Oh, thank goodness. What's he like?"

"Noakes? Oh, sort of stark and really intense. Big shoulders. Gorgeous. You know." Then Min wrinkled her brow with doubt. "Unless it was Boakes, Joe Boakes. Is there somebody called Boakes?"

Annie sighed and picked up the carafe of wine. Joseph Noakes-Boakes sounded a lot like her old boyfriend Jack. But now Min was off on something else, her latest work of art. "I call it *Millennial Woman*. It's almost finished. It's hubcaps, shiny hubcaps, rusty hubcaps, *thousands* of hubcaps. And you know what? It would look really fabulous on your lawn." Min reached across the table and gripped Annie's arm. "Look, why don't I truck it over? You could try it here and there. Special price for an old friend."

"Well, I don't know, Min," said Annie cautiously. "I was thinking more of a sundial."

On the way home she felt slightly tipsy. On Route 2 she stared straight ahead, widening her eyes, concentrating on the traffic rushing ahead of her, beside her, behind her, then ramming on her brakes when the car in front suddenly veered to one side and stopped with a jolt.

Something had run out on the road, some kind of animal. The driver yelled out the window, "Jesus Christ, what the hell do you think you're doing?"

He wasn't yelling at Annie, he was shouting at a small shape on the road. While other cars dodged around her and sounded angry horns, she threw open the door and ran to Eddy.

"Is that your kid?" bellowed the man who had nearly driven over him. "Criminal negligence," he shouted at Annie, as she hurried Eddy back to her car and pushed him into the front seat.

"Eddy," she said, working her way back into the slow lane,

"what happened? What were you doing out there on the highway?"

"Cambridge," he said, looking up at her, his voice trembling. "Going to Cambridge."

Oh, God, thought Annie, he had been trying to follow her to Cambridge. While she had been gossiping with Minnie Peck in the restaurant on JFK Street, poor old Eddy had been stumbling through the woods, fighting his way through the underbrush, heading for the highway. Why didn't Eddy's mother keep a closer watch on Eddy?

At home Annie brought Eddy to the Gasts' front door and confronted Roberta. "I was driving home from Cambridge on Route 2 when he ran out on the road."

Roberta said, "Oh dear." She took Eddy's hand and said faintly, "Thank you."

At home, in her own part of the house, after flinging down her bag, and tearing off her coat, Annie stopped to stare at the wall. The face was back. It was no longer the bleeding blank face of a woman with golden hair. This time it was dark and brutal, with pointed teeth, bulging eyes, and a bright-blue beard.

Chapter 17

❧

"**O**h, Flimnap," said Annie, "I forgot to tell you. Bob Gast wants to know if you could fix some things over there. You know, clogged drains, doors that won't shut."

Flimnap glanced at her. "Well, okay, fine." His voice was flat.

"And they say the trapdoor on the floor of the laundry porch is rotten."

"I'll do that first. It's not rotten, but I wouldn't put it past those people to fall through on purpose and sue you. Mrs. Gast's law firm specializes in that kind of thing."

"It does! They sue people? How do you know?"

"Ear to the ground."

It was a typically evasive Flimnappian remark. There were a lot of questions Annie wanted to ask him, such as, "Exactly what is your marital status?" But she knew he'd dodge around them somehow. The truth was probably something like, *Married and divorced, six children in child support.*

Flimnap asked Annie a question instead. "What does Bob Gast do? Is he another lawyer?"

Annie wasn't sure. "He's in some kind of real estate, I think. You know, land management, something like that."

Next day Flimnap began doing things for the Gasts, knocking on their front door, using Annie's key when they weren't at home. After replacing the trapdoor on the side porch, he climbed the stairs with bucket and pipe wrench to work on the stopped-up drain in the bathroom sink.

He was alone in the house. Bob and Roberta Gast were at work, the children were in school. Flimnap put the bucket down softly and began moving around among the bedrooms. One was an elegant master bedroom with a canopied bed. An-

other was a boy's room, Eddy's, rather spartan. A third was full
of dolls and swimming trophies, Charlene's.

There remained the small room on the north side. The door
was closed. Flimnap opened it boldly. The room was a study
with a desk, a filing cabinet, and an electric typewriter.

Slowly Flimnap walked up to the desk and looked down at
the rows of papers, neatly arranged in piles. Was this Roberta's
stuff, or her husband's? Or did they both use the room?

Big manila envelope, "Weingarten and Morrissey, Attorneys
at Law." That sounded like Roberta.

Legal-sized envelope, "Winchester, Board of Appeals." That
was more like Bob.

Folded plot plan, "Rolling Pastures, footprint." Footprint?
It was a land planner's term, the shape of a structure on a lot.
That was surely Bob Gast.

A sheaf of stapled pages, "Songsparrow Estates, Southtown,
Preliminary Estimates."

Flimnap picked up the sheaf and began to read.

❧

Bob Gast came home early from his downtown office. Roberta
was late. Eddy's driver had not yet brought him home. Charlene was at swimming practice. Bob ran upstairs to make a few
phone calls.

Sitting down at his desk, he picked up the phone. For a moment he held it in his hand, ready to dial, then put it down.

His papers didn't look right. "Songsparrow Estates, Southtown, Preliminary Estimates," what was it doing right there on
top? He had thrust it carefully underneath all the rest before he
left the house. His dealings with Fred Small were still in a shaky
state, and there was a tricky question about ownership. It was
too soon to go public.

Could Eddy have been messing around with his papers? No,
surely it wasn't Eddy. Charlene? Roberta? Not very likely. Gast

stood up and looked doubtfully out the window, as though an interfering marauder might be visible below.

ℒ

> *Fee, fi, fo, fum!*
> *I smell the blood of an Englishman;*
> *Be he alive or be he dead,*
> *I'll grind his bones to make my bread.*
>
> English nursery rhyme

Chapter 18

❧

*When he had crossed the water he found the entrance to Hell. It was
black and sooty within, and the Devil was not at home. . . .*
The Brothers Grimm,
"The Devil with the Three Golden Hairs"

"Sergeant? Is that you?"
"Professor Kelly?"

"Listen, I thought I'd head out your way and drop in on Fred
Small. Want to join me? And please call me Homer, for heaven's
sake."

"Well, all right, Homer. And my name's Bill. Sorry I can't join
you, I'm on traffic duty all day. Besides, Small would slam the
door in my face."

"Okay. I'll just barge in, the innocent bystander. All he can do
is throw me out. Where does he live, exactly?"

Kennebunk told him, but when Homer got to Southtown he
lost his way. *Out the Pig Road,* Kennebunk had said. Then he
had corrected himself, *Oh, no, it's Skylark now,* or something like
that. Homer drove around aimlessly, hoping to run into Skylark
Road.

Southtown was a village of annihilated farms turned into
housing tracts and shopping malls. After driving for miles down
a country lane lined with houses built in the 1950s, modest one-
storied cottages with big triangular gables, Homer stopped to
ask directions from a man who was washing his car.

"Skylark? Never heard of it." The guy lowered his hose and
the water ran out on the driveway. "Sorry."

"Thanks anyway." Homer turned his car around and went

back the way he had come. At a crossroads he took a right, just for the heck of it. At once he saw a carved sign, "Meadowlark Estates." Wasn't that what Kennebunk had said?

There were gateposts at the entrance to Meadowlark Estates, surrounded by dwarf Alberta spruce trees, Blue Rug junipers, and daffodils. The daffodils spoke up at once and addressed Homer sternly. *This is a pretty classy place. Are you sure you measure up?*

I'm afraid not, mumbled Homer, glancing nervously at the miniature castle behind the daffodils. It was a guardhouse. Like the daffodils, it asked a nosy question: *Do you have any legitimate business here, my friend? Are you acquainted with any of these important people?*

Homer rehearsed an answer in his head. *Can you tell me which house belongs to Mr. Frederick Small?*

But there was no one in the guardhouse. How lax, thought Homer, how careless. In the absence of the palace guard, anybody might walk in off the street, just anybody. An outside agitator like himself, for instance.

Homer grinned and drove slowly along the curving drive, examining the splendid houses left and right. The place was a jumble. There were fairy castles straight from Disneyland, French châteaux, and Grecian temples. Medieval crenellated towers and half-timbered Elizabethan mansions were cheek by jowl with Corinthian peristyles and Italianate balustrades. Homer thought about the abundant gushes of cash that had resulted in the building of these dream homes. He imagined husbands saying to their wives, "Honey, the sky's the limit, let your imagination soar." And the wives had answered quick as a flash, because they knew exactly what they wanted, they'd been dreaming about it for years, "Marble foyer, curving staircase, gold fixtures in the powder room." Were they happy now, the wives? Did they wake up joyfully every morning and leap out of bed with glad cries, or did they suffer from the ordinary anxieties of the rest of humankind? Did their husbands run around with other women, did their children flunk out of school?

Homer drove on, looking for a human being who could direct him to the house of Frederick Small. At the end of Meadowlark Drive, circling past an Ionic temple with a cupola on top, he was surprised to see a blot on the landscape. Behind the temple rose a rusty tower, a contraption of crumbling chutes and ladders. Surely this was not part of Meadowlark Estates? No, it was some sort of rattling, clanking commercial enterprise. Homer guessed at once what it was, the sand-and-gravel company belonging to Frederick Small.

His house must be here somewhere. Homer drove on, looking for someone to talk to. But the massive houses were blank, and the shades of the windows were pulled down. No children played on the faultless grass, no father washed his car, no dog barked. The houses looked abandoned, like monuments in the desert.

But not utterly abandoned. Homer put his foot on the brake and stopped his car. The garage door of one of the fairy castles was rising without the aid of human hands. A car backed out silently, a low sports car with swollen fenders.

Homer jumped out and hailed the driver, a faceless dark shape behind the tinted windows, but the car continued to back up, swerving out into the street, ready to take off. Homer ran in front of it, waving his arms.

Reluctantly the driver stopped. A window rolled down. A white male face in black goggles looked out at him and said, "How did you get past the gate?"

Oh, what a courteous welcome! What a hospitable reception to the stranger from afar! Homer bent down to the window and explained that he was looking for Frederick Small.

"Christ," said Black Goggles. "I hope you're an interested buyer."

"No, no, just an interested party." Homer glanced at the huge blocky houses up and down the street. "He's selling his place? Does he live around here?"

"Oh, God, no, he's on the Pig Road." Black Goggles wagged his head to the left. "Oughta be condemned. Here we are in these executive estates, gated properties, paying a lousy fortune in taxes, while he's got this phony agricultural assessment and pays zilch. Farmland, bullshit! And that fucking sand-and-gravel company, that's his too." Black Goggles jerked his head in the direction of the rusty towers. "Jesus, he swore it'd be gone by New Year's Day. You tell him we're gonna sue."

Magically the window beside Black Goggles moved upward. The sleek hips of the car silked past Homer. Gathering speed, it zoomed out of sight.

Chapter 19

∾

There was once a man who had beautiful houses in the city and in the country . . . But, unfortunately, he had a blue beard.

Charles Perrault, "Bluebeard"

Homer was still looking for Fred Small. As he drove out of the gated community called Meadowlark, he reflected on Small's name. It had the sound of one of those modest little men who are actually homicidal psychopaths. Hadn't there been a notorious Dr. Small who had poisoned his wife with potassium cyanide, prescribing it for gastric distress? And wasn't there another Small in Maine who had strangled his wife, set fire to the house, and gone off for a jolly weekend in the city? Only, unfortunately, his wife's body had fallen through the floor into the basement, where the local sheriff observed the cord around its neck? Maybe Fred was yet another homicidal wife-killing Small.

The next driveway was heralded by another impressive sign, "Songsparrow Estates." That was it. Kennebunk had not said Skylark or Meadowlark, he had said Songsparrow.

This driveway was unpaved. There were no gateposts and no daffodils, and the only house in sight was a dark little bungalow.

Homer pulled to the side and stared at the sign. Black Goggles had said nothing about Songsparrow Estates. He had called it the Pig Road. Then Homer discovered another sign on a tall metal pole, an official green highway sign. He squinted at it. The name had been smeared with mud, but the shapes of the letters were clear in the slanting light of afternoon: "Pig Road."

What did it mean, two signs with different names for the

same road? Pride, that was what it meant. "Pig Road" sounded agricultural and foul-smelling. One's nose wrinkled with distaste. Whereas there was a sweetly spiritual ring to "Songsparrow," shamelessly imitating the musical overtones of "Meadowlark" next door.

Homer parked beside the bungalow, got out of his car, and approached the front porch. The air had a high thin sound, as of birds chirping far away. Round leaves on a bush dangled and trembled. Directly in his path a crow flapped up from some dead creature, a field mouse or a shrew.

Climbing the porch steps, Homer told himself that of course he should have written an introductory letter, asking for an appointment. But it was not in Homer's nature to make appointments. He never called ahead or wrote a letter, he just blundered in. It was partly laziness, partly his habit of making impulsive decisions, and partly his belief in surprise, giving his quarry no time to clean up, to shove the body under the bed and wash the bloody knife and put the kettle on for tea.

He pushed the bell. It failed to ring. No one came to the door. He knocked loudly. Again there was no response, but as he turned away, the door opened softly behind him.

"Oh, good afternoon," said Homer, feeling like a Fuller brush salesman, "my name's Kelly. I'm looking for Mr. Small."

"I am Frederick Small." The man at the door was not built like his name. He was tall and broad-shouldered. The hands that hung from the sleeves of his sweater were like cabbages. Only his head was small, as though borrowed from the body of some undersized person. He sported a toothbrush mustache and a neat little beard. Behind his glasses his eyes were large and lustrous, like a rabbit's. "Are you here about real estate?" asked Frederick Small.

Of course Homer was here about real estate. "I understand you have land for sale. I'm—uh—looking for a lot. My wife and I—"

"Sorry," said Frederick Small. "The entire estate is—uh—subject to a purchase-and-sale agreement, to be signed in the very near future." But he backed up and held the door open.

The entrance hall was narrow and dark. The pictures on the wall were nearly invisible. Small's glittering glasses floated in the dark.

"I thought," lied Homer, making a frolicsome leap into the unknown, "there was some question about the title?"

"Who told you that?" said Small sharply.

"Can't remember," said Homer glibly. "Heard it somewhere."

"Well, there isn't." Small led the way into a narrow living room. At once a memory of the past welled up around Homer, because an old building was like a time machine. This one evoked memories of the 1920s. Not the fashionable decade of cloche hats and short skirts and cigarettes in long holders, but the one that appeared in old photographs—rooms crowded with brown furniture, women with odd haircuts sitting on porch swings, radios with matching veneer and lighted dials, chairs upholstered in brown plush. Some of Homer's aunts and uncles had lived in houses like this. They had sat in the dim light under sepia reproductions of *The Light of the World* and *Sir Galahad*, rooms in which the only spot of color was the Sacred Heart.

There was no Sacred Heart hanging on the walls of this room; in fact, the pictures—Homer turned his head from one to another—were quite extraordinary. He moved to look at one of them more closely, but Small was unrolling a map, spreading it out on a table, holding down the corners with a lamp, a couple of ashtrays, and a paperweight.

"What exactly are you looking for? The lots will not be available until the—uh—effectuation of the agreement with the developer. This is the plot plan of my—I mean *our* land."

Homer pounced on Small's slip of the tongue. At once he asked a nosy question. "You live here alone?"

"Yes," said Small, then, quickly, "No." His soft eyes blinked. "My wife's away."

"I see." Homer wanted to explore the house and find the room in which Bluebeard stored the bodies of his murdered wives—hadn't he been widowed several times? But Small was pointing to the map, running his finger around the pink area of Meadowlark Estates, spreading a proud hand over the broad rectangle of Songsparrow. "Ninety-nine acres, sixty-five lots accepted by the planning board."

"How much per lot?"

"Well, of course, that depends on the lot in question. Some are more desirable than others."

"But the average price might be—?"

"Oh, say, two hundred and fifty, three hundred."

"You mean three hundred thousand? Three hundred thousand dollars for a lot?"

"Yes, I'd say that was about average." Small had a way of looking around the room as he talked, frowning at the backs of chairs and the glass knobs of doors.

Homer trailed his finger over the map and stopped at the lot farthest from the highway. "How much is this one?"

"Oh, well, that's a very choice lot, looking out over the pond. I'd say four hundred for that one."

"Might I see it?"

Small looked surprised. "Well, I guess so. I don't see why not."

❧

The landscape of Songsparrow Estates was a monoculture of burdock. This year's growth was green and flowering, last year's bristled with burrs, which caught in the fabric of Homer's coat. Small evergreens emerged from the burdock, just visible above the prickly surface. "You planted those?" said Homer, pointing to a cluster of infant white pines.

"My wife—" began Small, then stopped and said feebly, "That's right."

"Ouch," said Homer, tripping over a lump of brick. He rubbed his shin and looked down at a low structure almost hidden by burdock.

"Feeding platform," explained Small. "This used to be a pig farm."

"Ah," said Homer, the light dawning. "Of course." He gazed around, imagining the landscape teeming with pigs. "How many did they have?"

There was a pause, as if Small were weighing the question, considering his answer carefully. "Oh, thousands, I think. They were long gone when my wife—when we came into possession of the property."

"Was the other place here then?" asked Homer inquisitively. "Meadowlark Estates?"

Again there was a wary pause. Then Small said, "No, Meadowlark is only about five years old."

"So, when your wife—when *you* got hold of this place, the whole area around here was rural? Aren't you sorry to see what's happened to it?"

"Sorry! Oh, no!" Small looked shocked. "Property values, they've gone way up." Instantly regretting this remark, he looked sidelong at Homer and took it back. "That is, the land is worth a little more. Individual parcels have more value."

"You're still classed as agricultural, is that right? So your town taxes are way down? Even though the pigs aren't here anymore?"

Small turned his flashing glasses on Homer. "Of course we're agricultural." He waved at the trees springing up through the burdock. "It's a tree farm. And I'm negotiating with a riding stable to pasture horses."

"Oh, do horses eat burdock?" said Homer innocently.

Small ignored the question. He turned away and waved an

arm. "This is the parcel you were talking about, from here to that line of trees."

"Ah, yes, with a view of the pond." Beyond the trees the sky opened up and the rusty towers of the sand-and-gravel company loomed beyond a chain-link fence. Homer went to the fence and looked down into the pit below. At the bottom there was a muddy pond between two huge heaps of gravel.

"Of course this operation is being closed down," explained Small, hurrying up beside him. Impulsively, as though it had just occurred to him, he said, "I'm going to dam it up. It will be, you know, like a lake."

Homer had had enough of Frederick Small and his grandiose plans for upmarket real estate. "Well, thank you, Mr. Small," he said, turning away. "Goodbye. I'll tell my wife all about it." Then Homer took his leave, hurrying back along the Pig Road ahead of Small.

As he got into his car the crow rose again from the ugly little cadaver on the rutted drive beside Small's house, and Homer remembered a story about twelve princes who had been transformed into ravens. Was this crow one of the brothers? Where was its sister, the princess, who was destined to restore it to its princely human form?

It was dark as Homer made the turn onto Route 2 on the way home. High in the sky to the west, he recognized a familiar star. *ARCTURUS SPEAKING—INHABITANTS OF EASTERN MASSACHUSETTS ARE KINDLY REQUESTED TO TAKE NOTE.*

Homer, to whom celestial objects often addressed remarks, was glad to see Arcturus again. Its appearance in the sky meant that spring was here.

He had been oppressed all afternoon by the tawdry aura of Southtown. In the presence of Arcturus his depression dissipated and blew away.

Chapter 20

❧

When Minnie Peck arrived with the colossal sculpture she called *Millennial Woman*, Annie was beginning to work on the third division of her wall. It was more wonderful every day, the wall, with its wild juxtapositions and crazy clots of unity.

She had forgotten all about Minnie Peck. But suddenly there she was, rolling up in a Rent-a-Truck. Bouncing out of the front seat, she hailed Flimnap O'Dougherty, who was doing something to a bush. Two heavyset Rent-a-Guys began undoing the ropes securing a large cloth-covered object in the back of the truck.

"Where do you want it?" said one of the guys, getting a grip on one end, looking over his shoulder at Minnie.

"Wait a sec." Minnie raced back and forth in Annie's front yard, looking around. "Not here—not here—what about here? No, that won't do. Ah, wait a minute, let's try it over here. Yes, this looks good. It was destined to be here from the beginning of time."

It was smack in front of Annie's new south windows. Flimnap pocketed his clippers, ambled across the grass, and tapped on the glass door.

"No," said Annie, coming outside, taking in everything—Minnie, the two guys, the giant cloth-covered object sailing forward in their arms, clanking and rattling. "Stop! Minnie, I don't want it. Take it back."

"No, wait," cried Minnie. "You've got to see it in place." She twitched at the cloth wrapping and it fell away.

The metal woman was twelve feet tall. She was entirely made of hubcaps. The concept was good, but the execution was faulty. *Millennial Woman* was a mess. Her iron armature

was a tangle of welded blobs. Her hubcaps dangled on short lengths of rusty wire.

"Please, Minnie, I don't want anything on the grass. Nothing at all. I'm sorry, but you've got to take it away."

Minnie laughed merrily. "No, no, you just need to get used to it. It has to settle in. You'll see. Later on we'll decide on a price, but not now. No obligation, honest." She scuttled away.

The Rent-a-Guys exchanged looks and glanced at Annie. Her mouth was open, but she was speechless. They shrugged, stumped off after Minnie, helped her into the truck, and disappeared.

Flimnap laughed. "Don't worry. I'll drag it over there, behind the compost heap. Maybe the woodchucks will appreciate it." He reached up and grabbed *Millennial Woman* under her iron arms. "Nothing to it. Come on, girl."

Annie watched him move backward in the direction of the wilderness, where orange peels and grass clippings were rotting into compost, and piles of pruned-off water sprouts lay in a twiggy mass. She told herself the truth, that the presence of Flimnap O'Dougherty was the overwhelming fact of her life.

It wasn't that he was bossy. No one could be more self-effacing. It was as though he exuded a vapor she couldn't help inhaling, some sort of airy potion that filled the inner spaces of her house, a delicate secretion that stuck to chairs and tables and clung to Annie's nose and hair. Once again she played with the fancy that he was an emanation of her painted wall, while she, Annie, went back and forth between her playful images and the grubby facts of the real world—her overdue bills, her parking ticket, her occasional indulgence in booze. Annie winced, remembering last week's embarrassing dinner in honor of a big important librarian, when she had drunk too much wine. When they had asked her for a few words, she had sprung up and talked too fast and giggled too much at her own jokes and sat down suddenly, nearly falling off her chair.

Of course Flimnap too had to navigate among the lumpy facts of commonplace life. He managed it very well, better than Annie. He could fix anything, make anything, do anything. And yet the Hitchcock chair he had repaired for Annie, gluing the rungs fast in their holes, now had a Flimnappian air. She liked to sit in it, as though his influence might flow up and saturate her soul.

Their relation as employer and employee had changed. Flimnap had begun to make up his own tasks, deciding for himself what needed to be done. Were they friends now, equals, partners? More than friends? Perhaps Flimnap didn't really like her at all. She was eager to know what he thought of her, but there was some sort of gap between them. Something was wrong. Flimnap was like a puzzle with a missing piece. And in his case the piece was crucial. Without it the rest of the linked pieces didn't hang together.

So things were on hold. Annie had become shy about looking at Flimnap directly. His light eyes seemed focused on things far away. Like her wall, he was a story without an end, like the enfolded tales of *The Arabian Nights*, told by Scheherazade to the heartless sultan. If Scheherazade were ever to complete the last of her stories, if her imagination ever faltered, she would lose her head. What was Flimnap's last chapter? Who was waiting for him with a headsman's ax?

❧

Praise be to God . . . whose purposes concerning me are as yet hid in darkness.   The Thousand and One Nights

Chapter 21

❧

The Gasts were having a party. All their friends came. Annie was invited, Flimnap wasn't.

They had put up a fence between the two front yards. Annie walked through the gate and joined the party. It was a lovely April afternoon, as warm as a day in June, and everyone had drifted outside. Charlene carried around a tray of snacks. Some of her friends from school helped with the trays, and then they all gathered in Charlene's room, and admired her princess doll and her swimming trophies and giggled and bounced on her bed.

A teenage babysitter had been provided for Eddy, but just when the talk and laughter were at their height, he appeared in the middle of the party, gaping up at the guests and clutching the front of his pants, which were wet. The teenager was indoors, helping herself to a glass of wine.

Roberta grasped Eddy by the collar, found the babysitter, hissed at her, and removed the two of them to the upper regions.

The party wound down and the guests departed. Annie went home, feeling sorry for Eddy. But as soon as she walked into her part of the house, she forgot about Eddy Gast. There was another unwanted face on her wall. Once again it was ugly and demonic. The eyes were fiercer than before, and the blue beard was matted with blood.

Annie stared at it, shocked and frightened. Who was doing this to her, who was invading her wall, disturbing her jolly visions of children's stories? Who else could it possibly be but Flimnap? Surely it was Flimnap O'Dougherty! Flimnap had a key to her house, he could walk on his hands and juggle six balls at once and keep three plates in the air (but not four). He could throw his hat in the air so cleverly that it came down on his head. Flimnap could do anything!

No, not quite anything, remembered Annie, exonerating him once again. It couldn't be Flimnap, because he couldn't draw at all. He couldn't draw, he couldn't write, he couldn't even make a diagram. He had no use for pencil and paper. It was one of the missing pieces in the puzzle that was Flimnap O'Dougherty.

This time Annie got rid of the ugly face herself, brushing over it a coat of quick-drying varnish and a layer of ocher-colored paint. As the staring black-ringed eyes disappeared, she heard a whimpering from next door. Through the open windows came the sound of crying and raised voices.

Eddy was being punished. Poor Eddy!

❧

The poor kid was certainly accident-prone. On the very day after the party, he had another misfortune on the highway. The door of his father's car flew open and Eddy tumbled out. Somehow the traffic behind the car missed him as he rolled over and over and sat up, dazed and bruised, in the middle of the road.

"You mean to say he wasn't strapped in?" said a self-righteous woman in the next car, stopping to criticize. "I think that's absolutely criminal."

Poor old Eddy! When he next came to Annie's door there was a purple lump on his forehead. But he was beaming. "Whassat?" he said, staring up at the wall, pointing at the mouse in Beatrix Potter's pocket and the rabbits at her feet. Annie explained about Peter Rabbit and his invasion of Mr. McGregor's garden. She found her copy of the story and showed it to Eddy. Then she gave him a sheet of her best paper and a collection of colored pens, and climbed her ladder and got back to work. Below her at the table Eddy's small head was lowered over his paper. A bright-green pad was clutched in his hand.

This time his picture took only half an hour. "All done!" cried Eddy, holding the picture over his head.

Annie came down the ladder to look. It was Peter Rabbit. His ears glowed pink, his jacket reflected the blue of the sky, and Mr. McGregor's garden was a corner of Paradise. "Oh, Eddy," breathed Annie, delighted once again, "how wonderful."

When Flimnap came in, he admired it too. "I like your pictures, Eddy," he said, lifting him onto his shoulders. "Come on. I want to show you something." Annie watched them swoop together out the door. Soon there were squeals of joy from the driveway. She looked out and laughed. Flimnap was still carrying Eddy on his shoulders, but now he was riding a unicycle. Around and around they went, Eddy whirling high in the air, shrieking with delight.

Roberta Gast witnessed this episode, coming unexpectedly out of the house. She stared, blank-faced, until Flimnap lowered Eddy to the ground and jumped down from the bike himself, grinning at her sheepishly. Roberta turned away without a word, climbed into her car, and sat behind the wheel for a moment, looking down. *She's making a note,* decided Annie. *Date, time, witnesses present.*

❧

That evening as they got ready for bed, Roberta and Bob Gast had another conversation about Eddy. Roberta stood in the bathroom doorway in her nightgown, watching her husband brush his teeth. "It's no good," she said. "Nothing works."

Bob spat and hung up his toothbrush. "What do you mean, nothing works?"

"You know what I mean."

"Oh, that," said Bob uncomfortably. He slicked back his hair with a comb.

Roberta changed the subject. She sounded shocked. "You know what, Bob Gast? You're getting bald."

"Oh, I know," said Bob. "Don't you think I know?" Because of course it was true. If he had taken the trouble to count them, the separate strands above his high receding hairline would have numbered only one or two thousand. They had once been a thick bushy mass. Embarrassed, he rubbed the shiny place in the middle of his scalp, which was growing larger and larger. *Rub, rub, rub. Oh, genie of the magic scalp, make my hair grow in again!*

Roberta watched him put the cap back on the toothpaste. At once she was struck by an idea. She waited until he was finished in the bathroom, and then she got to work right away.

She did not look at herself in the mirror, knowing she wouldn't like what she saw, a tired woman with pouches under her eyes. Instead she opened the door of the cupboard under the sink and took out a little piece of cardboard, handling it with care. On it lay a viscous drop of liquid. It was ant poison. Ants had become a problem on the kitchen counter and the bathroom sink. This nasty stuff seemed to do the trick. The ants were in retreat.

With delicate fingers Roberta put the square of poison down behind the cold-water faucet. Still more carefully she took a small toothbrush from the holder on the wall and laid it bristle side down in the drop of liquid, as though it had fallen there by accident. Then she washed her hands and went to bed.

She lay awake most of the night, staring at the shadowy ceiling. In the morning, just after she fell asleep at last, there was a shout from the bathroom, "What the hell?"

Roberta woke up instantly and opened her eyes. In a moment her enraged husband stood beside the bed looking down at her. "Eddy's toothbrush, it was in the ant poison!"

She sat up and said feebly, "Oh dear, it must have fallen in.

The ants were all over the sink, so I—" She didn't finish. She put her legs over the side of the bed and stood up.

Bob stared at her. Then he said roughly, "God," and went back to the bathroom. He wrapped the sticky toothbrush in toilet paper and threw it in the wastebasket, along with the square of ant poison. Then he scrubbed the sink with cleanser and washed his hands thoroughly, over and over again, his mind in a torment. An unlatched car door, a touch of ant poison, what was the difference? None, there was no difference at all. He shouldn't blame Roberta any more than he blamed himself.

❧

My mother she killed me,
My father he ate me,
. . . what a beautiful bird am I!
The Brothers Grimm, "The Juniper Tree"

Chapter 22

❧

At Weston Country Day the girls in the fifth grade were studying the Greek myths. Mary had written a play about Pandora's box. Amelia Patterson was Pandora and Becca Smith was Prometheus. Everybody else was an evil spirit released from the box by Pandora.

The first rehearsal in the auditorium was noisy and successful. The evil spirits threw themselves into it. Mary laughed and stood back while they hopped and howled. "Good, good. Now, why don't you run off the stage and make faces at the kids in the audience? That's right, Carrie. Good, Julie. Good, good, Beverly. Oh, Mrs. Rutledge, welcome. I'm sorry, are we making too much noise?"

"No, no." Mrs. Rutledge clapped her hands. "Sorry, you people. Charlene has just come in late and told us she won that big swimming meet last night in Danvers. We want to congratulate her in front of the whole school."

It was an impromptu assembly. All the classes poured into the auditorium. The headmistress told her news, and everyone applauded. Then Mrs. Rutledge called Charlene to the stage and congratulated her. Mr. Orth, the athletic coach, presented her with a bouquet. Charlene thanked him prettily and said, "I hope everybody will come to the swimming meet at Harvard next Friday night. It's the semifinals."

Mary sat in the back of the auditorium and clapped along with everybody else. She was interested in the way everyone in the school admired Charlene Gast. Already she was beginning to get a sense of the ruthlessness of ten-year-old tribal structure. It occurred to her that if all the fifth-graders in the school were to fill out a questionnaire ranking their classmates in order of popularity, Charlene Gast would come out on top. Even the outcasts would list her as number one. Even fat little Cissie Aufsesser.

The hierarchy was painfully visible on the playground. Young as she was, Charlene had perfected a system of total domination. She bound the others to her one at a time. She would take Becca aside and giggle with her and whisper in her ear. Next day Becca would be out and Carrie was the favorite. Then Carrie was forgotten and it was Joanna's turn. In the on-going drama of the spring semester in Mrs. Rutledge's fifth grade, hearts were broken, mended, and broken again, as Charlene tossed her favors this way and that.

On the day when it was Beverly Eckstein's turn, Mary was monitoring the playground. She saw Charlene approach Beverly with a beaming smile, she saw Beverly's joyful surprise. She watched as Charlene admired Beverly's new bike, and ran her hand over the narrow blue fender that sparkled with flecks of gold. She saw Charlene take something out of her jacket. She saw Beverly start with surprise. But she couldn't hear what they were saying.

The magazine was Beverly's. She had found it under her big brother's bed. It showed two naked women and a naked man intertwined like snakes. Charlene had discovered it in Beverly's desk, hidden under her English workbook.

"I'm going to tell on you," said Charlene.

Beverly's homely round face flushed purple. Tears ran down her cheeks. "No, no, oh, please, please. Oh, Charlene, please."

"Give me your bike, then, or I'll tell."

Beverly couldn't believe it. She clutched the handlebars. "Oh, I can't, Charlene. I just can't."

"Okay, then. I'll tell."

When the recess break was over, Beverly hurried back indoors ahead of everyone else. Mrs. Kelly spoke to her as she trotted past with a tear-streaked face. "Are you all right, Beverly?"

Beverly nodded, not trusting herself to speak. Inside the school, she ran down the basement steps to the building superintendent's office, next to the furnace. The room smelled of tuna fish and orange peel. It was dark in there, but Beverly did not switch on the light. For five minutes in the dim windowless room she tore out the pages of the dirty magazine one by one, wadded them up, and stuffed them in the big plastic waste barrel. Then she stirred the contents with both hands until the crumpled pages were thoroughly mixed up with greasy paper towels, dusty cleaning rags, used-up workbooks, and the remains of a hundred paper-bag lunches. Her bicycle was gone, but so was the magazine.

❧

"Why, Charlene," said Roberta Gast, "where did you get that beautiful bike?"

"Beverly gave it to me," said Charlene. "She got a new one for her birthday, so she gave me her old one. You know, because I won the swimming meet."

Roberta looked at the bike. "She got a new one? But this one looks perfectly new."

"No, no." Charlene pointed to a slight dent in the front fender. "See, it's old, really old."

Eddy was excited by Charlene's new bike. He made enthusiastic noises and tried to grab the handlebars.

Charlene jerked it out of his grasp. "Get away, dummy." She glowered at her mother. "If he so much as touches this bike, I'll murder him. I mean it."

❧

"Beverly," said her mother, "why did you come home on the school bus? I thought you were going to ride your bike to school from now on."

"I had this flat tire," said Beverly in a small voice.

"A flat tire already? Well, then, jump in the car. We'll pick up your bike so Daddy can fix it."

"No, no, Mummy. It's—it's in the gym, and everything's all locked up by now."

"Well, tomorrow, then."

After a miserable night, Beverly confessed that her bike was gone. "This big boy, he came to the playground and grabbed it and took it away."

"He stole your bike? A girl's bike?"

"Right. Like maybe he had a sister or something."

"What did he look like? We'll call the police."

So Beverly had to go on telling lie after lie. At school there were more lies. "Isn't that your bike Charlene's got?" said Becca. "It looks just like it."

"No, no, it's not my bike. I—uh—gave mine to my cousin. Didn't I, Charlene?"

"That's right," said Charlene, smiling sweetly at Becca.

ॐ

"Lord Fish, Lord Fish!" cried the fisherman, rowing in a circle, looking up anxiously at the dark clouds gathering in the sky.

The great fish appeared above the slowly heaving sea, and whispered, "Here I am."

"Oh, Lord Fish, forgive me, but my wife would like to ride in a golden chariot drawn by six white horses."

"It shall be as she wishes," murmured the fish. Leaping in a great arc out of the water, he plunged back into the deep.

Chapter 23

❧

"My grandmother, what big ears you have!"
"The better to hear you, my child!"
Charles Perrault, "Little Red Riding Hood"

"Listen," said Fred Small, "some guy was here the other day, wanted to look at a lot. I took him all the way to the end of the property, he said he'd talk to his wife."

"Did you get his name?" said Bob Gast. "When the deal goes through we'll send him a brochure."

"Kelly, I think. Homer Kelly."

"Homer Kelly! No kidding? Hey, he's my landlady's uncle. Big professor. Listen, when's Pearl coming back? Where is she? She's got to sign on the dotted line, or we can't get going. I mean, my expenses are colossal. You wouldn't believe—"

"Don't get so upset. She'll sign. I—uh—had a postcard yesterday."

"Where from? Where is she?"

"Albany, big hotel in Albany."

"Albany? I'll bet she's at the Regency, right?"

"I don't remember. I handed it over to McNutt. He's got those gossip columnists on his tail. You know, MISSING WOMAN WAS BATTERED WIFE. This'll shut 'em up."

"Well, great. Good for you, Fred."

❧

"Professor Kelly?" The voice on the line sounded familiar.

"Sergeant Kennebunk? Hey, how are you? Have you got the chief's job yet?"

Kennebunk cleared his throat. "Professor Kelly, Chief Mc-Nutt would like to speak to you."

"His Honor, Rollo McNutt, he's right there?" Homer made a derisive blubbering noise. "Well, okay, put him on."

There was a pause. Homer could hear a muffled explosion from McNutt and an apologetic mutter from Kennebunk. Then McNutt spoke fiercely into the phone. "Listen, Kelly, I got news for you. Mrs. Small, she's in Albany. Her husband got a post-card. You want I should read it to you?"

"Well, okay, go ahead."

McNutt read the postcard in a horrible falsetto.

> Dear Fred, this is a luxury hotel
> in the heart of downtown Albany,
> with 229 rooms, a London pub,
> a French cafe, a hairdressing salon,
> and an indoor pool. I'm exploring
> the fashionable shops located
> in the lobby. Love, Pearl.

Homer couldn't believe his ears. "Hold on. Just read that again."

McNutt harrumphed, then read it again very fast, in his own voice this time. "So you see, pal," he said, coming down heavily on the word "pal," "the woman is not missing, she's on a shopping spree in Albany. Kindly get lost."

There was a savage crash in Homer's ear. Wincing, he stared at the phone, then called back the police department in Southtown.

"Sergeant Kennebunk? Is McNutt still there?"

"No," said Kennebunk softly, "he's in his office."

"Well, listen, did you see that postcard? Is it the real thing? Was it canceled by the post office in Albany?"

"Oh, sure, it came from Albany, all right. There's a picture of the Regency Hotel on the other side."

"Tell me, Sergeant, did you ever hear anything so phony in all your life?"

Kennebunk snickered. "It sounded to me like a promotional pamphlet."

"Exactly." Homer gripped the phone and gazed out the window at the opposite shore of Fair Haven Bay, hazy now with pale-green budding leaves and a mist rising from the river. "Easy enough to check. We could call the hotel, find out if she's registered as a guest."

"Great, I'll take care of it." Then Kennebunk raised his voice. "Yes, ma'am, of course we'll look into your missing cat. I'll talk to the dog officer. She also handles cats."

"Thanks, Sergeant," whispered Homer, and put down the phone.

Chapter 24

❧

. . . the Dodo suddenly called out "The race is over!"
and they all crowded round it, panting,
and asking "But who has won?"

Lewis Carroll, Alice's Adventures in Wonderland

Charlene won in her age group at the New England Senior Swimming Championships at Harvard's Blodgett Pool. Most of the kids in her homeroom at Weston Country Day were there to watch her compete.

Mary went along to swell the participation of the school in support of its star athlete. Besides, she was still taking an interest in the sociopathology of the fifth-grade class in which Charlene had become so powerful.

Mary had taught at Harvard for ten years in a joint professorship with Homer, but she had never been to Blodgett Pool. She edged along one of the steep rows of seats in the bleachers, which were crowded with the families of the contestants. Sitting down, she tried to take it all in.

It was an unfamiliar world. Below her the pool was big and blue, its surrounding apron alive with adolescent contestants, slim girls in one-piece bathing suits, gangly bare-chested boys. Deafening music roared from the loudspeakers. For an hour the rows of patient parents watched their children practice in the roped-off lanes. The swimmers were slender fishes speeding underwater, surfacing to race for the turn and go bottoms-up, then pushing off again with strong thrusts of their feet against the wall.

"Hi, Mrs. Kelly." A procession of excited girls crowded in

beside her and sat down, pulling off jackets and scarves and craning their necks to look for Charlene. Were they too late? Had they missed her event?

No, they were just in time. There were squeals. "There she is!" "Charlene," screamed Alice Mooney, who had lost her doll to Charlene. "Charlene," screamed Beverly Eckstein, whose bicycle had mysteriously become Charlene's. "Charlene," screamed Cissie Aufsesser and Wilma Brownhill, to whom Charlene had never said a friendly word. "Charlene, Charlene," screamed Becca and Joanna and Carrie and all the rest.

Charlene looked up and smiled her queenly smile. She was standing with her competitors behind a row of low diving platforms along one side of the pool. The other girls had narrow waists, plump breasts and thighs. Charlene was still a skinny little kid.

The music stopped. The loudspeaker grated and scratched. "At this time," boomed the master of ceremonies, "please rise for our national anthem." At once everyone stood up. The young swimmers turned to face the flag hanging over the pool, and a hoarse recorded version of "The Star-Spangled Banner" bounced off the walls. When it ground to a stop, the voice roared again, "EVENT NUMBER THIRTEEN, THE WOMEN'S TWO-HUNDRED-YARD INDIVIDUAL MEDLEY."

Charlene's classmates clutched each other as she mounted her low diving block. There were eight contestants along the edge of the pool, waiting for the signal, nervously adjusting swimming caps and goggles, pulling at their suits, waggling their arms to loosen muscles.

The whistle blew. At once the eight girls bent over, ready to dive, and then, at the sound of a horn, they plunged into the water.

Charlene was in lane four. "Go, go, Charlene," screamed all the girls from Weston Country Day. Mary screamed too, "Go, Charlene, go!"

Charlene needed no urging. She was ahead of the pack from the beginning.

"What are they doing?" shrieked Mary to the woman sitting in front of her, as the eight girls rose and fell across the twenty-five-foot width of the pool. "The butterfly," shouted the woman. "Go, Debbie, go!"

There was no contest. Charlene's butterfly stroke was no more graceful than the rest, but it was faster. Her backstroke carried her yards ahead of her nearest competitor. With her breast stroke she was far in the lead, and in the beautiful stroke called "freestyle" she flew to victory. "CHARLENE GAST, THE YOUNGEST COMPETITOR, WINS WITH A TIME OF TWO-ONE-FORTY."

Mary stayed to watch Charlene receive her award. The eight girls had changed to sweat suits. They stood on a pyramid of boxes. It was just like the Olympics. Charlene stood at the top to accept her medal, while her classmates screamed her name, and screamed it again.

Mary applauded politely, then stood up to go. She brushed past the knees of Charlene's fifth-grade fans, smiling at them, saying goodbye. Looking back, she saw Roberta and Bob Gast way down in front, cheering their daughter. Eddy was not there.

❧

Annie woke up. Across the room the TV was noisy with excited music. A cheetah in a final burst of speed reached its prey. Cymbals clashed, the rhebok was dragged down. Annie hated wildlife shows. She clicked the remote control, put out her hand for the lamp switch, and gave a small shriek. There was a face at the window.

Oh, God, it was Eddy. What was he doing, wandering around in the dark?

She unfastened the screen and lifted him inside. "Eddy, what are you doing? Why aren't you in bed?"

There were tears on Eddy's cheeks, but he smiled at her, and gave her a rumpled piece of paper. It was a drawing of the emperor's nightingale. Annie had read him the Andersen story. Eddy's mechanical bird was a miracle of jewels and interlocking gears, while his live bird sang in the background with open beak. "For you," said Eddy.

"Oh, Eddy, thank you, it's beautiful. Come on, now, I'll take you home. Your mother will wonder where on earth you are."

The front door of Eddy's house was wide open, the way he had left it. No one was at home. There were no cars in the driveway.

What should she do? She could send him back upstairs to bed, but that would mean leaving him alone. She could take him back to her house and put him down on the couch and leave a note for the Gasts to explain where he was, but it would look like a criticism. Well, goddamnit, they deserved it. They might be indulgent parents for their talented daughter Charlene, but they were rotten caretakers for their retarded son Eddy.

Her dilemma was solved by the return of the Gasts. They came rocketing up the driveway in two cars. Charlene bounced out of the Bronco and ran past Eddy and Annie. At once there was a blare of noise from inside the house.

"It's the news," explained Roberta, hurrying in after her. "She's on the news."

"Charlene won," cried Bob, slamming his car door. "The youngest kid there, and she broke the record."

Annie stood in his way. "Here's Eddy," she said loudly. "He was wandering around outside."

"Oh, thanks," said Bob. He took Eddy by the shoulders and rushed him indoors.

There was a screech from Charlene. "Here it is, quick, quick. It's me!"

Chapter 25

❧

*"Oh dear!" said the poor Princess. And the three drops of blood heard
her, and said, "If your mother knew of this, it would break her heart."*
The Brothers Grimm, "The Goose-Girl"

"Homer, Annie's got problems."

"*Annie's* got problems?" Homer stared at his wife in
disbelief. "For Christ's sake, who cares? Not me. *I'm* the one
with problems. My teaching assistant's down with flu, so who
has to read two hundred papers? *I do.* And those poor kids in
prison, what about them? Talk about problems! *They've* got
problems, and who's going to help them out? Me again. Yours
truly. And what about my poor *book*? It's not getting *written,* for
Christ's sake, and, good grief, Mary Kelly, your friend Princess
Pearl, *she's* got a problem, because where the hell is she? She's
not really in Albany at all, did I tell you? Because that postcard
was the silliest thing you ever—" Homer scrambled his hair
with his fingers and looked wildly at his wife. "And now you
tell me poor old Annie has problems." Homer groaned. "Well,
all right, what is it this time?"

Mary looked at him pitilessly, and explained about the recur-
ring mystery of the face on Annie's wall. "It keeps coming back.
At first they thought it was just a blotch. You know, mildew or
something, but now it's clearly a face. Somebody's been getting
into her house and painting weird faces on her wall."

Homer showed no interest in the face on Annie's wall. "Well,
so what? What difference does it make, one face more or less
on Annie's wall, compared with a missing woman and two

hundred student papers and the abandonment of a truly significant book and the plight of six poor guys serving mandatory minimum sentences in the Concord prison?" Homer picked up his briefcase, slammed it on the table, and began stuffing it with books.

"And there's something else," said Mary ruthlessly. "Homer, listen, this is important. Annie's little neighbor, Eddy Gast, Annie thinks his parents are trying to get rid of him."

"They want to send him away?"

"No, no. Worse than that. He keeps having accidents. She thinks it's more than just carelessness on their part. She thinks it's deliberate."

Homer couldn't handle it. "Oh, God, I don't know. Don't you think she's just being melodramatic?"

"Well, possibly, but don't you think somebody should—?"

"Listen, I've got to go." Homer looked at his wife despairingly and zipped up his briefcase. "Later, we'll talk about it later." With a guilty *harrumph* he went out and slammed the front door. His feet pounded heavily down the porch stairs.

Mary tried to remind herself of Homer's good qualities, and couldn't think of any. Sighing, she gathered up her own books and papers, put on her coat and followed him out the door. It was time for her weekly class as Historian in Residence at Weston Country Day.

❧

For half an hour the house was empty. The phone rang and rang in the presence of curtains and rugs, tables and chairs, then stopped ringing. But when Homer roared back down the driveway in a rage, catapulted up the porch steps, and snatched up his forgotten lecture notes, it rang again.

Angrily he grabbed it, dropped it, picked it up, juggled it, and shouted, "HELLO."

There was a pause, while the caller recovered his hearing. "Homer, this is Bill Kennebunk."

"Oh, God, Bill, I'm sorry. How's Rollo McNutt today? Is he within earshot? Listening for compliments?" Homer raised his voice. "Hey there, McNutt, you're a sleazeball and an asshole."

Sergeant Kennebunk snickered. "No, no, it's okay. He's shut himself in his office to write reports. Actually, he goes in there every morning to take a nap. Listen, Professor Kelly, I mean Homer, I called that hotel in Albany. The name Pearl Small appears on the register, single room, number 609, April eighth and ninth."

"No kidding?" Homer pondered. "Of course, it doesn't mean—"

"That's right. Anybody could use a false name. The hotel people aren't about to ask for a birth certificate. So I asked for a description. Blonde, the guy said. Cute blonde, maybe thirty, thirty-five."

"Cute blonde? Does that sound like a princess? Remember, Bill, I told you Princess was her nickname, because she looked like one. You know, in a fairy story. Mary puts a lot of stress on her long golden hair. I like brunettes myself."

"The point is, somebody should go there. Right away."

"Go there! Oh, right. Go to Albany and interview the staff before they forget which guest was which." Homer winced, feeling the questioning glance of Kennebunk's brown eyes across fifteen miles of Massachusetts landscape—highways, fields, strip malls, and the miscellaneous sprawl of suburban Boston. "Well, I'm afraid it can't be me. I can't possibly get away. Couldn't you get McNutt to assign you to Albany to look into the whole thing?" This suggestion was answered by ironic laughter, and at once Homer saw the impossibility of his suggestion. "Well, no, I suppose you couldn't. But—oh, God, Bill— if you knew my schedule. I've just been explaining it to my wife. Oh, Jesus, Bill, I'll think about it. I know, I know, it's got to be done right away. Hey, I've got an idea. My wife will go." Homer rolled his eyes at the ceiling, imagining the domestic strife to come.

"Your wife?"

"Certainly. Mary's a good sport. She'll go. You'll see."

Chapter 26

❧

Humpty Dumpty sat on a wall. . . .
Lewis Carroll,
Through the Looking Glass

Annie's broker was on the phone, her old boyfriend Burgess. He had walked out on Annie a long time ago, but he made up for it by giving her investment tips from time to time. Annie trusted him. Burgess wasn't your typical suit-and-tie corporate kind of stockbroker, he was a sporting adventurer in business for himself, but his insane speculations usually paid off. "Listen, Annie, I'm going to take every single cent out of those mutual funds of yours. I've got a really hot tip."

"Well, fine, Burgess. Anything you say."

❧

Annie had forgotten about Minnie Peck's giant hubcap woman. She didn't think of her again until she brought a bag of garbage to the compost heap and stumbled over a heap of junk. Good God, it was *Millennial Woman*, stretched out on a pile of oak leaves. Annie called Flimnap and he came to look. He had been away—it was yet another of his mysterious absences—but now he was back.

"We've got to get that thing out of here before the vegetation closes in," said Flimnap. "Why don't I rent a flatbed truck?"

"Sure," said Annie, laughing. "And you'd better hurry. That vine crawling up her arm is poison ivy."

They didn't warn Minnie Peck that *Millennial Woman* was coming, not until they had dumped Min's giant work of art onto the bed of the rented truck with a clatter of colliding hub-caps. Only then, as Flimnap climbed into the driver's seat, did Annie phone Minnie to say her colossal sculpture was on its way home.

Minnie was furious, but there was nothing she could do. She had to clear a space in the middle of her studio, where she was welding together another enormous work of art.

As they backed up to her loading platform, she turned off her blowtorch and took off her welder's mask. "Hi there," she said, cheering up at once when she saw Flimnap O'Dougherty. "Come on up. Meet *Millennial Man*."

Annie gaped. Feebly she said, "Wow." *Millennial Man* was a construction of identical TV sets tuned to the same boxing match. All seventeen televisions had been glued and screwed together into a vague suggestion of the human body. Halfway down between the legs dangled a remote control and a couple of sponge-rubber balls. Minnie was launching herself fearlessly into the next thousand years.

Flimnap studied the seventeen screens, as blow after blow landed on bleeding flesh and the bloodthirsty crowd roared. "They're on a loop, right? So it plays the same thing over and over?"

Minnie had taken a fancy to Flimnap. "O'Dougherty, I need you," she said boldly. "Why don't you stay and give me a hand? I'm great on the creative side, but the engineering follow-through gives me a hard time." She glanced at Annie and said slyly, "Surely Annie doesn't need you anymore, and anyway housepainting isn't worthy of you at all. My stuff is *art*."

There could be two opinions about that, thought Annie, as they got to work removing *Millennial Woman* from the truck. With a racket of dingdonging hubcaps, they soon had her standing erect next to *Millennial Man*.

"Oh, don't they look *darling* together!" screamed Minnie.

❧

When Annie got home again she found Eddy Gast high up on her scaffolding, smiling down at her. He said a cheerful, "Hello, Annie!" and bounced on the wooden boards, which boomed and slid a little sideways.

She was dismayed. "Oh, Eddy, how did you get in? Come on down. Here, let me help you."

He had a picture in his hand. Clutching it, he was clumsy on the ladder. Annie supported him, and set him safely on the floor, and scolded him for coming in when she wasn't there.

But she couldn't be mad at Eddy for long. Joyfully he beamed at her and showed her the picture. It was Mother Goose astride a majestic bird, its wings spread wide over constellations of stars.

"Oh, Eddy," she said, "how marvelous."

Chapter 27

❧

"I will sing to you of the happy ones and of those that suffer. I will sing about the good and the evil, which are kept hidden from you."
Hans Christian Andersen, "The Nightingale"

Cissie Aufsesser was astonished when Charlene Gast spoke to her in school. Normally Charlene looked right through her, as though she were invisible, when actually Cissie was a solid mound of a girl, twenty-five pounds overweight.

"That's cool," Charlene said, staring at the brand-new camera hanging on a strap around Cissie's neck. "Is it automatic?"

"Oh, yes, Charlene," said Cissie. "It does everything. You just aim it and click." She took it off her neck and pushed a button to uncover the lens. "See, you just look through here." She handed the camera to Charlene, who lifted it to her face. "You don't even have to decide whether you need the flash or not. If it's too dark, the flash goes off by itself."

Charlene turned the camera over in her hand, then gave it back to Cissie. "It's really cool," she said again.

"Want me to take your picture?" said Cissie, greatly daring.

"Okay," said Charlene. She stood smiling while Cissie fumbled with the camera, her fingers trembling.

Charlene did not offer to take Cissie's picture. "Thanks," she said, turning away quickly. Wistfully Cissie watched her run away across the playground to Becca and Joanna and Carrie. Should Cissie offer to take everybody's picture? Maybe they would talk to her if she took their picture. Everybody liked to have their picture taken. In fact, although Cissie didn't know it,

her father had hoped his gift of a camera would improve her social standing.

But now she hung back. She was too shy.

"What a nice camera, Cissie," said Mary Kelly, who had seen
her with Charlene. "May I take your picture?"

"Oh, yes, Mrs. Kelly." Cissie's doleful face brightened. Mary
took a picture of her against a background of oaks and beech
trees, the pretty woodland beyond the playground on the north
side of the school.

❧

After the last class of the day, Cissie had to stay for remedial
help in math. She couldn't understand the concept of percent.
She sat at her desk, bowed over her workbook, alone in the
room with Mrs. Rutledge.

The first problem was impenetrable. "Mr. Green's coffee
shop earns $75,000 a year in gross income. If 8 percent goes for
rent, 10 percent for part-time help, and 5 percent for supplies,
what is Mr. Green's profit from his shop?"

Cissie didn't know where to start. Should she divide eight
into seventy-five thousand? Oh, it was too hard. Tears ran
down her cheeks.

She looked up as Mrs. Rutledge rose from her chair. "Cissie, I
have to make a phone call. Please stay until I come back. I've
left my purse in my desk drawer."

"Okay, Mrs. Rutledge."

Mrs. Rutledge was gone. The room was silent. No one was
passing in the hall. *Mrs. Rutledge's pocketbook was in her desk
drawer.*

Quietly and carefully, Cissie heaved herself up from her
chair. Her camera swung forward, and thumped against her
chest. Her heart thumped against the camera.

At once she found the right drawer. The shiny black patent-

leather pocketbook was right there in front. Cissie took it out
and opened it. An exotic fragrance billowed up around her
nose. There was a dusting of pink powder on Mrs. Rutledge's
billfold.

Someone snorted with laughter. Cissie gave a small shriek. It
was Charlene Gast, looking at her from the doorway.

"I'll tell," said Charlene.

ᐟ

Bus 2 was nearly empty. A few kids who had been kept after
school, like Cissie, sat in front, and three noisy members of the
field-hockey team plumped themselves down in the middle.
But as usual no one wanted to sit with Cissie. Sunk in gloom,
she made her way to the back of the bus.

How was she going to tell her father that her camera was
gone? As the bus rumbled in the general direction of her part of
town, Cissie bounced up and down, sniffling and trying to think.

ᐟ

Roberta Gast pulled up beside the Hayden Recreation Center in
Lexington, where Charlene swam three times a week. Her
daughter was waiting for her on the curb.

"Smile, Mummy."

The camera clicked, recording Roberta's blank face. "For
heaven's sake, Charlene, give me some warning next time."

Grinning, Charlene picked up her swim bag and got into the
car. "Look, Mummy," she said, showing her the camera, "it
does everything by itself."

Roberta pulled away from the curb. "Charlene, where on
earth did you get an expensive camera like that?"

"One of the kids in swim class gave it to me." Charlene
smiled smugly. "He likes me."

"Oho!" Roberta laughed, wondering if she should start worry-
ing about the beginnings of a childish interest in sex. "Is he cute?"

"Oh, no." Charlene giggled. "He's like really disgusting. You know, really fat and stuff."

❧

Cissie Aufsesser's father was a judge in the Superior Court of Massachusetts. Her mother was a nurse at Emerson Hospital. Cissie was their only child.

The truth was, Judge Aufsesser was a little disappointed in his daughter, who was not only fat but slow-witted. But he was a reasonably good father, and he pitied her friendlessness. How did kids live through a painful childhood like Cissie's? If only the poor kid would lose a little weight.

His gift of the camera had been an attempt to give her an interest, something that would take her out of herself. After supper on the day Cissie lost her camera to Charlene, he spoke to his daughter with false heartiness. "How's the picture-taking, Cissie? Are you having fun with the camera?"

"Oh—oh, sure, Daddy."

Judge Aufsesser guessed that something wasn't right. "What sort of pictures have you been taking?"

"Um—oh, just stuff at school." Puffing, Cissie leaned over and retied her shoes. Her eyes were hidden.

Something was certainly the matter. "Where is it, Cissie?" her father said quietly. "Where's the camera?"

It was the question Cissie had dreaded. "Oh, I'm sorry, Daddy," she said in a small voice. "I left it at school."

"Now, Cissie, I told you never to do that. Somebody might steal it."

Cissie's eyes filled with tears. "I—I'm sorry." And then she broke down and sobbed. Poor Cissie's life was so painful, the smallest additional misery sent her over the edge.

"Oh, it's already happened, has it?" said her father sternly. "I told you, Cissie. I told you!"

"No," wept Cissie, "I didn't leave it at school."

Her father was relentless, and in a few minutes he had the truth. He knew about Mrs. Rutledge's purse, he knew about the exchange of Cissie's camera for Charlene's silence.

"Don't tell Mrs. Rutledge," sobbed Cissie. "Oh, please, Daddy, don't tell Mrs. Rutledge."

"You've got to tell her, Cissie," said her father. "You've got to talk to Mrs. Rutledge if we're going to do something about that nasty little blackmailer."

"Blackmailer?"

"Your charming friend, what's her name? Charlene."

"Oh, but Daddy, you can't. You just can't."

"Can't I? We'll see about that."

Cissie trembled at what might happen, but she felt better. Her father was on her side.

Chapter 28

ᕽ

But as nothing remains hidden from God, so this black deed also was to come to light. The Brothers Grimm, "The Singing Bone"

Sergeant Kennebunk could not get permission to go to Albany. Homer Kelly refused to take the time to go to Albany. Mary fumed and fussed, but she went by train to Albany, and took a cab from the station to the Regency Hotel.

In fact, Mary was pleased to see Homer take an interest at last in the disappearance of her missing friend Pearl, wife of the abominable Frederick Small and once the golden-haired darling of her seminar on women poets. Something terrible had happened to Pearl. And she wasn't the first of Small's vanished wives. In the Bluebeard story there was a room crammed with their dead bodies. They hung on hooks around the wall, their clotted blood pooling on the floor. Mary was grimly determined to find the room and the wives and the reason for the disappearance of Pearl Small.

But when she walked into the lobby of the hotel she burst out laughing. It had been decorated by a comedian in the style of the 1930s. The leather chairs had a zooming shape, the sofas were outrageously overstuffed. There were designer bellboys too, tall good-looking kids in pleated black trousers, white shirts, and wire-framed glasses, their hair combed straight back. They strode about the lobby carrying gorgeous pieces of luggage—pigskin and gleaming saddle leather—probably stage props, decided Mary.

Sergeant Kennebunk had typed up an official introduction and faxed it to Mary from the Southtown Pharmacy. When she presented it to the clerk at the registration desk, he cooperated at once.

"Oh, yes, Mrs. Kelly, he called to say you were coming." The clerk was a dapper young man in a jacket with enormous padded shoulders. "What can I do for you?"

Mary showed him the newspaper image of Pearl Small. "I understand she was registered in this hotel for a few days last week. Can you tell me if this is the same woman?"

The clerk studied the picture and shook his head doubtfully. "I don't know. It's hard to say. She was very attractive, with long blond hair."

Mary opened her mouth to ask if the woman had the air of a fairy princess, then decided against it. "Might I see the room, number 609?"

"Certainly." The clerk dinged a little bell and raised a white-gloved hand. At once a dashing bellboy appeared at Mary's side. "Please escort Mrs. Kelly to Room 609."

The bellboy grinned at Mary and led the way to the elevator. *I can find my own way perfectly well,* thought Mary, but as the bell-boy pushed the button for the sixth floor, she felt for her billfold and extracted a dollar.

"This way," he said graciously, leading the way down the hall. "Uh-oh." Outside the open door of Room 609 stood a cart laden with cleaning equipment and linen. "Could you please re-move this stuff and do another room?" he said grandly to the chambermaid, who was reaching into the cart for a set of sheets.

The chambermaid was a cheerful-looking woman with golden-brown skin and chubby cheeks. "Sure thing," she said, putting back the sheets.

"No, wait," said Mary impulsively. She turned to the bellboy, thrust the dollar at him, and said, "Thank you. That's fine."

He looked surprised, glanced at the dollar, which was apparently inadequate, took it, and vanished with a toss of his cowlick.

Mary turned gratefully to the chambermaid and stretched out her hand. "Good afternoon. My name's Mary Kelly. I'm from Boston."

The chambermaid beamed at her and shook hands. "Just call me Molly."

"Molly—¿"

"Marshall."

"Go right ahead with what you're doing, Mrs. Marshall. I'm not staying in the hotel. I'm here to ask questions about a missing woman named Pearl Small, who stayed in this room a few days ago. I'm on assignment from the police department of Southtown, Massachusetts."

"No fooling?" Molly Marshall grinned and pushed the cart into Room 609.

Mary followed, and looked around appreciatively. Room 609 matched the lobby. There were ridiculous chairs and a bed with a headboard of matched veneer. Through the bathroom door she could see the steel sink, a cone rising from the floor.

Only one of the twin beds was unmade. Mrs. Marshall began pulling off the disordered sheets.

Mary watched her, rejoicing in the fact that women everywhere could talk to each other. They had a common language in their daily tasks—the cooking of meals, the cleaning of houses, the changing of beds. And of course a lot of women had their pregnancies to talk about, their labor pains, the births of their children. Mary had not given birth herself, but she had heard innumerable stories. It was their shared experiences of housework and pain that bound women together, even professional women and important executives.

"I'm so glad to have caught you," said Mary, beaming at the chambermaid. Carefully, leaving nothing out, she explained her

connection with Sergeant Kennebunk and the case of the missing woman named Pearl Small. "She had this room a week ago,
a pretty woman with yellow hair. Do you remember her?"

"Oh, sure, I remember. Usually I don't see folks, but I saw
her because she come in the first day she was here, while I was
doing the room. When she see me, she say, Excuse me, and go
away again."

Mary showed her the picture from the newspaper. "Is this
the same woman?"

The maid chuckled and shook her head. "Sorry, honey, I just
don't know. I only see her for a second or two. She had this
long yellow hair hanging down her back, I remember that."

Mary asked her childish question: "With all that golden hair,
did she look like a princess? You know, a princess in a fairy
tale?"

The chambermaid laughed. "Yellow hair don't make no
princess for black folks."

"No, of course not." Mary glanced around the room. "How
many people have used this room since she was here?"

"Nobody. Empty since she left. This here hotel, don't tell nobody, it's half empty most of the time."

"Tell me, Mrs. Marshall, could you explain what you do in
every room, I mean the whole routine you have to go through?
Do you have a list?"

"Oh, sure, we got a list. I'll show you." Mrs. Marshall turned
to the big bureau. "First we puts down a clean doily, and we has
to make sure the name of the hotel's in the front, and then we
puts out clean glasses with these here paper covers, and we
makes sure the lampshades have the seam in the back, and then
we got to check all the hotel cards and refill the booklet with
writing paper, and look in the closet because sometimes they
takes home the pants hangers, they's got to be six, and we got
to leave the thermostat cooling on low, and make sure the TV's
turned straight, and then there's the beds."

"Isn't this supposed to be a single room? Why does it have two beds?"

"Oh, it's a single all right. They's just twin beds. Double rooms, they got two double beds."

Mary watched Mrs. Marshall pull the sheets off the unmade bed and float a clean one over it. "How do you know the other bed's not been slept in? I mean, just because it's made up, that doesn't mean it wasn't occupied?"

"That's right. We got to check." Mrs. Marshall reached over and lifted a corner of the spread on the other bed. "Well, look at that, it ain't got no tuck. Somebody did sleep in it. See, we got our secret little tuck at the corner, and it ain't there. I got to change this one too."

Mary looked reverently at the chambermaid, who was a fount of wisdom. "Do you think they were pretending that only one person spent the night? So she left her bed unmade, and put the other one back together just so, only she didn't know about the tuck?"

"Well, I dunno." Mrs. Marshall giggled. "Maybe she just got tired of sleeping in one bed, so she got up and tried the other one. I dunno."

Mary watched her gather up the sheets and shove them in the hamper attached to the cart. Then, while the chambermaid's back was turned, Mary bent down with a sudden gesture and lifted something from the floor. It was a long blond hair.

Chapter 29

❧

Rapunzel had beautiful long hair that shone like gold.
The Brothers Grimm, "Rapunzel"

Back home from Albany, walking into the small house on Fair Haven Bay, Mary said, "No, no, I'm not tired at all, just hungry." At once she took a folded tissue out of her bag and showed the strand of yellow hair to Homer.

She had coiled it in a ring. Homer looked at it, and said at once, "Dirty blond."

"Oh, do you think so?" Mary held it to the light. "Well, maybe you're right. Surely Pearl's hair was lighter than this. I told you, she was like—"

"I know, I know, a fairy princess. Okay, then, her husband is lying. Pearl Small is still missing, and that postcard from Albany is a lie."

"Homer, there's something else. There were two people in that hotel room." Mary told him about the chambermaid's special tuck at the corner of the sheet. "It's a professional secret, so she always knows whether a bed's been slept in or not."

"Well, fine, good for her, but the trouble is," complained Homer, "we're no further along. If the woman wasn't Pearl Small, who was she? Do you suppose Small went to the trouble of hiring some woman with yellow hair to take a room in the hotel and send him a postcard?"

"But what if the other person in the room was Small himself? Maybe he was the mysterious roommate. Maybe he was romantically mixed up with some blonde in Albany." Mary uncoiled the strand of yellow hair and looked at it again. "Or maybe I'm wrong about the color of Pearl's hair. Maybe she was really there in that hotel, running away from her husband with a boyfriend."

"That's what Chief McNutt thinks," growled Homer. "I refuse to agree with McNutt. So tell me, if she ran away, why did she send her abandoned husband a meaningless postcard?"

"Oh, I don't know, Homer. What's for supper?"

It was a joke. Homer looked blank. Mary laughed and went to the kitchen to wrestle with her pots and pans, thinking about the chambermaid in the Regency Hotel. After a long day's work changing beds and rearranging doilies and scrubbing bathtubs, Mrs. Marshall too probably had to make supper for a hungry family.

❧

Next day Mary stopped off at Annie's on her way to work. "Any more ghastly faces on the wall?"

Annie unlocked the wheels of her scaffolding and rolled it sideways. "Well, yes, Aunt Mary, there was another one yesterday." She pointed to a freshly daubed patch on the empty plaster at the far right end of the wall.

"Where's your friend Flimnap?"

Annie rattled the ladder into place and locked the wheels and began to climb up. "I don't know. He's been gone for a day or two. Maybe he'll never come back."

Mary looked shrewdly at her niece. "Would that bother you?"

Annie thought about it, and told the truth. "Yes, it would."

"Not very considerate of him," murmured Mary, "to go off without telling you."

"I suppose not," muttered Annie. Resolutely she stepped off the ladder onto the first platform, then climbed higher still.

Mary abandoned the subject of Flimnap and gazed up at the wall. "My dear girl, it's wonderful."

Annie's tense face cleared. She looked at Mary and smiled. "Do you really think so?"

Together they looked at the great garden of folktales and children's stories that was blossoming on Annie's wall. In the foreground there were lifesize figures of the tellers of the tales. The Homeric bard was crowned with laurel, Beatrix Potter wore an old garden hat. Their stories teemed around them. Annie had finished the first two openings of her five-part arcade, and now she was beginning the third.

Mary pointed to a pair of pink legs sticking out of the mouth of a big gray wolf. "It's not Little Red Riding Hood?"

"Of course it is. It's the original story by Charles Perrault. The wolf gobbles her up, and that's the end of her."

"Oh, really? You mean the wolf just pats his tummy and belches and that's the end of the story? I didn't know that. Well, I never believed in that hunter anyway, slitting open the wolf so neatly and extracting Red Riding Hood and Grandma." Mary pulled on her coat and said goodbye.

No sooner was she gone than Annie had another visitor. "Whassat?"

She turned around carefully on the top shelf of the scaffolding and looked down, startled. There was Eddy Gast, back again, pointing up at the Mole and the Water Rat from Kenneth Grahame's *Wind in the Willows*. "Whassat, Annie? Whassat?"

"Oh, Eddy, how did you get in? I thought I locked the door. Now, look, Eddy, dear, I'm going to Boston, and you mustn't come in while I'm gone. I'll lock everything up. I'll be back late this afternoon. Then you can come."

Eddy held up a sheet of Annie's best watercolor paper. "I made it for you."

"Oh, good, dear. Just leave it on the table and I'll look at it later." Annie opened the door for him, then locked it firmly. Five minutes later she left by the front door, locked it carefully behind her, and went to her car.

Eddy trotted home obediently. His father met him at the door. He had watched Annie disappear down the driveway. "Where's Annie going?" he asked Eddy.

"Boston," said Eddy, proud to know the answer. "Annie's going to Boston."

Chapter 30

❧

"This man is not my son, I drive him forth, and command you to take him out into the forest and kill him."

The Brothers Grimm, "The Three Languages"

But he couldn't wait for Annie to come home. Eddy loved Annie's wall. He had seen her lock the door, but he came back anyway to look through the glass. To his surprise he found the door ajar, and the screen propped open with a stick.

Gladly he walked in. Was Annie home again from Boston? But no one welcomed him. No one said, *Hello, Eddy!* and offered him a big piece of paper and a paintbox. Flimnap wasn't there either, Flimnap who found gumdrops in Eddy's ears, who could catch a ball in his mouth and carry Eddy high in the air on his funny bike.

He was alone in Annie's magical house. There on the table was the new picture he had drawn for Annie, and high on the wall her new animals glowed at him—two funny ones in a boat. He had to come closer. He had to see. He would be so careful! He mustn't hurt anything that belonged to Annie.

Carefully Eddy went to the ladder and climbed up to the place where Annie sat to work on her pictures. The ladder was shaky. When he got to his feet on the platform, he had to throw out his short arms for balance, because the scaffolding was rolling sideways. Then it stopped. He looked up. The new animals were higher still.

Grasping the second ladder, Eddy went up slowly, setting both feet on every rung. He put his knees on the upper board and crawled forward until it was safe to stand up. Then he moved cautiously to the right, with the board shifting beneath his feet, and stopped in front of the little river scene. There before him was a big mouse standing up in a boat and holding a pair of oars, and another funny animal with glasses perched on his long snout. It was the Water Rat and the Mole from *The Wind in the Willows*, and it was the last wondrous vision of Eddy's life.

❧

Charlene saw everything. She heard the thundering racket and Eddy's cry, she felt the vibration as his body struck the tile floor, she witnessed the final blow. Then there was no sound but weeping, and the rasping voice of a crow in the faraway field, *caw-caw, caw-caw.* The shutter of Cissie Aufsesser's camera had made no sound at all as it opened and closed. Nor was there a sudden flash of light, because the brilliant sunshine of midday flooded the room from Annie's four tall windows.

Charlene put the camera in her pocket and said, "I'll tell."

Only then did her father turn around, his shoulders shaking with sobs, and see his daughter standing in the doorway.

❧

"Oh, my Lord Fish," said the fisherman, calling to him above the rumble of thunder, "my wife is still unhappy."

The great fish gazed up at him from the water and said softly, "But she is rich and young and beautiful. Is that not enough?"

"I am sorry, Lord Fish, but she wants to be Queen of the land."

The fish looked at him gravely, and murmured, "Go home. It shall be as she desires." And then he sank down into the deepest part of the sea.

Part Two

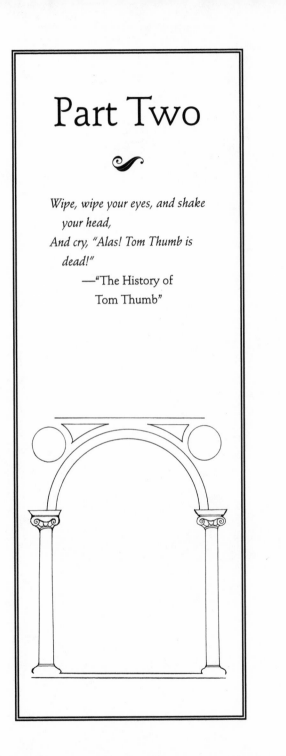

*Wipe, wipe your eyes, and shake
 your head,
And cry, "Alas! Tom Thumb is
 dead!"*
— "The History of
 Tom Thumb"

Chapter 31

❧

Annie lugged her books from the car to the front door. She had to set them down on the broad stone step in order to unlock the door and push it open. Then she transferred the books to the hall table, hung up her coat, and dodged into the laundry, where she took the wet towels out of the washing machine and shoved them into the dryer.

It was a routine job, postponing for a moment the discovery that her life had taken a new and disastrous turn. Not until she picked up the books and carried them into the living room did she see what had happened. At once her arms went limp, and the books fell to the floor.

In the general wreckage of collapsed ladders, fallen boards, and smashed jars of paint she did not at first see Eddy, because his small body was obscured by her big plastic tarp. But when she came closer, cursing, there he was, and she cried, "Eddy, oh, Eddy," and fell to her knees beside him.

It was clear that he was dead. His small round head was flattened against the tile floor in an ooze of blood. Annie wrenched herself around and stared at the French door. It was open, it was wide open, swinging a little in the cool spring breeze. But she had locked the door, she had locked it!

But there it was, wide open, and Bob Gast was running into the room, followed by three men in uniform. When he saw Annie, he shouted at her, "Get away from my son. You killed him, you bitch, you killed him."

Annie opened her mouth to protest, but she had no voice.

"Move out of the way, miss," said the sergeant in charge, coming closer and looking down at Eddy. "This is your house?"

"Yes." Shaking, Annie stood up, stumbling over the fallen

ladder. One of the uniformed officers took her arm and drew her out of the way, beyond the big littered table. There was something unfamiliar on the table. It was Eddy's new picture, the one he had given her that morning, saying, *I made it for you.*

Annie picked it up. It was a portrait of herself. There she was in her denim workshirt with every button glowing like a pearl, and her face—her face—Annie put the picture down and began to cry.

The sergeant stared at the wrecked scaffolding and ignored her. "He's laying on top of all this mess. Wheels on the apparatus, must've rolled. Look, see, the wheels aren't locked." He looked up at the painted wall and spoke to Annie. "This is your work?"

Annie mopped her sleeve over her face and looked up too. There, high above the place where Eddy's body lay on the floor, were the new figures she had painted that morning, Rat and Mole in their boat on the river. Eddy had climbed the ladder to see them, trusting the scaffolding to hold him, but it had not.

The sergeant turned to Bob Gast. "What was the youngster doing here? Why wasn't he at home?"

"Ask her," said Gast angrily. "She taught him to climb that shaky ladder and bounce around on those narrow boards." His voice mounted in fury. "He was always over here. He could come in anytime. She went away and left the door open. She killed him. It's her fault. She killed my little son."

Annie pulled herself together and spoke up, her voice sounding shrill in her own ears. "But I locked the door before I left. I did, I swear I did. I always lock the door when I go out. I lock both doors."

"Then how come it's open?" Gast was shouting now. He pointed at the door. "You went away and left it open so my innocent little son could come in, and so of course he did, and of course he climbed the ladder, and you hadn't even locked those goddamn wheels, so the thing rolled right out from under him." Gast whirled around to the detective sergeant, who was looking at him mournfully. "What do you call it? There's a legal term for it, 'attractive nuisance.' She enticed Eddy over here day after day, and she didn't do a damn thing to protect him, my poor helpless little boy. She's no better than a murderer." He was crying now. He turned back to Annie. "I'll sue you. I'll sue you for every cent you've got. You murdered my little son."

"No, no, I didn't, I didn't." Annie was overwhelmed by a nightmare sense of unfairness. Her grief for Eddy turned to anger. She clenched her fists. "It was your fault. You didn't care what happened to Eddy, you and Roberta, you didn't care at all."

"Who else has keys to this place?" said the detective loudly, trying to restore order.

"He has a key," said Annie, pointing a trembling finger at Bob Gast. "I gave you a key, remember? That weekend I went away? I gave Roberta a key."

"We gave it back," shouted Gast.

So they had. It was the key with a tag, "Annie's house," lying in a tangle of other keys in a kitchen drawer, along with the pliers and the hammer. "My aunt, Mary Kelly, she has one."

"Homer Kelly's wife?" said the police sergeant. "She's your aunt? Anybody else?"

Annie tried to think. Her mind was a blank. She shook her head.

"Nobody else has a key to this house, just you and your aunt?"

"That's right."

They all turned their heads. There was a noise, the small rattle of a key in a lock, the sound of the front door opening and closing. Flimnap walked in from the hall.

"Oh, of course," said Annie lamely. "I forgot."

Chapter 32

❦

"Have you not seen Death go by, with my little child?"
Hans Christian Andersen, "The Story of a Mother"

They were finished with Annie, they were finished with the wreckage in her house. A couple of medical technicians carried Eddy's body outside on a stretcher. Bob Gast, his face streaked with tears, followed them out the front door. Roberta brought up the rear, weeping, holding Charlene by the hand. Charlene's eyes were dry.

Only the three police officers remained, tall dignified men in blue uniforms with leather holsters attached to their belts, and keys that jingled when they moved. With the departure of the Gasts, they gathered around Flimnap. They were dissatisfied with his refusal to explain where he had been. "Okay, Mr. O'Dougherty, it's a simple question. We just want to know where you went, and what for?"

"I had things to do," Flimnap said softly, and in response to their exclamations of ridicule he said nothing more. He stood stubbornly silent, facing three representatives of the state, highly trained and responsible men who were trying to bring order out of the muddle created by erring humankind. His expression was vacant. He looked sidelong, as if concentrating on quiet words spoken in another room.

Annie watched with mounting anxiety. *Say something, Flimnap, say anything. Why don't you lie?*

But Flimnap said nothing.

Frustrated, the four officers moved aside to mutter among

themselves, glancing over their shoulders at Flimnap. He was obviously a nutcase, but why the hell would he come back right now, with a police cruiser in the driveway, if the kid's death was his doing? Before long they gave up and left, shaking their heads and promising to come back.

At once Flimnap looked at Annie. "Call your Uncle Homer."

"Oh, yes," said Annie, and she plucked the phone off the kitchen wall. Eddy's picture of the White Rabbit was taped to the wall beside it, and for a moment she couldn't see. Then the sound of Mary Kelly's comfortable family voice produced a flood of tears. It was a minute before Annie could explain, and ask for Homer.

"I'll get him. Oh, Annie, my God."

Homer started for Annie's house at once. He wasn't surprised at what had happened, because Mary's niece was always getting into some kind of terrible trouble. But now his affection for the girl rose up and hit him hard. Poor old Annie!

As he headed down Route 2, he saw the police ambulance coming toward him, and he swore under his breath. He was too late. He had missed getting a look at the poor kid lying exactly where he had fallen. It was too bad. Homer had a theory that the first glance at a scene of trouble could tell you everything, if you could only register it on your brain and sort it out.

With Mary's key he unlocked Annie's door and walked into her big living room. It was empty. The scaffolding still lay in a clutter of fallen boards on the floor. Homer glanced up at the storytellers on Annie's wall. There were a lot more of them than he remembered. They stood in clusters, serenely disregarding the wreckage below. Their arcaded gallery was like a splendid extension of the room, an opening into another world, in which the death of one small boy was an insignificant event. Homer tore his eyes away. Where was Annie? Where was Whoseywhatsis, Flimnap?

He crossed the hall and lifted his hand to knock on Annie's bedroom door, but she opened it at once and clutched him. "Oh, Uncle Homer."

Homer had known Annie ever since she was an excitable little girl skipping rope on the grass in front of the old farmhouse on Barrett's Mill Road. It just happened to be the house in which a tall young woman named Mary Morgan was living with her sister and brother-in-law. Now Homer held Annie close and murmured in her ear, "It's okay, honey. Tell me what the hell happened."

"The door was locked," sobbed Annie. "They were both locked. I swear they were locked."

"Okay, Annie, it's all right." He pushed her gently down on the bed and pulled up a chair. "Tell me."

"He's going to sue me. And his wife is a litigation lawyer. She works for Pouch, Heaviside and Sprocket. They'll sue me for everything I've got, that's what he said."

"Pouch, Heaviside and Sprocket! Christ almighty, they're the sleaziest dirtballs in Boston. I've had a few grim encounters with them myself. Homer shook his head in melancholy wonder. "Look here, tell me about Eddy. Tell me everything you can remember about that poor little kid."

Annie began haltingly, then caught her breath and hurried on. She began with Eddy's delight in the stories she had been painting on her wall. "He loved to come here and hear about Little Red Riding Hood and, you know, the Emperor's nightingale and all the rest, and look at the wall." *Whassat, Annie? Whassat?*

Homer had a sinking feeling. "He liked your wall?"

"Oh, yes. I doubt his parents ever read to him. He was hungry for stories. And, listen, Homer, I'm convinced they were trying to kill him. You know, without actually using a gun or anything." Annie told Homer about Eddy's horrifying ride down the hill in one of the Gasts' cars. "Actually, it was an extra car, an old wreck of a car, not one they used very much." *Only when they wanted to make a certain kind of impression on their future landlady,* thought Annie bitterly. "They wouldn't have wanted to destroy one of their good cars. So they encouraged Eddy to play in this old car. I'll bet they released the brake themselves."

"You don't know that for certain. Where's the car now?"

"I don't know."

Homer looked at Annie sadly. "You said Eddy liked your wall?"

"Oh, yes. He wanted to know about everything, the hare and the tortoise, Wilbur the pig, Peter Rabbit. He wanted me to tell him all the stories." Annie looked at Homer with tears in her eyes. "That was when it all began. Listen, Homer, this is the plain truth. That little kid, you've seen what he could do." She pointed at the wall beside her bed where she had hung some of Eddy's paintings, newly matted and framed. "I gave him good paints and good paper, and look at the marvelous things he did with them. His death is such a waste. Oh, God, Homer, do you think it was my fault?"

Grimly Homer took her hand and squeezed it. "Carry on. Tell me more."

"He began to come here. Almost every day he'd show up at the door. If it was locked, he'd knock. If it wasn't, he'd just walk in. Once he came in the middle of the night."

"Did he ever come when you weren't here?"

"Yes, once or twice. Once I came home and found him up on the scaffolding, like—like today." Annie got up and reached for her box of tissues and mopped at her face. "That was when I began locking the doors whenever I went out. Oh, I always lock the front door, but at first I didn't bother with the other one. Then, after Eddy got in that day, I began locking that too."

"What about Flimnap? Did he have a key? Was he here sometimes when you were out?"

"Yes, he had a key, and of course he was often here when I was out. You'll have to ask him about Eddy."

Homer stared at Eddy's glowing pictures and said slowly, "He was fascinated by what you were doing? You were enriching his life, discovering the artist in him?"

"Yes, that's right, that's right! He was thirsty for it. And I helped him. I was glad and grateful to help him, he was so gifted."

Homer's melancholy deepened. "Annie, you're making it worse, don't you see? The more he wanted to come here, the more you look like an attractive nuisance. They'll say you enticed him here to his peril."

"That's what Bob Gast said just now. But I didn't, I didn't. Oh, God, perhaps I did, only it wasn't to his peril, it was just the opposite."

It was worse and worse. Homer shook his head. There was no comfort to be had. "Look here, you're going to need a good defense attorney. If they really do sue you, I'll try to persuade Jerry Neville to take your case. He's given up active practice to write a book, but he's the best trial lawyer in Middlesex County. Or the entire country, or maybe the world."

Chapter 33

❦

. . . at every step you take it will feel as if you were treading upon sharp knives, and that the blood must flow.
                    Hans Christian Andersen, "The Little Mermaid"

"**B**ob?"

There was a pause, and then Bob Gast said, "Here."

"Hey, are you okay? You sound kind of strange."

"I'm okay." Gast pulled himself together. "What is it?"

"Pearl's signature, I've got it. She signed the release."

"She signed? Well, fine. Send it to me, okay?"

"Well, sure, only I've got to make copies. It may be a few days."

"You're sure she signed? No kidding?"

"Oh, sure, she signed." Fred Small stared at the practice sheet in front of him, on which he had at last perfected the swift upright signature of his murdered wife. "I've got it right here in front of me."

❦

In the woods in Northtown, Flimnap knew a trail leading back into the thickest growth of trees, where tall white pines grew out of a cellarhole. No other trace of the original house remained. Had the farmer abandoned it to pan for gold in California? There were still a couple of spindly lilac bushes beside the hole.

On his second day in the woods Flimnap ventured out for a *Boston Globe*, and found a mention of Eddy's death on page 43. The story included a picture of the Gast family in happier days—a grinning Bob, a smiling Roberta, a beaming Charlene, and a solemn Eddy. Annie's painted wall was mentioned, and so was the rolling scaffolding, but there was no picture of Annie and no accusation of carelessness on her part. There was nothing in the article about keys, nothing about a handyman called Flimnap O'Dougherty.

Flimnap stayed in the Northtown woods through fourteen *Boston Globe*s, just to be on the safe side. He spent his time exploring the remoter parts of the wilderness, identifying shrubs and trees and looking for wildflowers. One day, in a sheltered corner under a rocky cliff, far from the place where he had parked his truck, he found something unexpected. He stopped short and heaved aside a pile of dead branches. Then, grimly, he went back to his truck for a shovel.

❧

The long creamy envelope appeared in Annie's mail precisely one week after the death of Eddy Gast. The return address was menacing—"Pouch, Heaviside and Sprocket, Attorneys at Law, 7 Federal Street, Boston, Massachusetts 02108."

She read the terrible paragraph within the envelope, dropped the letter on the floor, and snatched up the phone. "Two million, Uncle Homer. They're suing me for two million dollars."

"Two million!" There was a horrified pause, and then Homer said angrily, "Isn't it interesting the way some people maximize their good fortune? Not only did the Gasts get rid of their embarrassing little son, they mean to get rich at the same time."

"But that's what's so awful, Uncle Homer. *They* were the ones who were careless. It was almost as if they wanted him to get lost, or—listen, did I tell you what happened on Route 2?" Annie described the near-accident on the highway, when Eddy had almost been run over. Then her voice faltered. "He was coming after me, I'm afraid. I told him I was going to Cambridge, so he walked all the way through the woods to Route 2.

He was trying to follow me to Cambridge. But, Uncle Homer, it wasn't my fault. It was because they didn't watch over him. They didn't care what happened to Eddy."

Homer's heart dropped into his shoes. It was worse than ever. The boy had obviously been fixated on Annie. "Look," he said, "I'll call Jerry Neville right away."

"Listen, Uncle Homer, I've got insurance. I've got a big personal-injury policy. Won't that cover it?"

Homer's dejection deepened. "Don't pin your hopes on it, honey child."

⌇

Jerry Neville did not lighten Homer's gloom. He listened politely to Homer's account of Annie's troubles, then made a noise of harsh discouragement. "Impossible case. She can't win. And those sharks, Pouch, Heaviside and Sprocket, they'll gouge and gouge, and leave her with nothing. And I mean nothing."

"Oh, Lord. Poor Annie."

"Her only hope is to settle out of court. Tell you what, Homer, I'll do my best. Maybe we can save something."

"Oh, God, Jerry, thank you. In the meantime I'll see if I can find out anything that might help. Annie swears she locked her doors, to keep the kid from getting in. She's absolutely sure."

"Well, fine. Do what you can."

"Listen, Jerry, Annie's got insurance, Paul Revere personal-injury insurance. Won't they pay up?"

Neville uttered a cynical snort. "If she hires an expensive lawyer and sues the company, maybe they'd pay a few thousand."

ᴄ

Oh! John, John, John, the grey goose is gone,
And the fox is off to his den O!

Mother Goose rhyme

ᴄ

Next morning, when the phone rang, Annie had another shock. It was her old boyfriend Burgess the stockbroker, the whiz kid, the boy wonder. "Listen, Annie," said Burgess, "don't worry about a thing."

"Worry? Why should I worry?"

"Oh, I thought you might be following the Dow Jones."

"The Dow Jones! You mean it's gone down? That computer stock you said I should buy? It's gone down?"

"Way down. Way, way down. But it's bottomed out, Annie. I've got inside information. Hang in there. You'll soon be sitting pretty, I swear."

"Oh, Burgess, my God."

"Trust me."

ᴄ

It was springtime around Annie's house. But the season was rushing by too fast. Why didn't it show a little thrift? Why didn't it save some of its blossoms and bring them on one kind at a time? No, it was behaving as if there were no tomorrow, spending all its flowers at once—magnolias and forsythia, daffodils and bleeding heart, lily of the valley and the sweet-smelling daphne she had transplanted beside her front door.

Trying to cheer herself up, Annie wandered down the hill into the wilderness at the bottom of the lawn. From the house she had seen white clouds of shadblow flowering among the weedy oak saplings and sprawling honeysuckle. Struggling among the briars, she lifted a blossoming twig to her nose. There was no fragrance, only the freshness of a thousand expanding leaves.

It didn't help. She was still too sickened by Eddy's death and too fearful about her own financial peril. What if her invested capital disappeared altogether? And what if she lost the suit and had to pay Bob and Roberta Gast all that money? She would lose the house and the hillside and the vegetable garden and the thorny wilderness and every tree and bush and flower. And her wall! She would lose her painted wall.

Annie went back up the hill, picked up the phone, found the number for the central offices of the Paul Revere Mutual Insurance Company, and worked her way through the electronic labyrinth in search of Jack.

When she found him at last he was delighted to talk to her. "Oh, hi there, Annie. What's the matter, you want to upgrade your policy? Listen, I thought at the time you ought to add a little something to cover all that valuable furniture."

"No, no, Jack, it's not that. Oh, Jack, I'm in awful trouble." Quickly Annie explained what had happened to young Eddy Gast in her new house. "They think it's my fault. They think I left the door open so Eddy could come in when I wasn't there. But I didn't, Jack, I didn't. I locked it. Anyway, his parents are suing me for two million dollars. But you sold me that big personal-liability policy. Oh, thank you, Jack. I'm so grateful. Paul Revere will cover it, won't they, Jack? The whole two million?"

Jack hemmed and hawed. "Now, hold it, Annie. Just a minute. Let me look into it. I'll call you right back."

Instead of calling, Jack turned up in person. When Annie came home from a trip to the library and the post office and the supermarket, she found him napping on the sofa.

She dumped a bag of groceries on the counter and stood over him angrily. "Jack, how the hell did you get in?"

Jack woke up, looked at her lazily, closed his eyes again, and muttered, "Stole a key last time I was here."

"You stole one of my keys?" Annie was flabbergasted. "How?"

"Nothing to it. It was in your pocketbook. Right there on your pocketbook hook." Drunkenly Jack began to sing, "You got a hook for your hat and a hook for your coat and a hook, hook, hook for your pocketbook." Groggily he tried to sit up. "Hey, gimme a hand."

Annie made a pot of strong coffee. She needed an insurance agent with a clear head. "Okay, Jack, now tell me. Will Paul Revere deliver on its promise?"

"Promise?" said Jack evasively. "There wasn't any promise, Annie."

"Of course there was a promise." Annie banged her cup down on the coffee table. "What's the *point* of having an insurance policy if you pay premium after premium and then, when you need help, the company doesn't deliver?"

"Well, of course, decisions about claims aren't really my department. It'll be up to an adjuster. Oh, the company will help, of course they'll help. But you can't expect— Listen, Annie, *you* left the door open. You knew the child was a half-wit. It was your fault."

"It wasn't, it wasn't." Annie stared at him, outraged. "And it doesn't matter anyway if it was my fault. Personal-injury insurance is supposed to cover cases like that, isn't it? Isn't it? What's it for, if it doesn't pay when somebody breaks a leg by slipping on your front step?"

"For Christ's sake, Annie, don't get so upset."

"Upset? Upset? They're suing me for two million dollars, and I shouldn't get upset?"

༄

It was clear that Jack would be no help. The Paul Revere Mutual Insurance Company would try to wriggle out of it.

Annie called Uncle Homer, and he said he'd look into it. "But there's no point in talking to Jack. It's not in his interest for Paul Revere to lose a couple of million on a policy he sold you. And how do you think they got so rich in the first place? They've got a whole floor of crafty lawyers diddling people out of their rightful settlements. Every time one of them saves the company a million dollars he gets a bonus." Homer said he was sorry. Annie thanked him and said goodbye.

She got back to work, trying not to think about her plummeting software stock, or about the suit against her. But she couldn't forget about Eddy, the only member of the family who had appreciated her wall.

Come on, now. Concentrate. There was still so much to finish. The last two sections of her arcaded gallery were entirely blank, and the center section only half done. She had been saving a space for Tom Sawyer, lost in the cave with Becky Thatcher, but she didn't feel like painting a terrifying labyrinth, not today. It was too much like the dark tangle of her own life. Instead she'd get to work on Sam Clemens himself, leaning against a pillar in his white suit.

Annie climbed the ladder. Her hands were shaking. It took nerve to climb out on the scaffolding again, even though she had put all the boards back in place and locked the wheels.

Flimnap was gone again. He had said nothing about leaving, but on the day after Eddy's death he had taken off. The detective sergeant wanted to know where he was. Was it not Flimnap O'Dougherty who had put the rolling scaffolding together in the first place, who knew how to lock and unlock the wheels? Maybe the whole thing was his fault.

❧

Mary Kelly was working overtime as Historian in Residence at Weston Country Day. She made a batch of slides, using a camera stand to photograph pictures in books—the temple of Poseidon at Paestum, the Parthenon, the temple of Artemis at Ephesus. It was a lot of work, especially tricky because Homer had cluttered up the floor. He was putting together a documentary history of the town of Concord, and his papers were distributed in a hundred piles all over the rug, one for each year of the nineteenth century. Mary had to tiptoe around the edges, and watch her step as she handled the camera.

When the slides were ready, she arranged them in the right order and carried her projector into the classroom, dropping a book on the way in, stooping to pick it up, dropping another book.

"Sssh," said Mrs. Rutledge, looking up from the story she was reading aloud to the class, *The Flying Family.* In her opinion it was a great classic. Mary had heard some of the chapters before. The family in the story had discovered a magical tree in their front yard. When they jumped off its branches they could fly.

"Joan stood on the highest branch of the enchanted tree," read Mrs. Rutledge. "She wasn't afraid, and when she jumped off, she turned a somersault in the air, just to show Jim her new trick. 'Isn't this fun?' she called to Mom and Dad, who were smiling up at her from the lawn. Then Jim jumped too, and turned a double somersault. Mom and Dad laughed and clapped their hands."

The class was mesmerized. They gazed at Mrs. Rutledge. Some had their mouths open.

Mary put down the projector and waited until Mrs. Rutledge closed the book and stood up to make an announcement. "Class, I have something very sad to tell you this morning. There has been a death in Charlene's family. Last week there was an accident, and her little brother was killed." There were real tears in Mrs. Rutledge's eyes. "Eddy was eight years old. He was going to a special school. I'm sure you will all want to show your sympathy for Charlene."

Everyone looked inquisitively at Charlene Gast. Charlene stared straight ahead and said nothing.

"It was so brave of you, dear, not to miss a day of school," continued Mrs. Rutledge. "But we all know what a courageous young woman you are." With relief she changed the subject to something jollier. "Charlene, is it true that a big swimming meet is coming up soon?"

Charlene's impassive expression disappeared. She beamed. "Next week it's the New England championships in Providence. After that I go to Orlando, Florida, for the Eastern Division Finals. The three top swimmers get to compete in the Junior Olympics."

Breaths were sucked in. How exciting! Charlene would soon be an Olympic swimmer! Mrs. Rutledge clasped her hands. "Is this the one I read about, with Cindy—?"

"Foxweiler." Charlene grinned. "Oh, right. But it's okay. I can swim faster than Cindy Foxweiler."

There were squeals of delight. Applause. Becca Smith waggled her hand in the air. "I saw her on TV! Cindy Foxweiler!"

"All right, class," said Mrs. Rutledge. "Now, just calm down. Thank you, Charlene. You know we'll all be cheering for you. Now, girls, quiet down, please, for Mrs. Kelly's thrilling slide talk about—what is it about, Mrs. Kelly?"

"Greek architecture," said Mary grimly.

"How exciting! Cissie, would you close the curtains? Now, girls, you heard what I said, *quiet down!*"

The news of the death of Charlene's little brother hardly made a dent in the consciousness of the fifth-grade class at Weston Country Day. Later that morning Mary watched them run around the playground. Her amateur psychological study of fifth-grade sociopathology was still in progress. It was obvious that an alarming virus was spreading among these eighteen ten-year-old girls. Mrs. Rutledge was nominally in charge, but in truth she was only a figurehead. Charlene Gast was commander-in-chief. She towered over the rest. They clustered around her, circling and giggling, vying for her attention.

Today Eddy's bereaved sister seemed especially gleeful.

Chapter 35

❧

"Go to the right, into the dark forest of fir-trees; for I saw Death take that road with your little child."
                    Hans Christian Andersen, "The Story of a Mother"

Homer looked at his watch. It was ten o'clock on Saturday morning. He was bored with his documentary history of the town of Concord, tired of waiting for news from Bill Kennebunk, sick of being nagged by his wife to do something about her niece's troubles.

But Annie's troubles were terrible enough to nag him on their own. Homer gazed out the window at the bend of the river. No wind ruffled the surface of the water. The red haze of the trees on the other shore had given way to a delicate veil of green leaves. Homer drummed his fingers on the table. What if he were to pay those lovable Gasts a friendly visit? Once again it amused him, the idea of barging in uninvited, lifting up a rock to watch the loathsome bugs scamper away from the light.

Now he stood up cautiously and minced around the papers on the floor, only once losing his balance and sending the notes for an entire decade sailing across the room.

❧

Roberta Gast opened the door, and said, "Oh."

"Hi there," said Homer cheerfully. "I just thought I'd pay you a call." He looked past Roberta at the front hall. "I've always liked this house. My nephew John used to live here." When Roberta still stood immobile, staring at him, he said, as if it explained everything, "Annie's brother."

"Oh," said Roberta again. "Well, come in." She stood back, and Homer walked past her into the hall. In spite of his familiarity with the house, he hardly recognized it. In John and Helen's time it had been dignified and bare, with only a few pieces of furniture making stark patterns against the walls. Now it was fussy with carpets, curtains, and bric-a-brac. Over a mantel hung a huge mirror with a fantastic gilt frame. The rest of the furniture was handsome too, but somehow phony—expensive replicas of antiques.

Furtively he inspected the seat of his pants, then sat down on a spotless sofa, *George III Chippendale, serpentine cresting, claw-and-ball feet, circa 1760.* Roberta sat opposite on a splendid side chair, *Williamsburg, Queen Anne, cabriole legs, vase-shaped splat.*

She looked wary. Her lip was firmly buttoned. By a trick of optics her face appeared before him twice, once across the room and once in the shining mirror. *Mirror, mirror, on the wall, who is wickedest of all?*

Roberta offered nothing in the way of comfortable small talk to the fumbling guest. Homer rattled on about the old days. Foolishly he mentioned John's spider collection, and asked if she ever came across descendants of John's dear old barn spiders. "Sort of fuzzy creatures, with big round webs?"

Roberta shuddered. "God, no. My cleaning lady comes twice a week."

Homer leaned forward and turned sober. "My wife and I are so sorry about your boy."

Roberta grimaced, and said, "Thank you."

Homer blundered on, as though entirely unaware that the Gasts were suing Mary's niece. "So strange, the way he got into Annie's house. You people didn't have a key, did you? Children are so curious. Eddy might have found a key somewhere, and used it? You know, the way a child might do?"

Roberta bridled, and said, "Of course not." The button on her lip had become a closed zipper.

Homer floundered around in his head and produced another question. "I gather there were other incidents. Could you tell me any other things that happened, unavoidable accidents?"

Roberta no longer had a mouth at all. The lower part of her face was a block of cement. She stared at him venomously.

Homer stood up, and chuckled. "Well, I'd better be going. I'll drop in on Annie, and see what she's up to."

Roberta did not accompany him to the door. He shambled out, shouting cheerful farewells, and walked around the house to Annie's front door. Annie answered his knock at once and let him in. She looked drawn and pale.

"I should have remembered," said Homer. "That woman is some kind of lawyer, right?"

"What woman?"

"Mrs. Gast."

"Yes, unfortunately. She's with the firm that's suing me. Come on in, Uncle Homer."

"I just stopped in over there. She didn't exactly roll out the red carpet. I asked her if they have a key to your place, and she said no."

"My God, Uncle Homer, what nerve! Did you expect her to answer a question like that?"

"Well, probably not. But you said you loaned them your key, right? So before they gave it back they could have had it copied. Have you still got it?"

Annie went to the kitchen counter and opened a drawer. "Here it is. It's got a tag."

Homer looked at the tag, which said "Annie's house," and stroked his chin. "When was this?"

"Last month sometime. Before—" She reached for her calendar. "Yes, here it is." She showed it to Homer, the scrawl across the spaces for March 27 and 28. "I went to New York with my little sister. Miranda and I saw a couple of plays."

"Ah," said Homer, "just three weeks before Eddy's death.

How very interesting. May I keep this key for a while? You don't happen to have a picture of those people, do you?"

"The Gasts? Why, yes, I think so." Annie took a shoebox from a bookshelf. "I ought to paste these in a scrapbook, but I never get around to it." She groped in the box and pulled out a picture. "I took it just after they moved in." Her voice hardened. "When we were all such jolly friends."

It was a family picture. There they were, the Gasts, lined up before their new front door. Roberta's mouth, now so firmly cemented shut, was wide open in a toothy grin. Bob was smiling too, and so were Eddy and Charlene. "What a *sweet* young family," murmured Homer.

"Adorable."

Homer pocketed the picture, patted Annie's back awkwardly, and said goodbye. In his car on the way home he thought about all the places where a key could be copied. Oh, Christ, there were so many.

Impulsively he ignored the turnoff for Fair Haven Road, turned left on Route 62, and parked in front of Biggy's Hardware Store in West Concord.

It was an upmarket hardware store. Besides the usual tools, grass rakes, lawn mowers, trash cans, weed killers, and other murderous substances, it had an interior-decorating department with custom-mixed paint in colonial colors and samples of upholstery fabric. Homer thought of Roberta Gast's flossy furniture. This was surely her kind of hardware store.

"Do you people make keys?" he asked the guy at the counter.

"We sure do. Hand it over."

"No, I don't need a key." Homer pulled out the picture of the Gast family. "I'm looking into a case of B and E, breaking and entering—you know, burglary—and I wondered—"

"You a cop?"

Sighing, Homer produced the well-worn card that identified him as a lieutenant detective, the one dating from many years back. Displaying it as legitimate accreditation was increasingly ticklish. This time the guy behind the counter looked at it carefully and glanced up at Homer suspiciously. "Hey, fella, this isn't you."

"Oh, that was before I grew whiskers," said Homer, grinning foolishly.

"And the date, this card's no good. What are you trying to pull?"

Homer put the card away and tried a fallback approach, telling the truth. "Look, the people in this picture are suing my niece, claiming she's responsible for the death of their son. They say she left the door open while she was out, and the little kid got in and had a fatal accident."

"Oh, yeah, I read about it in the Concord paper. Kid was retarded, right?"

"Down's syndrome. Tell me, did you copy a key for these people?"

Doubtfully the hardware-store clerk looked at the key. "I didn't copy anything with a tag. Maybe Ron did. I just work weekends. And I don't recognize anybody in this picture. Come back Monday. Ask Ron."

At Vanderhoof's Hardware, on the Milldam, it was the same. "Sure, sometimes the keys have tags, but I don't remember this one." The proprietor bent over the picture. "I think that guy comes in here sometimes." He called to his clerk. "Do you recognize this guy? Didn't he buy some antifreeze in here one time?"

"Right. He's been in here a couple of times. Bought a bunch of twenty-five-watt candle-flame bulbs. Couple dozen, for a chandelier."

Homer dangled the key in front of him. "Can you remember if he had a key copied?"

"Not as far as I know," said the proprietor, glancing at the clerk.

"Nope," agreed the clerk. "I didn't cut a key for him. I'd remember it if I had."

Homer went out to the sidewalk, telling himself Gast would have been a fool to have his key copied smack in the middle of town. He went home and showed the key and the picture to Mary, and growled about his suspicions.

"There's a hardware store in Lexington," said Mary. "You could try that one. And there must be others in Bedford and Sudbury. Probably every town around here has a hardware store. And don't forget Boston. Roberta works in Boston."

"Oh, good. That's just great. My God." Then Homer noticed an appalling orderliness in the living room. "Good Lord, what happened? You didn't pick up my papers?" He looked around in a panic. "Where are they? Where the hell are they?"

"Now, now, Homer, don't worry, they're fine. Look, I bought you a file box and a lot of file folders. A hundred folders. I spent all morning putting labels on them. I mean, really, Homer, we had to get the room back. I was tired of tiptoeing around the edges."

Grumpily Homer ran his finger over the orderly row of folders, inspecting the labels and the neat disposition of his papers. "Well, I don't know. If only we had a library like Annie's, I could spread out in all directions."

"You're jealous, are you, Homer?"

"Nothing to be jealous of, I'm afraid. The poor kid's going to lose it all."

Chapter 36

"Open everything, go everywhere, but I forbid you to enter this little room." Charles Perrault, "Bluebeard"

Sergeant Kennebunk's voice on the phone seemed to come from the distant past, all the way back to last week, when Homer had been interested in the disappearance of the battered wife of Frederick Small.

"Oh, Bill, hi there," said Homer, trying to sound cheerful, failing.

"Say, Homer, that was great, the way your wife interviewed the maid in that hotel."

"Oh, right. But we still don't know if the blond woman in that room was really Pearl Small."

"No, that's right, we don't. So I thought you might like to join me in a little research project."

"Research project?"

"Examining Small's house. He seems to be elsewhere. I can't find him. His phone's been disconnected. I think McNutt knows where he is, but he just blusters and says it's none of my business, it's a free country, Small's a law-abiding citizen. Anyway, I thought I'd just take a look at the premises."

"Don't tell me you've got McNutt's signature on a search warrant?"

"Are you kidding?"

"Oh, I see." Homer was delighted. "You're ready to sacrifice your entire career as a law-abiding police officer and future candidate for the job of Rollo McNutt, in order to make a case against that monster Small? Well, good. I'm your man."

When Homer drove into the Pig Road, he had to fit his car into an opening beside three heavy pieces of machinery—a backhoe, a bulldozer, and a gigantic rig with an enormous toothed jaw. Beyond the machines stretched the ninety-nine burdock-infested acres of Songsparrow Estates. At the end rose the rusty towers of Frederick Small's sand-and-gravel company.

Homer found Kennebunk leaning against his car in the driveway behind the house. He was wearing a pea jacket and khaki pants. Homer nodded at the three big machines. "What's going on?"

"I don't know," said Kennebunk, "but I think we're too late. Look, the back door's wide open. I think he's about to move out. Come on."

They spent the rest of the morning roaming from room to room in Small's house. It was unrewarding. There was a dresser in one of the bedrooms, but the empty drawers were stacked on the floor. The drawers of Small's filing cabinet rattled open at Homer's touch, but they too were empty.

"Maybe he put all his papers in these boxes on the floor." Kennebunk opened the boxes one by one. They were tightly packed with books.

Homer looked at the books curiously, running his finger over the titles. "Nothing but gardening books. Disappointing. I wouldn't have thought Small was interested in gardening."

"Not Fred," said Kennebunk, extracting one, "his wife." He showed Homer her name, "Pearl Small," on the flyleaf. "Look at this, *Propagating Evergreens.* She was really serious about all this stuff."

Homer picked up another book. "Did I tell you what Small said when we were walking along the Pig Road? I asked him about the little trees growing up in the middle of the burdock. He said his wife planted them. And then he corrected himself. He said, *We planted them.* But I'll bet it was Pearl." The book in Homer's hand was a text on the uses of ground cover. He opened it and found Pearl's name.

Kennebunk knelt beside the boxes and extracted book after book, with murmured exclamations of pleasure. "What a collection." He glanced up at Homer. "I propagate a lot of stuff myself. I've got a cold frame attached to my garage."

The rest of the upstairs room had been stripped of everything but furniture. As Homer and Kennebunk went from room to room, their footsteps echoed sadly in the hollow spaces. The mattresses were bare. The closets were empty.

The downstairs rooms too had been stripped of curtains and bric-a-brac. Only one picture remained on the dining-room wall, as though forgotten, a drawing of birds in flight, two intersecting flocks. Homer stared at it. "You know, that's nice, really nice. I wonder what happened to all the rest."

There was a box on the floor here too, but it contained only heavy winter coats, not pictures.

But once again Kennebunk was interested. He took the coats out one by one and examined them, feeling in the pockets. "Look at this jacket, Homer. It's covered with burrs."

Homer plucked off a burr and stuck it rakishly on the collar of Kennebunk's jacket. "No question where they come from. Small must have been inspecting his magnificent estate, figuring out how to divide it up into three-hundred-thousand-dollar parcels, complete with pig bones, tin cans, and feeding platforms. Come on. I've seen enough."

"Wait."

Homer stood in the open back door and watched while Bill Kennebunk took a small plastic bag out of his coat pocket and plucked leaf fragments from the woolly fabric of Small's jacket. "A forensic botanist will know what these are," he said, depositing them carefully in the bag.

"A forensic botanist? How could a botanist identify a

piece that small? Are you sure they're not just cigarette tobacco?"

"No, no, they're leaves, all right. And those botanists can do amazing things."

They went outside. The machinery still stood beside the house. "Well, so long, Bill," said Homer. "I don't know if we learned anything, except that Small's about to move out. Where the hell do you suppose he's going? We'd better find out."

"McNutt probably knows. Maybe I can get it out of him." Then Kennebunk took a firm grip on Homer's arm. "Why don't we take a walk up the Pig Road? Half an hour, that's all it'll take. We'll just see if there's any place back there with freshly turned dirt."

"You think he killed his wife and buried her back there, is that it? Oh, God, it reminds me of a sad little case in the town of Nashoba, a couple of years back, a guy who planted his wife in a tomato patch."

Kennebunk set off through the burdock. "We've got to cover every square inch. Walk diagonally like this, then go back over the same ground in the other direction."

Homer groaned. It would take all day. But he set off gamely after Kennebunk, tramping this way, then that, on one side of the Pig Road, while Kennebunk explored the other. Thorny brambles tripped him up, burrs attached themselves to his

good pants, and he barked his shin on the corner of a feeding platform.

At the far end of Small's ninety-nine acres, Kennebunk stopped to admire a cluster of evergreens growing along the property line, bushy little white pines, narrow spires of red cedar, hemlocks with light tips on their fernlike branches. "Look at them, Pearl's plantings. I guess she wanted them to grow high enough to hide the towers of her husband's sand-and-gravel works." He shook his head sadly, and moved to the left along the chain-link fence. "We haven't done this corner yet, and then there's the other corner over there."

It took them two and a half hours. Homer stayed to the bitter end, thinking regretfully about the papers stored so invitingly in his new file folders. They had found nothing. Bill Kennebunk was disappointed. "Sorry, Homer. No soap."

They walked back to Small's house, and found a big van parked beside the rear door. A heavy couch was coming out, lugged by a pair of moving men. They lowered it to the lift on the back of the van and pushed a button. With a whine the couch moved upward.

Homer exercised his ever-present curiosity. "Where are you guys taking all this stuff?"

"Northtown," said the brawny kid in the truck, jumping down. "Warehouse in Northtown."

Kennebunk was surprised. "You mean Mr. Small's not moving to another house in Southtown?"

"I don't know any Small. General contractor, Max Plank, he called us."

Homer's head was spinning. "Max Planck, you mean the physicist?"

"Physicist? I don't think so. Big hairy guy, fat?"

Chapter 37

❧

A nnie's perfect new house, the newly built wing that was the fulfillment of all her dreams, had taken every cent of the advances for her two successful picture books. For future living expenses she could depend on substantial royalties. For security in the future—in illness and old age—there was the comfortable reserve of her invested funds.

What invested funds? There were no mutual funds anymore. That madman Burgess had cashed in Annie's savings and dumped everything down a hole called LexNet Software. And instead of bottoming out and zooming upward as Burgess had promised, the company went belly-up. It was not snatched up in a merger with a re-evaluation of its assets. It merely sold them off, distributed the profits to top management, and disappeared from the market.

As if that weren't bad enough, Annie's future royalties vanished too. She had a letter from her publisher. But instead of good old CURTIS PUBLISHING COMPANY, INC., the letterhead was a bunch of crazy tippy letters, FATCAT FUN BOOKS, with a crazy cartoon feline grinning at the top of the page. Curtis Publishing had been bought out.

Dear Ms. Xwann,
  It has come to our attention that the foll9wing titles

JACLK ANMD THE BEANSTALK
The OWL AND THE PUSSYCRAT

are being remaindered. 25,000 copies OF EACH are abvailable
at 25 c a piece. This offer xpir4s June 22.

> *Tiffany Shrike*
> *Sec'y to Boris Chirp, v. Prexzident*
> *Fatcat Enterp[ises*
> *Providence, R.I. 02902*

Annie didn't believe it. There was some mistake. She called
her agent in New York.

His voice on the phone was sepulchral. "Just another publishing takeover. I'll get your rights back and then we'll try to sell it
to somebody else, but it's the same everyplace. I'm thinking of
getting out entirely and raising mushrooms in Vermont."

"Raising mushrooms! You're kidding."

"Of course I'm kidding. But it's kind of intriguing." The
agent's lugubriousness changed to excitement. "You just order
these little packages of spores. Then you grow them in your cel-
lar and ship them to Boston. No investment, all profit."

"How about rabbits?" said Annie sarcastically. "You start
with two, pretty soon you've got a thousand."

Her agent took the joke seriously. "Right! Rabbits too! I've
thought about rabbits."

The news from attorney Jerry Neville was worse, far worse.
Annie sat in Jerry's office and listened as he explained the out-
of-court settlement with the Gasts.

He looked exhausted. "I'm sorry, dear. It was the best I could
do. You lose the house, but nothing else."

"The house! The whole house?"

"The whole house. But you can go on living in the new wing
as a tenant at will."

"As a tenant! Oh, Jerry, my God."

He looked at her dolefully. "You don't have to pay rent, just
utilities, if that's any comfort."

"Goddamn them anyway."

"Right. Goddamn them straight to hell. Listen, do you know if Homer's come up with anything? He told me those people were really careless with their kid. He said he'd look into it."

"I don't know. I'll ask him."

Annie looked so desolate, Jerry said once again, "I'm sorry, honey. I'm really sorry."

Jerry Neville was an old-fashioned American male, given to fatherly endearments. Annie didn't mind. "Oh, forgive me, Jerry. I know you did better than anybody else could possibly have done. I'm really grateful."

"Here, dear, I'm afraid I've got some papers for you to sign, agreeing to the whole thing."

"Oh, God, Jerry, I don't want to."

"I know." Jerry laid the papers tenderly on the table.

"Shit," said Annie, but she signed.

Jerry took the papers and stood up. "I just happen to have a bottle of scotch in the back of the file cabinet. I think of it as reverse champagne."

"Reverse—? Oh, I see. For the opposite of celebrating. Have you got champagne in there too?"

"Of course, filed under 'R' for 'Rejoicing.' We'll get it out one day for you, Annie dear. Don't despair."

❧

Charlene Gast won her backstroke event in Providence. But a week later she lost by two-tenths of a second in the two-hundred-yard medley to Cindy Foxweiler in Orlando, Florida. As one of the three fastest swimmers she would still be a contender in the Junior Olympics, but she was deeply disappointed. She couldn't believe it had happened. Neither could her classmates.

Mrs. Rutledge was appalled. She took Mary Kelly aside.

"How are we going to deal with it? Poor Charlene! We've got to show her we love her just the same."

"Oh, don't worry about Charlene Gast," said Mary with a dry laugh. "She'll survive."

Charlene had an explanation about her loss when she came back from Orlando, after missing two days of school. "Cindy Foxweiler has her own indoor pool, that's why she won. She can practice every day, like all the time. That's what you've got to have, your own indoor pool."

❧

"Oh, my Lord Fish," shouted the fisherman, his words nearly blown away in the howling wind, "my wife is still unhappy."

The great fish rose from the tumultuous sea and cried, "What favor does she ask for now?"

"She wants—forgive me, Lord Fish—she wants to rule an empire."

"Go home. She is emperor already."

C h a p t e r   3 8

❧

. . . When the sky began to roar,
'Twas like a lion at the door. . . .
                    Mother Goose rhyme

Sergeant William Kennebunk was an amateur horticulturalist and botanist. He was knowledgeable about all the trees and wild shrubs that grew in the fields and woods and swamps of Southtown, even on the fringes of parking lots and strip malls. He had found a *Stewartia koreana* with exfoliating bark in an abandoned garden behind a Wal-Mart on Route 72, and he himself had planted dawn redwoods on the conservation land around a cranberry bog.

Kennebunk knew how to identify trees and shrubs and wildflowers, but he didn't know anything about forensic botany. Fortunately, as a police officer he knew how to find a forensic botanist. On the day after exploring Small's property with Homer Kelly, Bill Kennebunk spent four hours directing traffic around a construction site, and then drove all the way to Boston, to the Bureau of Investigative Services. In the botanist's office he handed over the leaf fragments that had been caught in the woolly fibers of Frederick Small's coat.

The forensic botanist looked at Kennebunk's little plastic bag doubtfully. "I don't know when I'll get around to it. We're pretty goddamn busy. Whole department, we just been downsized. Me, I'm one of the lucky ones, only I don't know about luck. I'm supposed to handle everything four, five guys took care of before. They're out there on unemployment, going to

Florida. One guy, no kidding, he's in Paris, France. Me, I'd go to Italy. I've got aunts and uncles in Italy."

"Well, would you call me when you've had a chance to look at it? My phone number's inside the bag."

The botanist looked vaguely at the bag. "You're in South-borough, right? Lieutenant Kennedy?"

"Southtown. Sergeant Kennebunk."

"Oh, right, Sergeant." The botanist's gaze wandered away to the wall, where there was a calendar with a picture of gondolas in Venice. "Sure, I'll call you."

❧

Homer didn't know what the hell to do about Annie. Those shyster lawyers were tearing at her like a pack of dogs.

His pursuit of her possibly copied key was a trivial piece of research, but it made him feel he was doing something to help. And it didn't take much time to drop into hardware stores here and there.

So far nobody had recognized the faces in his picture of the Gasts. On the first of May, he went back to Biggy's in West Concord, hoping to talk to Ron, the weekday clerk.

"Oh, sorry," said the guy behind the counter, "he's not here. He's on vacation in the Caribbean."

"The Caribbean! But you said—"

"He won't be back for a couple of weeks."

"A couple of weeks!" Homer stared at the clerk, who gave up on him and went looking for a grass rake for another customer. "Wait, wait. Do you know where he is in the Caribbean?"

"God, I don't know." The clerk raised his voice, and shouted toward the back of the store. "Hey, Mitch, where's Ron? You know, where did he go in the Caribbean?"

"Ron? He's in St. Martin. Lucky stiff. You been there? I been there. They got nude beaches, time-share condos. I told him about this really great hotel, the Caribbean Princess." Mitch appeared, his arms dragged down by two gallons of paint, and beamed at Homer. "You want the address? No kidding, you ought to go."

"Oh, no thanks," said Homer, then changed his mind. "Wait a minute, I do want the address. Have you got the phone number of the hotel? I'll call him up. Hey, I could fax him the picture. Do you think the hotel has a fax machine?"

Homer took down Ron's full name and the address of the hotel, imagining the vacationing hardware-store clerk basking on the sand in St. Martin, gazing at the turquoise sea, or frolicking on the nude beach, tossing a Frisbee to a beautiful naked islander, his private parts jiggling up and down. Had Ron made a duplicate of Annie's key for Robert Gast, so that Gast could slyly unlock the door of Annie's house to allow little Eddy to walk in?

By midafternoon Homer had used all the technology available in Concord, Massachusetts, to send Annie's photograph of the Gasts to one Ronald Barnes, a possible guest in the Hotel Caribbean Princess on the island of St. Martin.

He waited around for a while beside the fax machine in the drugstore, hoping for an instantaneous response. None came. Ron was probably out there on the nude beach, enjoying a cookout with all the other naked guys and gals. Or snorkeling in the turquoise water, gazing at exotic fish in Day-Glo colors and beautiful sea anemones, opening and closing their gorgeous petals.

Chapter 39

❧

When the door began to crack,
'Twas like a stick across my back.
Mother Goose rhyme

Flimnap was there when Annie came back from Jerry Neville's office, after trading her house for the agreement by the Gasts to drop the court case against her. There was Flimnap, big as life, standing in the driveway juggling plates. When Annie got out of her car he dropped one, and said, "I'll never get the hang of four."

Annie lost all dignity. She fell on Flimnap's neck and sobbed out her wretched story.

He held her gently and said, "Bastards," and led the way inside.

Annie had decided firmly that she was not in love with Flimnap. You couldn't be in love with somebody who had a big hole in the middle, a lost piece of himself. Still, it was amazing how much she had missed him.

With her back to Flimnap, she put a kettle on the stove and said, "I'm sorry, Flimnap, but I can't afford you anymore. I guess you'll have to find work somewhere else." This was such a terrible thing to say that she leaned on the counter and started crying again.

"Look," said Flimnap quickly, "I don't want to work for anybody else. I want to work for you. Why don't I hang around for a while? You don't have to pay me." Then, as if this selfless remark made him uncomfortable, he looked up at her wall and changed the subject. "The face, it's back."

"What?" Annie looked at the wall and saw another demon staring down at her from the place where so many others had been painted out. It was the worst one yet. Worse than the giant she had invented for *Jack and the Beanstalk*, with its sharp teeth and bulging eyes, its hulking shoulders and clutching hands. "Punishment," wept Annie. "It's punishment, the whole thing is punishment."

"Punishment! Punishment for what?"

"For windows thirteen feet high, that's what for. For a wall thirty-five feet long." Once again the floodgates opened. Flimnap took Annie gently in his arms and held her carefully, patting her on the back like an uncle or a brother or a father, not like someone she might possibly be in love with, no, nothing like that.

❧

Mary Kelly had long since regretted becoming Historian in Residence at Weston Country Day. Not only did it take far too much time to teach the great age of Greece, but the great judge, on whom she had a foolish crush, did not occupy a desk in Mrs. Rutledge's homeroom. Mary's only connection with Judge Aufsesser was her concern for his fat little daughter, Cissie.

What Mary did not know was that Judge Aufsesser himself did feel strongly connected to his daughter's classroom. He had not forgotten Cissie's sordid little story. It was a classic case of blackmail. But of course she would have to pay for her mistake. "I'm sorry, Cissie, but you've got to apologize to Mrs. Rutledge," her father told her gravely. "Then that girl won't have any hold over you."

Cissie wept, but she agreed. Her father made an appointment, and together they entered the fifth-grade classroom after school, the massive figure of the distinguished judge with his timid little daughter.

"Oh, how do you do, Judge Aufsesser! What an honor! Cissie

dear! Won't you both sit down?" Mrs. Rutledge fluttered around her desk, arranging chairs.

"Cissie has something to tell you, Mrs. Rutledge," said Judge Aufsesser, in the voice of God.

Cissie's voice by contrast was a tiny squeak. "That time you asked me to guard your pocketbook, Mrs. Rutledge? I took it out of your desk drawer. I wanted to steal money from your billfold."

"Why, Cissie!" Mrs. Rutledge looked shocked. Then she brightened. "But how brave of you to confess!" She turned to the judge. "I'm sure Cissie will never do such a thing again. Oh, parents are so important in a case like this."

Judge Aufsesser was still solemn. "Go on, Cissie."

Cissie blinked, and whispered, "She saw me. She said she'd tell if I didn't give her my camera."

Mrs. Rutledge was bewildered. "Who saw you? I don't understand."

"Charlene. Charlene Gast."

There was a horrified pause. Mrs. Rutledge gaped at Cissie. "Oh, Cissie, surely you're mistaken."

Cissie shook her head violently, tears streaming down her cheeks.

Her father's eyebrows descended, condemning Mrs. Rutledge. "I know my own daughter. She is telling you the truth."

"But it can't be," spluttered Mrs. Rutledge. "It just can't be true."

"And she's got Beverly Eckstein's bike," squeaked Cissie, taking courage from the powerful presence of her father.

Mrs. Rutledge was deeply distressed. "No, no, that's not true at all. Charlene explained it to me. Their bicycles just happen to be the same make, that's all."

"But Beverly's is missing," said Cissie quickly. Her tears had dried. She felt something new rising up in her, the strength to fight back.

There was a pause. Mrs. Rutledge stood up. "I—I'll look into it, of course. I'll speak to Charlene. Thank you, Cissie. Thank you, Judge Aufsesser. I so much appreciate your coming here today. But I can't believe—" She stopped, and waggled her hands beside her head, as if to say, *It's too much, I can't handle it.*

Judge Aufsesser scowled. "Good day, Mrs. Rutledge. Come on, Cissie."

Outside the school he strode angrily toward his car. "It's not good enough. She's waffling." Cissie had to run to keep up.

❧

Mrs. Rutledge liked to communicate with her students by sending them little notes. "Excellent spelling paper, Becca!" "What a pretty sweater, Amelia!" Notes to Charlene went flying from her desk. "Charlene, your French paper was *très bon!*" "Charlene, you are excused from Special Projects to take charge of school visitors." "Charlene, would you read aloud the next chapter of *The Flying Family*?"

Mrs. Rutledge often called on Charlene Gast, because the child was so reliable and mature. And she was a superb reader, the best in the class, because she read with such expression. She would pick up a book and at once the story came alive. " 'Come ON, Bitsy,' declared Joan, helping her little sister climb to the HIGHEST branch of the tree. 'We'll fly TOGETHER. All right now, JUMP!' "

Mrs. Rutledge didn't know what to do about Judge Aufsesser's complaint. She would have let it slide, if Mary Kelly hadn't complained too. "You should speak to Charlene, Dorothy," said Mary. "She's a bully."

Privately Dorothy Rutledge was disappointed in her new colleague. Oh, Mary Kelly could teach, all right, you'd have to give her that. Once she got going on the temples and the gods and Athens, and so on, she had the kids in the palm of her hand. But she seemed to have a grudge against Charlene Gast.

"A bully! Charlene? But that's absurd."

"No, really. Watch her. She's a tyrant. She's got the rest of them cowed. She dominates. She's got an in-group and an out-group."

"Nonsense! She's a natural leader, that's all."

"Speak to her parents. Really and truly, she needs to be restrained. She's too powerful."

"Powerful! A ten-year-old girl?" Mrs. Kelly was jealous, decided Mrs. Rutledge, jealous of her own friendship with the star of the class.

But after two warnings she had to do something. She called Charlene's mother and asked her to come in after school.

Roberta Gast complained that as a working woman she found it difficult to make daytime appointments during the week. But at Mrs. Rutledge's insistence she made an exception. She came to Weston Country Day and sat in the chair so recently occupied by Judge Aufsesser, expecting to hear of some new honor for her daughter.

Mrs. Rutledge began with her own sorrow at the death of Charlene's little brother. "Oh, Mrs. Gast, the whole class offers you their sympathy."

"Thank you," said Roberta coldly.

Flustered, Mrs. Rutledge changed the subject to Charlene's strong powers of leadership. "The truth is, Mrs. Gast, sometimes she's apt to go a teeny bit too far. My colleague Mrs. Kelly complains of a slight tendency on Charlene's part to dominate the other girls."

"Dominate!"

"I feel sure that Charlene will one day go into politics, or become the president of a university."

"Mrs. Kelly complained about Charlene?" said Roberta Gast. "Mary Kelly? I see."

There was a note of disapproval in Roberta's voice. Mrs. Rutledge capitulated at once. "Perhaps I shouldn't have listened to her." Then Mrs. Rutledge squared her shoulders. There was still the matter of Judge Aufsesser's accusation. "I also want to speak to you about her camera. Cissie Aufsesser makes a rather audacious claim. She says Charlene blackmailed her, and took her camera. I know it sounds ridiculous, but children do say such extraordinary things."

"Cissie Aufsesser? The little fat girl?" Roberta Gast's voice was sharp.

Mrs. Rutledge tittered. "That's right. She's the one."

"I see." Roberta rose from her chair. "I'll look into it," she said, and strode out of the room with a pain in her heart. There was nothing she could do about Charlene. Her daughter was completely out of her control.

Chapter 40

❧

When my back began to smart,
'Twas like a pen knife in my heart.
                    Mother Goose rhyme

Homer combed his mop of bushy hair, trying to remember a word. It was right on the tip of his tongue. *Disbungled, bughundled.* Concentrating, he stared into the mirror and stuck out his tongue, but no word appeared on the end. His tongue was large and thick and quivering. How could so gross an object articulate human speech?

Gloomily he washed his face and mopped his beard with a towel. It was dismaying how often he found himself losing words lately, perfectly ordinary words in constant use. It was like being in the Garden of Eden, partaking of the childhood of humankind. The thing in its essence stood before you, the whole meaning of the word you were looking for, but without a name, like an animal in the Garden of Eden. *Large and striped with sharp teeth and claws? "Tiger,"* Adam would say, *naming it for the first time. "You're a tiger."*

"Homer," called Mary from the kitchen, "come and get it."

Still complaining, he sat down at the breakfast table and stared at his plate. "Dismungled," he said. "Grundundled. I'm trying to find a word."

Mary was fresh from the shower. Her shirt was freshly ironed. Her cheeks glowed, she smelled of soap. She poured him a cup of coffee. "Well, what does the word mean?"

Homer stared fixedly at her, thinking hard. The word poised for a minute in the air—he almost had it!—and then it fled.

183

"Goddamnit, it means the way you feel when you can't find it, goddamnit."

"Bad-tempered?" suggested Mary. "Irascible? Cantankerous?"

"Not as strong as that. It's more a feeling inside. You know, when you can't find your car keys, or some student asks a question and you don't know the answer. Dis—dis—?"

"Discontented? Disembodied? Dismembered? Come on, Homer. I'll drop you at the prison and do my shopping, and then I'll pick you up. And remember, you've got to be right there in the parking lot at ten-twenty so we can get to Cambridge in time for class." She slapped the dishes into the sink and together they hurried down the porch stairs.

Then Homer couldn't find the car keys. But his face was wreathed in smiles. "Disgruntled," he said happily. "Of course, that's it. Disgruntled."

∽

His second meeting with the six inmates of M.C.I. Concord was much like the first. They were all there. No one had failed to come back. They were still anxious, still in a hurry to get out of this fucking place. The mandatory minimum sentencing law had them by the balls. *Gawd!* It was only a little cocaine, for shit's sake, and the judge, she said she had no choice, she had to put you away for twenty years, *twenty fucking years. Without parole, for shit's sake.*

Homer agreed with their indignation, he agreed with their obscenities. But his sympathy would do them no good. They needed retrials, they needed a change in the law, they needed popular support outside the walls, they needed a governor more interested in justice than re-election. It was a vengeful and rancid time, and these poor bimbos were victims as well as offenders.

Gordie was still worried about the taxes he might have to

pay on the money socked away in his girlfriend's bureau drawer.

Hank still had not received payment for services rendered, and again he was unwilling to specify what those services had been.

Homer had pursued the matter of Jimmy's greedy wife. He had found her just as the twenty-eight-cubic-foot refrigerator was being manhandled out the door by a couple of husky men. Jimmy's wife came out carrying a large lamp.

"Stop," Homer said, "you've got to send those guys away." And Jimmy's wife had been mad as hell.

Homer had also obtained the records of Ferris's trial, and discovered that Ferris was right. His court-ordered defense counsel had been incredibly stupid. "Maybe I can persuade them to give you another chance in court."

"Well, thanks," said Ferris, pleased and surprised, because the news from outside was usually bad.

As for Barkley, he now had fifteen precedents to put on the table. He had found three cases in which the sex of the child and that of the molester were the same as in his own case, and so was the age of the child.

"Just what were the age and sex of the child in your case?" said Homer.

"Four-year-old female," said Barkley. "Just like in that other case, you know, *Commonwealth* versus *Kettle*."

"Four years old!" Homer could hardly control his disgust.

"You bastard," cried Ferris. "Animal," shouted Hank. They fell on Barkley and knocked him out of his chair.

Homer had all he could do to restore order. After class the supervisor of prison education spoke to Homer. "How's it going? I thought I heard a commotion in there this morning."

"Oh, no, it was fine," said Homer, smiling feebly, hurrying away to meet Mary in the parking lot. "It was absolutely fine."

Chapter 41

ॐ

When my heart began to bleed,
'Twas death and death and death indeed.
Mother Goose rhyme

"**B**ob? This is Fred."

"Fred Small! My God, where have you been? I've been trying to get hold of you. Your house, it's supposed to come down tomorrow. Pearl's signature on the papers, I've got to have her signature before they'll do anything. They can't touch the house without her name on the dotted line."

"The papers? Oh, sure, I've got them right here."

"Well, for Christ's sake, get 'em over there. Ted Hawk, he'll be there by seven A.M., he'll want the papers. He's been bugging me. Where the hell have you been?"

"Oh, all over the place. The fact is, I'm looking for somebody."

"Looking for somebody? You mean Pearl? You mean she's really a missing person? I thought you said she was in Albany, you got her signature."

"No, no, I'm not looking for Pearl. Never mind. I'll be there tomorrow at the site with the papers. Seven A.M., right? Right. So long."

"Wait, Fred, hold it. Where can I get in touch with you? There's things we have to decide." The phone went dead. "Shit," said Robert Gast.

ॐ

"Daddy?" said Charlene.

Her father was watching a basketball game. The Celtics had run up a score of 110, but the New York Knicks had rushed up from behind. In the fourth quarter they were two points ahead. "Sink it," shouted Bob Gast, as Hubie Buckle made a feint to the left, slammed down his enormous shoes, and pivoted to make the throw.

"Daddy!"

"Not now, Charlene."

Charlene came closer and muttered something in her father's ear. In spite of the roar from the television as the ball circled the rim of the basket, he heard her all too clearly.

He stared at her, and said, "Oh, Jesus, Charlene."

❧

For Bob Gast it was a problem of cash flow. The property in Southtown was finally freed up, but from now on he would need a lot of ready cash, a big loan. There would have to be more percolation tests, a couple of paved roads, a heavy-duty drainage system, and the removal of every trace of occupation by pigs. All those gruesome feeding platforms would have to be bulldozed out of there and the whole ninety-nine acres plowed under to remove the burdock. And all the new little trees too, because they didn't fit the landscaping scheme of the classy new land manager.

Classy! He was classy, all right, and extremely expensive. But you had to have a really professional land manager, Bob Gast knew that.

"What about an entry?" the land manager wanted to know. "Are you planning a formal entry?"

"Oh, of course," said Gast, thinking of the elegant gateposts and plantings at Meadowlark Estates.

"And what about the environmental-impact statement? Do

you want us to handle that? Those environmentalists on the planning board, they're going to say some of those lots are wetland. So you've got to have a professional analysis of the soils and get the results of the perc tests, how long it takes rainfall to drain away from the soggy places. What you do is, you wait for a really dry week before you do the testing. And don't forget the wildlife."

"Wildlife! You mean the pigs? The pigs are gone!"

"No, no. Raccoons, deer, pheasants, birds. Those people, they're really serious about nesting sites for birds. How about meadowlarks and song sparrows?"

"Song sparrows! God! The only birds around Small's place are crows."

It was all very exciting, but also very scary. Bob Gast had never been so deeply in debt. And now there was this goddamn thing of Charlene's. Of course, compared with developing from scratch a ninety-nine-acre piece of prime real estate, the cost of an indoor pool was peanuts. The only question was where to put the damn thing.

After Charlene went to bed, Bob talked it over with Roberta. At first she was shocked, but then, as usual, she came up with a solution. "Tear down the wing."

"The wing? You mean Annie Swann's new wing?"

"It's not hers, it's ours."

"But she's got a lease. My God, Roberta!"

"Talk to my boss. He'll fix it up. Talk to Dirk Sprocket."

❧

"No problem," said Sprocket, waving Gast's doubts aside. "Piece a cake."

"Are you sure?" said Gast nervously, smoothing down the 999 hairs that remained on his balding head. "But it was part of the out-of-court settlement. I signed it. Roberta signed it. *She* signed it. We agreed she can stay in the house as our tenant."

"Wrong," said Sprocket, leaning back in his chair, grinning, poking the air with his cigar. "Tenant *at will.*"

"At will?"

"At *your* will." Sprocket put his cigar in his mouth and chewed it sideways. "You want her out? She's out."

"Well, thanks," said Gast feebly. He couldn't summon the spiritual conviction to smile. "That's just great."

"I'll get an eviction notice," said Sprocket. "I got a judge in my pocket. We'll serve the papers this afternoon."

∾

"What?" cried Annie, staring at the envelope. "No, I won't accept it. Take it away."

"You gotta accept it, sister," said the process server at her door. "Contempt of court."

Annie put her hands behind her back. "No, no, I won't. Go away."

The man grinned and tossed the envelope over her shoulder. It landed in the middle of the hall floor and slid into the big room beyond. Annie chased after it and snatched it up, meaning to throw it back, but the front door banged shut with a shivering slam. By the time she wrenched it open, he was leaping into his car. The engine was running. He zoomed away.

Reluctantly she opened the envelope and read the official language of Sprocket's court order. Outraged, she tore it in half and called Homer. There was no answer, only the polite language of the message machine. Annie was so angry she could hardly speak. Her message was a string of obscenities, but its meaning was clear.

Homer's first words when he called back were as wrathful as her own. "Don't leave," he shouted into the phone. "Whatever you do, don't move out."

"You bet I won't move out. I'm here to stay. So what can they do to me, Uncle Homer?"

"God, I don't know. I'll find out. In the meantime, hang in there."

Annie put down the phone and stared at her painted wall. Legally it belonged to the Gasts. Now they wanted her out. Well, she was not going to leave, she was never going to leave. How could she abandon her wall to the tender mercies of Robert and Roberta Gast, who would hide the five arches of her painted gallery under a dozen rolls of Williamsburg wallpaper? They didn't give a damn about her wall.

❧

"Is she gone?" said Charlene.

"Not yet," said her father. "But she's got to obey the court order."

"It's that painting of hers," said Roberta. "She's sentimental about that big painting on her wall."

"But it's not her wall anymore," said Gast. "It's our wall. We can do whatever the hell we want with that goddamned wall. You know what it is, that wall?" He swallowed hard, as a vision of the painted wall rose in his mind, bright with color and flowering with stories. "It's self-indulgence. Pure self-indulgence."

"You can knock it down, right?" said Charlene. "You'll have to, because my swimming pool's got to be, like, really, really big. I got this book out of the library. You've got to have radiant heating and automatic ventilators and a shower room and a towel closet and—"

"Oh, God, Charlene," said Bob Gast, dropping his head in his hands, "sometimes I think we should just—"

Charlene did not wait to hear what he was going to say. Once again she moved in close and whispered in his ear.

"Oh, God, I know," said her father. "I know, I know."

Roberta Gast did not ask what it was that her husband knew. She knew what he knew. She leaped up and began pulling things out of the refrigerator for supper, trying not to think about the future.

❧

"Lord Fish, Lord Fish!" shrieked the fisherman, struggling to keep his boat from foundering in the tormented sea. "My wife is not happy being emperor."

"Perhaps," croaked the fish, gazing up at him from the boiling whirlpool below the boat, "she would like to rule the world."

"Oh, yes, Lord Fish! How did you know? She wants to rule the whole entire world."

The eyes of the great fish glowed back at him. "Go home, my friend. Your wife is ruler of all the continents on earth and all the islands in the sea."

Part Three

London Bridge is falling down,
Falling down, falling down.
London Bridge is falling down,
My fair lady.
— Mother Goose rhyme

Chapter 42

❧

By now Bob Gast was well acquainted with Ted Hawk, proprietor of Hawk Wrecking and Demolition, owner of the big machines that were now demolishing Fred Small's house in Southtown and grinding their way across his ninety-nine acres of burdock, uprooting hundreds of small hemlocks and white pines and crushing an entire nursery of pasture juniper and mountain laurel. Originally Bob had chosen Hawk's outfit from an ad in the Yellow Pages—

HAWK WRECKING AND DEMOLITION
COMMERCIAL * RESIDENTIAL * INDUSTRIAL
24 HOUR EMERGENCY SERVICE
7 DAYS A WEEK
LICENSED * BONDED * INSURED
Braintree Mass
848-5555

So now he knew just where to go for this job here at home. On the phone to Hawk he explained the problem. "It's a wing attached to my house. It's only the wing that is to be—uh—removed. The house is to remain intact."

"Well, sure, no problem. Why don't I come out and take a look?"

Ted Hawk was a tall, dignified man in a business suit. He walked around the new wing with Bob Gast. As they strolled past the south side, Annie was plainly visible within, sitting on her scaffolding, twisting around to look at them.

"Somebody's living in there now?" said Hawk.

"Oh, sure, but she's getting out. Don't worry."

"You positive? She hasn't got a lease? You've got a deed, says you're the owner? We've got to see the deed. Like at Southtown, we don't want any trouble. You'd be surprised the kind of things that happen."

"Oh, everything's fine, perfectly legal, all according to Hoyle."

"Well, as you know, there's paperwork. We've got to prep it, do utility disconnects, get all the fluorescent tubing out because of, you know, PCBs. Notarized permission letter, building inspector informed. You got any tax liens on the property? Mortgage? Bank's got to sign off too." Again Hawk looked appraisingly at the wing of the house that no longer belonged to Anna Elizabeth Swann. "It's a small job. Take a day, maybe two with site clearing. When will your tenant be out, all her stuff?" Hawk's voice was loud. He was staring straight into one of Annie's big windows.

Embarrassed, Gast drew him aside. "In two weeks. She's got to be out by May twenty-first."

Hawk consulted his pocket notebook. "Right. Say May twenty-third. That okay with you?"

Gast cleared his throat and stared at Hawk with bulging eyes. "How much is this going to cost me? I mean all together?"

"It's a small job." Hawk rubbed his chin. "Twenty thousand? Round figure."

"Jesus Christ! Small's house, it was only fifteen."

"Well, this one's tricky, separating the two parts. It's like dividing Siamese twins, you gotta be careful."

"Well, okay, go ahead, God!" Bob added up figures in his mind. It wasn't just the original sum of his mounting debts, plus this extra twenty thousand, it was the accumulating interest. *One hundred dollars a day, one hundred dollars a day, one hundred dollars a day.*

Chapter 43

❧

Build it up with needles and pins,
Needles and pins, needles and pins!
Build it up with needles and pins,
My fair lady!

Mother Goose rhyme

"I told you," said Bob Gast, standing at Annie's front door, "you're to be out of here by the twenty-first."

"I'm not going," said Annie.

Gast restrained an impulse to take her by the arms and drag her out. But Annie was a big woman, taller than he was, and probably stronger. And that weird character O'Dougherty was visible outside the window, glancing in their direction. Yesterday Bob had seen him turn six handsprings on the lawn, one after another, his body making impossible contortions, springing higher with every bound.

And anyway, things were bad enough. Violence would only get him in trouble. "In that case I'll be forced to call the police."

"And I'll be forced to call the newspapers."

Gast blanched, then said sarcastically, "I don't think an article in the *Concord Journal* would make much of a stir."

"One in the *Boston Globe* would make a stir." Annie pawed around in her head for the name of a famous columnist. "Gabe Garibaldi, he'd be interested."

"Gabe Garibaldi!" In spite of himself, Gast was choked with doubt. He had read Garibaldi's column. The man was a master of sentimental hardship cases. "Mother-to-be fired without cause." "Elderly ripped off." "Widow robbed of life savings."

He knew exactly what would happen. Garibaldi would write a phony column about Annie that would make her landlord look like a bastard. Bob could write it for him, every lying word. "Cruel landlord evicts famous artist. Masterpiece destroyed."

"God*damn* you, Annie Swann," he said, with an intensity that welled up from his bowels and sifted pathetically down from the 752 remaining hairs on the top of his head.

In Jerry Neville's original out-of-court settlement with the Gasts, Annie was not required to pay rent. But now she was eager to pay. She produced a handful of hundred-dollar bills. "Here, this is for next month."

He shouted at her, "You won't be here next month."

Annie tossed the bills at his retreating back. They flew up, then fluttered down into the pachysandra bordering the north side of the house. Some of them blew across the driveway.

She went inside and slammed the door.

It began to rain, beating down on the roof of Annie's house and the driveway and the pachysandra, plastering the unclaimed greenbacks to the pavement, thrusting them into crevices between the shiny leaves of the ground cover. Later on, when the sun came out, Charlene discovered them and picked them up, pouncing on one after another. It was like an Easter-egg hunt, but with hundred-dollar bills instead of jelly beans. That afternoon she flipped through the catalogue from the pool company and picked out a poolside chaise and sent the money in cash. Later on, when the big box was delivered by UPS, her mother said, "Charlene, what's this?" and Charlene said, "It's okay, Mummy, I found the money on the driveway," and Roberta, scandalized, said, *"What?"* But of course this time Charlene was telling the truth.

❧

"They can't knock anything down if I'm in the way, can they?"

Flimnap looked at Annie soberly. "Superior force. A couple of

big cops, that's all it would take. They'd haul you out of here."
He glanced up at the endangered wall. "Who's that in the big
chair?"

Annie looked up too and smiled. "Charles Dodgson. You
know, Lewis Carroll. He's reading to Alice Liddell."

Flimnap stared at Dodgson. Annie waited for him to say
something complimentary. Instead he began talking about
moral force. "Look, Annie, it's all you've got to fight with. You
need publicity, a protest movement. They've got the law.
You've got righteousness, justice, and truth."

She laughed. "You sound just like my Uncle Homer. He loves
big sweeping abstractions. But you're right. I'll write a letter to
the *Globe*."

"Let me take care of it," said Flimnap. "I know somebody
there."

So it was Flimnap, not Annie, who went to the *Boston Globe*.

His friend at the paper just happened to be the executive editor, Harvey Broadstairs. When the editorial assistant mentioned
the visitor's name, Broadstairs summoned him at once and listened to his story sympathetically.

"Great stuff," said Broadstairs. "Sob story. Worth its weight
in gold. Sure, it's Garibaldi's kind of thing, but not just
Garibaldi. When does the bulldozer arrive? Good. We'll have
somebody out there. Color shot."

"Well, thanks, that's great. Oh, say, there's just one thing.
Don't use my name, all right?"

"Why not? I should think it would carry weight. Why don't
you capitalize on it? No? Well, all right, if you say so."

❧

The story in the *Boston Globe* did indeed create a stir. And Gabe
Garibaldi's column oozed with sympathy. Garibaldi knew noth-
ing about the death of Eddy Gast. His outrage was directed at
Eddy's father, who was threatening the safety of a work of art.

Moral force, Flimnap said, *it's all you've got to fight with,* but Annie couldn't see what good his publicity was doing. Everything was in such a mess. A new unwanted face had appeared on her wall, even more savage than before, and those bastards were about to bring in their machines and knock her house down.

In despair Annie decided she would die before she'd allow them to destroy her wall. Just let them try! They'd have to destroy Annie Swann at the same time. Melodramatically Annie told herself that the people who believed in the publicity value of moral force could take a picture of her mangled body and publish *that.*

Then Minnie Peck, the found-object sculptor, and Trudy Tuck, the creator of artistic candles, saved the day. Together they roused the countryside.

Chapter 44

Pins and needles bend and break,
Bend and break, bend and break,
Pins and needles bend and break,
My fair lady.

Mother Goose rhyme

"**I** just wondered if you've had time to work on the sample I brought in last week," said Sergeant Bill Kennebunk, at last connected by phone to the forensic botanist in the Bureau of Investigative Services, after jumping over a series of electronic hurdles.

"Oh, that one. You mean the sample from Southborough? You're—uh—Patrolman Kensington?"

"Southtown, not Southborough. And my name's Kennebunk." Sergeant Kennebunk's faith in the scientific accuracy of the Bureau of Investigative Services plummeted. How could he trust anything this bungler came up with?

But there were still no findings. "Sorry, Kensington, we're still way behind. Our chief just retired, and his replacement, he's a new broom." A tone of bitterness crept into the botanist's voice. Kennebunk suspected he had been passed over for promotion. "He wants us to clean out all our old files. So we've been throwing out stuff. Not your stuff, of course. At least I hope not."

Kennebunk called Homer Kelly, and explained the delay.

Homer was used to bureaucratic foot-dragging, and anyway he had forgotten the point of Kennebunk's botanizing. "Any sign of Frederick Small? Where did his furniture end up?"

"Storage warehouse in Northtown. Nobody seems to know where he is himself. McNutt just grins and won't tell me anything, but I think he knows. Oh, say, Homer, his house has been torn down."

"No kidding! I suppose it wasn't elegant enough for Songsparrow Estates. The better class of buyers might turn up their noses."

❧

Like most construction workers, demolition expert Ted Hawk rose early. This morning he was up at four-thirty. There was always a lot to do, mobilizing a job. You had to haul the forty-ton excavator up onto the low-bed trailer with a hydraulic lift and lash it down with chains and get it out on the road by five-thirty, because, Christ, during commuting hours you couldn't obstruct the highway with two slow-moving heavy trucks and a tractor trailer lugging a monster machine.

Therefore, it was only six-thirty when his car pulled into the Gasts' driveway, followed by the two trucks and the tractor trailer with its colossal burden. Hawk was dismayed to find the scene of his day's work already teeming with the friends and relatives of Annie Swann. They were carrying signs—

BARBARIAN, GO HOME!
GET LOST!
STOP THIS MADNESS!
SAVE THIS ARTISTIC TREASURE!
PRESERVE THIS WORK OF ART FOR THE NEXT
MILLENNIUM!

Flimnap O'Dougherty was nowhere in sight, but someone had braced the north side of the house with props, heavy wooden beams like flying buttresses on a church. Homer Kelly too was somewhere else, trying to wake up a judge and get an injunction.

The protestors shrieked at Hawk and jiggled their signs up and down. Minnie Peck turned on her boom box, and a chorus of thousands began roaring "The Star-Spangled Banner." Thunder-claps of patriotic music battered Hawk's windshield. A video camera was aimed in his direction. Somebody else was taking pictures.

Hawk dropped his hands from the steering wheel and said, "Oh, fuck."

Hawk's passenger, his subcontractor, said, "God almighty."

"I told the guy we didn't want any trouble," said Hawk. "Look at those sons a bitches."

Someone opened the car door. It was one of Hawk's truck drivers. He gestured with his thumb. "There's a guy inside, see?" Hawk craned his neck, and saw Bob Gast beckoning from a window. "He's scared to come out," said the truck driver, grinning.

They followed Gast's pointing finger to his front door and went inside, while Annie's friends hooted and booed.

"They're just bluffing," said Bob Gast, his face white. "Go ahead. Get the machine down off the truck. Start it up. They'll disappear in a hurry."

"No way," said Ted Hawk. "A couple of those people, they've got cameras. You said there wouldn't be any trouble."

"There won't be, I tell you." Gast was frantic. "Go ahead and get started."

"I'm sorry, Mr. Gast, but protesters are bad news. We're leav-ing, so that'll be two thousand dollars, okay? For our time, and tying up the equipment."

Gast was scandalized. "*What?* But you haven't *done* anything yet."

"Mobilizing fee. Six guys, couple of trucks, and all this equip-ment, creeping down 128 thirty miles from Braintree and thirty miles back, and then three guys have to get the machine down off the flatbed again, whaddayamean, that's not doing anything?" Hawk took a rumpled form out of his pocket, slapped it on the kitchen table, and scrawled on it with his pen. "So I'd like a check right now, if it's all the same to you."

❦

After school Charlene was disappointed to see Annie's part of the house still standing. "Hey, Daddy," she said, "what happened? Aren't they going to knock it down?"

Bob Gast felt driven into a corner by women. Young or old, they were all the same. Stubborn, demanding, they never let go. "Don't worry, I'll get her out. We'll hire another wrecking company. She'll have to pack up and leave."

"Well, I wish she'd hurry up. Look, Daddy, here's the catalogue from the swimming-pool company." Charlene flipped it open so that he could admire the Olympic-sized indoor pool. It was full of jolly swimmers, children, mothers, and fathers. A model in a scanty suit lay on an inflated mattress. A serious swimmer clove the water with a powerful backstroke. There were ladders, slides, diving boards, track lighting, and huge windows, poolside tables and chairs, a garden with tropical plants and gigantic blossoms. The water was aquamarine.

Charlene's father looked for a price. It was nowhere to be seen.

❦

"Lord Fish, Lord Fish!" cried the fisherman, screaming above the tempest, as the towering waves washed over his foundering boat. "My wife has another request."

For a moment the enchanted fish did not appear above the churning sea. When at last he thrust up his great head he glowered at the fisherman and said, "Your wife rules the world. What more can she ask of me?"

"Oh, Lord Fish, forgive me, but she wants to be pope! She wants to sit on the throne of St. Peter!"

The sea foamed, the sky split with lightning and thunder. The fish hissed his answer, "So it shall be. Your wife is mistress of the Holy See."

Chapter 45

❧

Build it up with wood and clay,
Wood and clay, wood and clay!
Build it up with wood and clay,
My fair lady!

Mother Goose rhyme

Next morning the *Boston Globe* had a color shot of the protesters defying Ted Hawk's enormous demolition machine. In addition, the local TV news ran the story.

Bob Gast was disgusted with the publicity those people were
managing to whip up. It was all on the side of Anna Swann. She
was supposed to be some kind of heroine for defying his eviction order. He had to keep reminding himself that the law was
on his side, not hers. He wrote a huffy letter to the *Globe*, making this point, but of course the damage was done.

Nervously he flipped through the Yellow Pages again, and
began calling other wrecking contractors. The first three had
read about the confrontation and wanted no part of it. The
fourth demolition expert seemed ignorant about the whole
thing. Apparently he never read the paper or watched the news
on TV.

"I'll pay you overtime if you'll do it late at night," said Bob
Gast.

But late at night or not, Flimnap O'Dougherty was alerted by
the shuddering noise of the hydraulic lift and the scream of the
chain, as the big machine with its grappling jaw descended
from the low-bed trailer. He bounced out of bed in his gypsy
caravan, which was hidden in a leafy thicket deep in the

woods. Seizing his telephone, he made a call, then raced down the hill. He found Annie standing at her door pulling on her coat, her hair flowing over her nightgown in a tangle.

Behind Flimnap, Annie could see the glaring headlights of the big excavator wobble up and down as it headed around the corner, plowing headlong through a blossoming viburnum bush. Frantically she turned back into the house. "I'll call Uncle Homer. He was going to get a restraining order."

"I called him already," said Flimnap. "He's calling Minnie Peck. They're all coming."

A pale face swam up in the dark. It was Bob Gast. "She's got to get out," he said angrily to Flimnap, flourishing his copy of the eviction notice as another set of headlights floundered up the driveway.

"Excuse me," said Flimnap dreamily, reaching out in the dark. "I think you've got something in your ear." He held it up delicately between finger and thumb. It was an egg.

"What's he doing with an egg in his ear?" said Homer Kelly, looming up beside him, sounding puzzled, trailed by his wife Mary.

"The injunction, Uncle Homer," cried Annie, as the racket of the huge machine grew louder and its headlights sent a ray streaking through the house, "have you got the injunction?"

"You mean this thing?" Homer extracted a folded paper from his pocket and showed it to Bob Gast. He showed it to Flimnap. He showed it to the wrecking contractor.

It was a contest between two pieces of paper. Homer's paper won.

"That'll be thirty-two hundred for our trouble," said the contractor, handing Gast another piece of paper, while Minnie Peck's friends tumbled out of cars. The installation artist was there, Henry Coombs, along with his wife Lily, who made pretty pictures with dried flowers. They were joined by poet Henrietta Willsey and potter Perry Chestnut. Minnie had also summoned Wally Feather, the plaster-cast man, and Trudy Tuck, who made ornamental candles. All of them gathered around Gast and Homer and Mary and Annie, and grinned and made rude remarks. Trudy took more pictures.

Nearly insane with anger and frustration, Bob Gast scrawled another check, steam fizzing out of his pen, and abandoned the field. Annie invited her supporters in for a drink.

They were triumphant, noisy with the spirit of the barricades. Mary Kelly was excited too, but she couldn't help hearing a note of hysteria in Annie's loud laugh. "To Annie!" shouted Homer, raising his glass. "Long may she wave!" And in no time at all he had guzzled down three whiskeys, while his wife looked on indulgently and reminded herself to take the wheel when the party was over.

Before long Annie had imbibed at least two whiskeys herself. She was leaping from sofa to sofa. Homer beamed at her, then glanced up at her insane and wonderful wall. Nutty the girl might be, but you had to give her credit for achieving something truly amazing.

When the party broke up, Homer too was standing on one of the sofas, making oracular pronouncements. Mary cut him short and stuffed him into his coat and took him home.

Trudy Tuck wasn't ready to go to bed. She extracted the film from her camera, held it high, and exclaimed loudly, "I'll take it to the *Globe* right now."

"But Trudy, it's three in the morning," cried Annie.

"I don't care what time it is. So long, everybody." Trudy's coat swirled dramatically as she made a rush for the door.

"That's Trudy all over," said Minnie Peck jealously. "The swashbuckling gesture. Hey, could somebody drive me home?" She looked around for Flimnap. "Where's O'Dougherty?"

"He was here a minute ago," said Annie, looking around too.

"We'll take you," said Henry Coombs. "You're right on our way." Henry put down his glass and glanced up at the splendid images on Annie's wall. He had seen them before, at her house-warming party. They had all seen them before. But now the wall was much more complete. Annie's painted storytellers stood in a stately row. They were at once homely and imposing. Behind them their stories romped all over the landscape: Huck and Jim drifting down the Mississippi on their raft, the old witch threatening Hansel and Gretel, Cinderella on her way to the ball, and the emperor in his underwear. The background shimmered with detail.

Annie's friends put on their coats and looked at the wall, admiring it, making suggestions and criticizing—Henry and Lily Coombs, Wally Feather, Minnie Peck, Henrietta Willsey, and Perry Chestnut. Novelist Albert Flood looked at it too, and weaver Lindsay Jiggs, who had driven up too late to see the action. But whether they found fault with her wall or not, whether they approved of Annie's sense of design and choice of subject matter, it represented something they all believed in, something endangered by the might and majesty of the law. Somehow or other it must be saved.

Chapter 46

Wood and clay will wash away,
Wash away, wash away!
Wood and clay will wash away,
My fair lady!

Mother Goose rhyme

But of course Robert Gast eventually found another willing company in the Yellow Pages—Quincy Contractors, Wrecking Demolition Specialists, Serving All New England, Interior/Exterior Demolition, 24-Hour Emergency Service, Buildings, Tanks, Towers, Chimneys, Heavy Industrial & Civil Dismantling, Disposal of Debris, Licensed, Bonded, Insured.

Quincy Contractors didn't give a damn about protesters. "We'll mow 'em down," said the contractor in charge. "Just joking, of course." But there was a surly undertone in his voice, as though he wasn't joking at all.

Homer tried and failed to get another injunction. "Sorry," said the judge. "The man's got a deed. He owns the entire building. He has a perfect right to knock it down if he wants to." Privately he admitted to Homer that Gast was scum, but unfortunately there was no way the law could stop him. "Just go on shaming him before the world," he suggested kindly. "I don't know what else you can do."

Once again Annie's supporters answered the summons, along with a lot of strangers who wanted to be part of the best story of the day and see themselves on the evening news. Homer was there too, although he protested to Mary that her niece's problems were taking too much of his time.

"Oh, Homer, for heaven's sake," said Mary. "We can't abandon her now."

This time the pugnacious president of the demolition company meant business. Following his beckoning finger, the operator of the huge grappling machine floundered around Annie's house to the south side. A small crowd of newspeople and photographers trailed after him, along with a horde of Annie's friends, relatives, and camp followers.

Things looked bad. The driver of the machine had a thick bull neck and an expressionless face. Homer suspected he would flatten anything in his path if the boss gave the order—a herd of sheep, a flock of children. His giant grappling machine lurched and swiveled across Annie's lawn, leaving deep gouges in the grass. When he pulled a handle in front of his knees, the Caterpillar track on the left side churned around, its heavy plates driven by a roller and a chain of sprocket-driven wheels. The excavator with its massive toothed jaw careened in a quarter-circle until it faced the four tall windows on the south side of Annie's house.

For a moment the operator sat unmoving in the shimmying seat. The sun shone straight into the house from halfway up the sky, illuminating Aesop's sandaled feet, Charles Dodgson's small black boots, and Little Red Riding Hood in the jaws of the wolf. Annie herself was nowhere to be seen.

The sun shone on something else, a large wooden object. "What the hell is that?" said Robert Gast.

"It's O'Dougherty's," said Mary Kelly. "It's the roof from the back of his truck. Annie's inside it."

"Oh my God." Bob Gast shook his head in disbelief. The preposterous presence of a crazy piece of a ridiculous truck inside his deranged tenant's living room was just another surrealistic detail in what had become a continuing nightmare. Gast's stomach was in a constant state of convulsion. His hair fell out in handfuls. This morning his wife had stared at him and voiced her shock. "I never thought I'd be married to a man who was completely *bald.*"

Roberta was upset too. She refused to stay and watch the destruction. She hurried out to her car and drove off to work. Only Charlene was in top form. "They'll wreck it today, won't they, Daddy? I want to see!"

The decisive moment had arrived. With his heart in his mouth, Bob Gast shouted, "Go ahead, get on with it."

At once the bull-necked driver released his brake and opened the throttle and began wallowing forward.

"Come on, you guys," cried Trudy Tuck. She ran across the churned-up grass and took a defiant posture in front of Annie's windows.

"Oh, God," said Homer, as Mary jerked his arm and ran after Trudy.

Minnie Peck came too, along with all the other protesters, forty-three supporters of artists' rights, beauty, creative genius, and revolution, as well as a number of people in favor of any sort of excitement, while television cameramen and *Globe* photographers had a field day. Annie's friends lined up in a crowd before the house, facing the great reaching arm and jaw of the machine. They shouted and shook their fists and waggled their signs. Behind the oncoming juggernaut Mary Kelly caught a glimpse of a white-faced Robert Gast and his awestruck little daughter. Unnoticed at one side, the president of Quincy Contractors nodded his head and crooked his finger.

The driver saw the nod, he saw the encouraging finger. Relentlessly he ground forward, refusing to slacken speed. The threatening jaw on the end of the machine's long arm wobbled to within six feet of Minnie Peck before she screamed and fled. The others scrambled after her.

Window glass shattered. Posts and beams collapsed. Bookcases crumpled. A thousand books tumbled to the floor. The edge of the roof gave way with a shriek of ripped-out nails, and part of the ceiling fell in a shower of plaster.

There were screams and boos from the sidelines. Annie's dream house, the glorious room she had designed with her own hands, her beautiful high windows and perfect kitchen, her perfect, perfect house—it was all being shattered and destroyed by the great dragon teeth of the wrecking machine, as it opened its jaw and crushed and tore and turned and came back for more.

Annie couldn't bear it. Sobbing, she cowered under the wooden roof of Flimnap's truck, wondering why in the hell he wasn't there. He had known the crisis was coming, he had prepared for the worst, he had unscrewed the roof of his gypsy caravan and dismantled Annie's scaffolding, and then he had reassembled the pieces, making a shelter against the collapse of the roof, a barricade in front of her painted wall. And then, once again, he had vanished. *Oh, where the hell are you, Flimnap?*

The dozer driver's red face stared down impassively at the wrecked south side of Annie's house, and then he pulled on his stick to swing the grapple to the right.

"Christ," muttered Homer. Galloping across the ruined grass, he mounted the high step of the cab and yelled at the driver, "Look, give her time to move out." Stumbling down again, he shouted at Bob Gast, "Come on, we'll move the furniture out. Give us a little time."

"Well, for Christ's sake, you've had all the time in the world." Gast jerked his head at the machine. "Five hundred dollars an hour, this thing is costing me. You want to pay for it? Be my guest."

"We'll manage," said Homer curtly. "Don't worry about it."

"Well, okay, then." Bob looked at the wrecking contractor, who nodded at the operator. The heavy throbbing of the engine died away and the machine fell silent. The driver took off his hard hat and heaved himself out of the cab. Glowering, Gast disappeared, tugging behind him a reluctant Charlene.

The cause was lost. Annie's friends looked at each other mournfully. "Come on," said Mary. "Let's take everything out the front door."

Annie didn't like it. When Mary and Homer stumbled around the wreckage and looked in at her under Flimnap's roof, she grasped Mary's hand and whispered, "Never mind about the furniture. Let him knock down everything. Everything except my wall. I don't give a damn about the rest. Let him do his worst. I'm not leaving. He'll have to kill me before he knocks down my wall." Her eyes were glittering, her hair was wild.

Mary knelt beside her and put her arms around her. Homer was exhausted. But he knew perfectly well that Annie's resistance wasn't mere surface flamboyance like Trudy Tuck's. She spoke from a granite core. She meant what she said. Gast's hired machine would crush her under its tracks before she would abandon her wall. He pleaded with her: "Oh, come on, Annie. We might as well save what we can."

"Listen, Annie," said Mary craftily, "that highboy belonged to your great-great-grandfather, and you know what? He was my ancestor too. You've got to save it. And what about Eddy Gast's pictures? You can't let anything happen to them."

"Oh, all right," said Annie, her voice thick with tears. "Well, okay. Just keep those cameras out of here." She kicked at a heap of fallen books, and began picking them up. "There are a lot of empty boxes in the laundry."

Everybody helped. Even the rubberneckers lent a hand, lugging out carton after carton while Mary barred the door against inquisitive gate-crashers with cameras. Let Annie's house stay private, at least for the few moments it continued to exist.

The driveway was soon littered with her possessions. "What about the fridge?" said Henry Coombs. "It'd be a shame to let it go to waste."

"It's on little wheels," said Annie. Desperately she grasped one side while Henry took the other. Rocking the refrigerator this way and that, they pulled it out from the wall.

Perry Chestnut unearthed a Phillips screwdriver, and like a good sport he got to work on the dishwasher. "It's just a matter of a few screws, and then you pull out the hose."

"Annie, what about all these jars of paint?" said Henrietta Willsey.

At this Annie broke down. "No, no, don't take them away. I need them. I'm nearly done. I've got to finish. I've got to finish my wall."

Chapter 47

Build it up with gold and silver,
Gold and silver, gold and silver!
Build it up with gold and silver,
My fair lady!

Gold and silver I've not got,
I've not got, I've not got!
Gold and silver I've not got,
My fair lady!

Mother Goose rhyme

It was only a pause in the storm. The grappling machine was still parked on the south side of the house, its long arm folded back on itself, its jaw resting on the ground, its three upper teeth meshed with the two below.

The operator of the machine had taken himself off. He sat on the stone wall with his feet dangling among thorny canes of blackberry. When he jerked on the pull-top of his can of beer, it fizzed out and frothed all over his lap, and he said, *"Mierda."*

Robert Gast showed up to complain that somebody might have the courtesy to hire a moving van. "You've got the entire driveway cluttered up with furniture. What the hell are you going to do with all this stuff?"

They were down to the rugs and the contents of Annie's linen cupboard. Henry and Lily Coombs picked up the last of her books and blew on them to remove the plaster dust. People sat yawning in the sunlight on Annie's upholstered chairs. A television cameraman wandered around lazily, recording the scene. He was waiting for real action, the collapse of the house. Of course it wouldn't be like the fall of an entire high-rise building, with thousands of tons of steel and concrete gently descending in slow motion, but in a milder way it would have the same charm—order followed by chaos.

The removal of Annie's furniture was almost done. Homer and Mary parked the headboard of her bed against a tree, and Homer mopped his forehead with his sleeve. "What are we going to do with all this stuff? We can't take it to our place. Our house is too small."

"Oh, ugh," said Mary. She was worn out. Her back would never be the same. "There's a storage place on Route 2A." She stretched out on the grass. "Of course, there's always my sister's barn, there on Barrett's Mill Road. But poor old Gwen, we can't crowd more things in there while she's away. She's already storing Freddy's boat, and Miranda's boyfriend's stuff, and John's old muscle-building apparatus, and your old files, remember, Homer? You promised to remove them as soon as you got organized, and that was ten years ago."

"Oh, Lord, I keep forgetting." Gasping, Homer sat down beside Mary. "Look, the furniture's no problem. What are we going to do about Annie?"

"Oh, Homer, it's not her fault."

"The thing is, she swears she won't leave. She's going to sit right there in front of that wall while forty tons of machinery comes straight at her."

"Well, maybe being stubborn will work." Mary looked at him defiantly. "Homer, she won't be alone. I'm going to sit right there beside her. The guy won't go through with it. No matter how many court opinions Gast has on his side, it would be murder if anybody got hurt. Besides, if she can hold out long enough, maybe we can get something on the Gasts." Mary sat up and grasped Homer's arm. "Hurry up, Homer. Find something. I know it wasn't Annie's fault that little Eddy died."

"Oh, I see," whined Homer, "it's all up to me."

Gast was back. "Okay, that's enough," he said loudly. "Now get that woman out."

Annie's friends came back to life. They jumped up, prepared to witness the collision between an irresistible force—the grappling machine—and an immovable object—Annie Swann and her wall. The television crew came alive too, as did the reporter from the *Globe* and the one from the *Boston Herald*.

Gast glowered at Mary Kelly. "She's your relative, right? Get her out of there."

Mary turned her back on him, and walked in the front door. "Annie, are you okay?"

Annie was alone in her ruined living room, using a broom to sweep broken glass into a heap. It was a housewifely action, as though she were still surrounded by four solid walls, as though one side of her house were not gaping open to the wind and weather.

"I'm okay," said Annie, sweeping too vigorously, sending fragments of glass whizzing across the floor.

"Oh, goddamnit," said Homer, coming in after his wife, resigned to the necessity of joining Annie's death-defying stand against the monster machine. He grinned at her. "Why didn't I marry into a sensible family?"

Annie laughed. "Sorry, Uncle Homer. That was your big mistake."

The enormous grinding whine of the diesel engine began once more, and the scream of the hydraulic pumps sending oil into the pistons at high pressure. Minnie Peck was there again, along with Trudy Tuck, Lily and Henry Coombs, Wally Feather, Henrietta Willsey, and Perry Chestnut. This time they were not whooping and shouting. Their warlike spirit was gone.

They stood silently at one side, watching the swing of the grappling jaws and the rocking rotation of the massive counter-weight. Delicately, as if he were reaching out his hand, the operator opened the grapple over the corner of the kitchen wall and closed it again, biting off a chunk of Annie's kitchen cabinets. A forgotten tin of sardines shot up in the air. A section of the ceiling caved in and collapsed.

Annie, Homer and Mary huddled inside Flimnap's wooden shelter. "Come on out, you guys," shouted Wally Feather.

"Come out, come out!" cried Trudy Tuck.

"Get out of there, you people," shouted Bob Gast, his voice trembling. "Come on out, I mean it."

"Mrs. Kelly," screamed Charlene, "get out, get out!"

"We're not leaving," roared Homer. He put one arm around Annie and the other around Mary. Together they crouched under Flimnap's wooden roof as the teeth of the grappling machine bit down and tore at joists and rafters with a grinding racket of splintering wood.

"Oh, God," muttered Mary, "there goes the kitchen."

"It's okay," whispered Annie, as the corner post went down and the east window buckled out of its frame. "Let him, let him. It's okay."

"Christ," muttered Homer, wondering what demonic forces in his life had led inevitably to this crisis, what tendencies ingrained in him since childhood. What ghastly flaw in his character pointed directly to this moment when he would find himself crouching inside a collapsing building? Good Lord, what was Annie doing? She was jumping up, standing out from under the sheltering wooden roof to look up at her painted wall. "Come back, you idiot," cried Homer. "You'll get yourself killed."

She couldn't hear him, she wasn't listening. She was staring at her wall.

So far it seemed all right. There were no cracks. The lifesize figures were nearly hidden under plaster dust, but they were intact. The ghostly ship on her painted horizon was still afloat. Under a white film the Owl and the Pussy-cat still rowed their boat serenely.

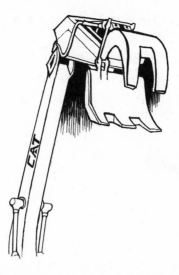

As the grappling machine rolled back over the heap of wreckage and swiveled on its massive turntable, Annie crawled into Flimnap's house again and said shakily, "It's okay so far."

Robert Gast was in torment. Once again he yelled at the three fools who had holed up in his doomed house: "Get out, you morons, get out of there!"

"Morons!" echoed Charlene, screaming at the top of her lungs.

The machine groaned forward. Minnie and Trudy, Henry and Lily, Perry and Wally shouted, "No!"

"You're witnesses," yelled Gast, his voice cracking in a high shriek. "If anything happens, it's their fault. I won't be held responsible."

But he would be held responsible, and he knew it. Terrified, he watched as the grappling jaw yawned and gulped down another piece of roof. The south end of the kitchen was gone, the bedroom, the bathroom. Homer, Mary and Annie huddled under their wooden umbrella as another piece of the ceiling collapsed. Their friends screamed at them, "Come out, come out!" But they bowed their heads and hunched their shoulders and hung on.

Gast had endured enough. He shouted at the driver to stop.

"No, no, Daddy," cried Charlene, snatching at his arm, battering his chest with her fists. The fate of her Olympic pool hung in the balance, with its turquoise water, its red-and-blue deck chairs and colorful jungle plants.

The wrecking machine shivered a couple of times, then clanked to a stop and fell silent.

Chapter 48

Set a man to watch all night,
Watch all night, watch all night!
Set a man to watch all night,
My fair lady!

Mother Goose rhyme

"If we can't leave, we can at least make ourselves comfortable." Mary made a list of all the things they were going to need, like sleeping bags, blankets, bottled water, and a microwave oven.

Homer shook his head. "A microwave won't do us much good without electricity."

"Oh, we've got to have electricity." Mary grinned and poked him in the chest. "Go out and get us some electricity, Homer."

Fortunately, Flimnap O'Dougherty turned up just then. "Oh, God, Flimnap," said Annie, looking up at him from the dark cave of the wooden shelter he had detached from the back of his truck, "where have you been?"

For once he didn't dodge the question. He knelt on the gritty floor and said softly, "The fact is, I don't like cameras very well."

"I see," murmured Annie, although she didn't see.

The trouble was, the cameras were more and more in evidence. The story about Annie's refusal to move out of a condemned house had gripped the imagination of the newspaper-reading, television-watching nation. Some people sided with Annie, who was painting some sort of mural on the wall of a rented house and couldn't bear to see it destroyed.

Others were all for legality. "It's her own fault. It's not her house. Why would any sensible person paint a picture on the wall of a rented house?"

So there were more newspeople every day. Fortunately, the lay of the land and the shape of the house provided protection. Annie's friends could rattle the knocker of her front door and slip inside, but everybody else had to watch from the driveway. The wrecked south side of Annie's house was shut off on one side by a vast thorny patch of blackberries, and on the other by the fence and padlocked gate that had been erected by the Gasts. Far away, across the cornfield, Annie and her friends could see Baker Bridge Road, where the traffic came and went, looking like Matchbox cars, but immediately below her small front yard there was a bristling wilderness.

"They can't get through *that*," gloated Mary Kelly, who had tried it. "It's like the hedge of thorns around Sleeping Beauty's castle."

❧

It was true that Flimnap O'Dougherty did not like cameras. He came and went with care, appearing after nightfall or early in the morning, doing an odd job or two, then vanishing.

With his usual skill he solved the problem of electric power. He sent Homer out to buy an adapter for the cigarette lighter in Annie's car, then ran a long wire through the front door to a lamp with a bent silk shade. The lamp shone down on a card table belonging to Henrietta Willsey. Wally Feather was a camping enthusiast in his spare time, and he produced a pop-up tent. Mary brought over a television set, and Flimnap soon had it glowing in the dark hollow of the shelter. Then, ever the practical handyman, he built an old-fashioned privy in the bushes and provided it with a garden fork and spade.

The problem of guard duty was taken care of by Lily Coombs, the creator of pretty arrangements of dried flowers.

Lily worked out a schedule. She soon had all her time slots filled with stalwart defenders of Fortress Annie. Homer and Mary came and went, taking their turns.

And then, for a while, things settled down. Life was bizarre, but a routine developed. Before long a weird normalcy prevailed in Annie's ruined house.

And it wasn't just her friends who cheered her on. It was the images on her wall. They were still there, wraithlike under their coating of white dust, looming figures presiding over Annie's ramshackle domestic arrangements. They belonged to her, they needed her, they must not be allowed to die. "It's amazing," said Mary to Homer, "the way Annie hangs on. Tough, that girl is tough. We've got to back her all the way."

So it was a standoff. For the moment, Robert Gast was stumped. He had succeeded in destroying three-quarters of Annie's house (which was not really her house at all). But the north side remained intact, because the goddamned woman had put her body in the way. It was an absurd emotional gesture, but it meant going back to law.

"Don't talk to *me* about it," said Roberta, throwing up her hands. "Talk to Sprocket."

"Oh, God, Roberta."

"Hurry up, Daddy," insisted Charlene. "We've got to schedule the pool company early, or they won't come until next year."

"Honestly, Charlene," moaned her father, "sometimes I wonder if we should really go through with it. It's become such a big deal."

Charlene fixed him with her eye. "Dad-*DY?*"

"Well, all right, all right. Okay, I know."

Harassed by cameras and inquisitive reporters, Gast bought himself a toupee. It sat on the top of his head like a doily, making a sharp curve too low over his face. On television he looked pale and frightened. His protestations of perfect legality were unheard. All the sympathy went to Annie. COURAGEOUS ARTIST DEFIES WRECKING MACHINE, that was the gist of the reporting, and Gast resented it.

And how strange, the way they wrote about her all the time but never showed a picture of Anna Swann in the flesh.

༄

"Get her," said Harvey Broadstairs, executive editor of the *Boston Globe*. "It's insane, all that stuff about her on page one, and no picture."

Seven staff photographers were crowded around his desk. Tim Foley said, "How about the back flap of one of her children's books?"

"No picture," said Broadstairs. "We tried her publisher, but they're out of business. Big takeover. You guys have got to do something. I don't care what you do, but come back with a picture of Anna Swann."

Behind the seven photographers pressing up against the executive editor's desk there was an eighth. Bertha Rugg was crowded out. She couldn't squeeze between the hips of the young women and the shoulders of the young men. She stood in the back and listened with all her might.

Chapter 49

❧

. . . at the edge of the forest is a great lake. Behind it stands a tower,
and in the tower sits a beautiful princess . . .
          The Brothers Grimm, "The Skilful Huntsman"

"Why doesn't she come out?" said Tim Foley, button-
holing Mary Kelly in the driveway. "She's your niece,
right?"

"Why should she come out?" said Mary stoutly. Supporting a
blueberry pie on the flat of one hand, she banged the knocker
with the other. "She's fine in there. Just fine."

The door opened a crack and Trudy Tuck looked out. Mary
slipped past her, and the door closed, scraping the floor because
everything was out of plumb.

Tim sighed with frustration. He was one of the small army of
photographers who were trying to take a picture of the contro-
versial Anna Swann and show her to the world, because everybody out there was taking more and more of an interest in her
protest. The wire services transmitted the story far afield. The
TV cameramen were there every day, waiting for something to
happen.

Time was suspended. Bob and Roberta Gast came and went,
poker-faced, hiding away in their side of the house, from which
no living sound emerged. Annie and her friends camped in front
of her painted wall, wondering when the protest would come
to an end. Any day now a crowd of riot police would show up
with an arrest warrant and drag Annie out. Then Gast would
bring in his machines and obliterate Annie's wall. The time
would certainly come. Her wall was doomed.

Around the house the green biomass of late spring burgeoned in the trees. On the topmost twig of a dead elm in the field a mockingbird hurled tunes at the sky—*come and get 'em, no two alike.* In the late afternoon a robin repeated his own cheerful song over and over. The two birds were behaving exactly like the humans in the disputed house, claiming some patch of field or hillside or wilderness as their own.

In the mad circumstances of life in a nearly demolished dwelling, Annie felt it, the sense of approaching disaster, as though the puffy clouds of summer were inscribed with exclamations of warning. Defying the clouds, she assembled her chalk, her brushes, and her colors, and got back to work.

The fifth and last section of her painted gallery was only half finished. Edward Lear occupied one side of the arched opening, a bearded man with round spectacles and a stovepipe hat. Robert Louis Stevenson stood jauntily erect on the other side, with a parrot on his shoulder. The space between them was blank.

It was the dangerous spot where the mysterious face had returned so often. It had been empty for over a month. The ugly
face with its terrible teeth and horrible eyes had not come back.
What if she painted something on purpose in that spot? The
mysterious face might never show up again. Annie imagined a
ghostly image drifting up to the wall and saying, *Whoops, sorry,*
and fading away forever.

"Why don't we clear up this awful mess?" said Lily Coombs,
poking her foot at the pile of wreckage mounded on the floor
and all over the crushed grass outside—fallen timbers, shattered
glass, mangled clapboards, chunks of plaster, and torn strips of
asphalt roofing. On top of the heap, like a vulgar piece of sculpture, Annie's toilet lay on its back, gaping at the sky.

Homer was stubborn. "It's Gast's responsibility. He made the
mess. Let him clear it up."

"The wrecking company," said Henry Coombs. "It must be
part of their contract, to clean up the site."

Homer glanced in Annie's direction and lowered his voice.
"They haven't finished the job, that's the trouble. They're expecting to come back and knock down the rest."

"Well, maybe we shouldn't wait," said Lily, frowning at
Homer. "Why don't we clear it out ourselves? Hire a Dumpster
and carry stuff out in buckets through the front door? It'll give
us something to do."

It was a good idea. Soon everybody was scooping bits of
wreckage into wastebaskets and paper bags. Slowly the pile of
broken clapboards and chunks of plaster and fragments of glass
diminished, but only slightly.

Annie ran a borrowed vacuum cleaner around the edges. It
made a lot of noise, shrieking as it picked up plaster dust and
slivers of glass. Within the shriek Annie heard human voices,
high-pitched arguments and shouts.

There were no arguments among the guardians of Fortress
Annie. Eight of them were taking turns with Annie, bringing

food, bottled water, clean laundry, and news—Homer and Mary Kelly, Henry and Lily Coombs, Wally Feather, Henrietta Willsey, Trudy Tuck, and Minnie Peck.

Minnie was especially faithful. She was delighted to be prominently on hand. She loved bouncing out of her car beside the van from CBS and granting an interview. After all, she was ten times more telegenic than Annie, and as a fellow artist she had been close to the scene from the beginning. It was soon apparent to the assembled gatherers of information that Minnie was *au courant* with Annie's artistic *raison d'être,* and, more important, that she could answer questions about Annie's love life. Minnie conned one of the network people into interviewing her in her studio against a background of *Millennial Woman, Millennial Man*, and *Millennial Child.*

"This guy who disappeared," said the interviewer, "the handyman, who is he? Is he her lover?"

"Oh, I don't know," said Minnie carelessly. "Once there was Swann, then Burgess, then Jack, and now it's O'Dougherty. She sort of goes from man to man."

Then old lover Jack turned up in person. To Mary Kelly's astonishment, he appeared in the driveway one day, talking into a camera. She watched him expand with self-importance. He was eager to capitalize on his relationship with Annie. "She's a little unstable, I'm afraid. A wonderful woman, of course, but seriously unstable."

Jack should have been more cautious. The interviewer had done his homework. "Is it true that the personal-liability insurance you sold to Anna Swann did not cover her liability, when the time came?"

"Well, you have to understand, these things are difficult. An insurance company has its limits. We can't exactly—"

"Is not the Paul Revere Mutual Insurance Company notorious for refusing compensation until the claimant brings suit?"

"Of course not," blustered Jack.

The legal owners of the house, Roberta and Robert Gast, were less forthcoming. They dodged from house to car in the morning, and from car to house in the evening, without saying a word.

But at the offices of Pouch, Heaviside and Sprocket there were whispered conferences between Roberta and her boss, Dirk Sprocket, who was suggesting another lawsuit. This time the Swann woman would be sued for disturbing the peace of the neighborhood, for the severe emotional trauma endured by the Gast family, and for the mounting cost of the delay.

"Oh, God, I don't know," said Roberta. Her face was drawn. She hadn't had a good night's sleep for weeks. "I'm just so sick of the whole thing."

Only Charlene seemed strong in a crisis, buoyed by the vision of her indoor pool. She badgered her father. "Why don't the police get her out? Why don't you *do* something, Daddy?"

Then, without asking permission, she called up the swimming-pool company. Delighted, they sent out an eager salesman. Charlene ran to the door to greet him, but he was pale and shaking. A couple of cameramen had swarmed up around his van, with its big logo—

POOL AND PATIO
RESIDENTIAL AND COMMERCIAL
FREE DESIGN SERVICE

Too late, the salesman identified his potential customers as the notorious Gast family of television fame. And when he learned that he had been summoned by a ten-year-old girl, he had an excuse to back out.

"Get your father to call me," he said, and hurried back to his van.

But Bob Gast was not yet ready to order a swimming pool for his daughter. The heavy machinery that was at this moment

heaving its way across the ninety-nine-acre property belonging to Frederick and Pearl Small in Southtown was costing him an arm and a leg. In his head, night and day, he heard the clattering roar of the bulldozer, the grinding smash of the concrete pulverizer, the whine of the excavator, and worst of all a high keen ringing that pierced through all the rest, arising from no single source, an unbearable shrill scream in the same frequency range as the cry of herring gulls, the screeching of blue jays. But all the birds had vanished from Small's place in Southtown—except of course for the scavenging crows, ranging overhead, peering down, always on the lookout for something recently dead.

"I don't know, Charlene," said Gast. "I just don't know."

"But, Daddy," complained Charlene, "you promised. And don't forget what I said!"

"Oh, God, Charlene," groaned her father, sinking into a chair and putting his head in his hands, "you just don't understand."

The tension of waiting for an end to the crisis was unbearable. Gast went to the chief of police, shoved his copy of the eviction order under his nose, and demanded, "Come on, get her out of there."

The chief had been watching television and reading the paper. He had no intention of becoming the villain in this drama. "Okay, okay," he said, "I hear you."

"Well? Are you going to do something about it or not?"

The chief bristled. His hair-trigger irascibility came to his aid. "Listen, friend, kindly do not tell me how to run my department. I've got to consult counsel. I've got to know what the hell I'm doing. The media, they're savages. They'll roast me alive and serve me up on a platter. No, no, you heard what I said." The chief stood up. "I've got to consult town counsel."

As soon as Gast left, the chief did just that. Town counsel advised him to lie low.

Chapter 50

❧

She told him that if he could reach the place where the end of the rainbow stands he would find there a golden key.

George MacDonald, "The Golden Key"

R on was back. Homer had almost forgotten about the vacationing hardware-store clerk. But when he made another routine call to Biggy's in West Concord, the clerk on the line yelled, "Hey, Ron, guy wants to talk to you."

"Hello?" said Ron.

Homer almost dropped the phone. "Oh, Ron, is it really you? Listen, hold it, I'll be right over."

It turned out that Ron was not a tanned Lothario who had spent his vacation in St. Martin on a nude beach. He was tanned, all right, but he was a pudgy sixtyish man who had stayed with an old buddy and spent all his time fishing for tuna.

With trembling fingers Homer showed him Annie's snapshot of the grinning Gasts—Robert, Roberta, Eddy, and Charlene.

"Oh, sure," said Ron, "I made keys for that guy. He wanted half a dozen of the same one. Didn't trust me. Said half the time they didn't work."

Exultant, Homer showed him Annie's key. "Did the key you copied have a tag like this?"

"Yeah, that's right. That's the one. He wanted keys, bought some tools."

"When, Ron, when was it?"

"Oh, I dunno." It was obvious that the ocean horizon of the Caribbean was still hazy and blue in Ron's head, the outboard still loud in his ears, slamming his sportfisherman across the turquoise waters of the bay.

Homer prompted him. "Do you remember the little kid who died in a fall? It was in the *Concord Journal*, a story about—"

"Oh, right, the retarded boy. Sure, I remember."

"Well, was this before that? Do you remember whether you made the key before or after?"

"Heck, no."

"Well, *try,*" said Homer, exasperated. "Try to remember."

Ron struck a pose of mock concentration, eyes crossed, finger to forehead. "Sorry, fella, it's no use."

"Hey, Ron," called the other clerk, "you got customers backed up."

"Just one more question. What kind of tools did he buy?"

"God, I don't remember. How many tools you think we sell every week?"

Homer thanked him and drove away. It was raining. He was depressed. True, he had succeeded in finding out that Robert Gast had copied Annie's key, but what good did that do? There was no law against copying somebody else's key, and Gast could say it was merely a neighborly precaution. Suppose he saw smoke from Annie Swann's part of the house, and she wasn't home?

At Annie's fortified camp a few patient media people sat in their cars, waiting for something to happen. Surely another wrecking machine would roar up the driveway one of these days, accompanied this time by law enforcement. There'd be a confrontation, the Swann woman would be physically removed, her wall would be knocked down, her friends would do a lot of yelling, but then they would give up and go away, and the whole thing would be over.

But so far nothing was happening. They were bored. The rain came down.

Mary opened the gate in response to Homer's shout. "Lunch, Homer? I made some really good liverwurst sandwiches."

From the door of Flimnap's shelter Annie's welcoming smile was a tense constriction of facial muscles. "Come on in, Uncle Homer. You're getting soaked."

"Just a sec," said Homer, mopping his dripping face. He walked across the muddy churned-up grass to Robert Gast's fence and stared at it. The gate was padlocked. At one end the fence was attached to the house near the rip in the clapboarded wall where Quincy Wrecking had severed the two parts of the house. At the other end the ground fell away into a thorny tangle.

Oh, Jesus, he'd have to climb over in the middle. Homer shouted to Mary for a chair.

She looked at him doubtfully. "Homer, what fool thing are you going to do now?" But she reached into the shelter and pulled out a folding chair.

Homer took it, set it up beside the fence, and pushed its flimsy legs down into the rain-soaked dirt. Then he hoisted his six-foot-six-inch, 250-pound frame up onto the seat, wobbled left and right, and grabbed frantically for the tops of the fence-poles. Clinging to them uneasily, he explained, "I just want to take a peek into Bob Gast's tool room. Oof!" Gasping, he threw one leg over the fence, lost his foothold on the chair, and slithered to the ground on the other side, landing in a muddy heap.

Mary called, "Homer, are you all right?"

"Umph," said Homer, struggling to stand up.

"Homer, dear, you're trespassing. Come back."

"Just a goddamn minute." Homer limped to the house and peered in the nearest window, holding his hands beside his eyes. His wet hair streamed into his face.

He was looking directly into Gast's workshop. It was neat as a pin. There was a place for everything and everything was in its place. A table saw and a drill press stood on the floor. Tools hung on a pegboard. Gast had used a marking pen to outline the hammer, the coping saw, the wire cutters, the wood saw, so that you could see exactly where to put them back. It was altogether admirable. Homer was envious. His own shop was a mess, with the tools heaped all over the workbench. He frowned, and hunched closer to the window.

One tool lay on the bench, uncategorized, unorganized, unfitted into Gast's perfect collection. There were no clever little supporting gadgets waiting for it on the pegboard. No black outline had been drawn around it, to show where it belonged.

It was a sledgehammer. Even within the dimness of an unlighted room on a rainy day Homer could see the price tag pasted on the handle. Instantly he made up a scenario—Gast had provided himself with a key and a sledgehammer at the West Concord hardware store. He had used the key to unlock Annie's door. He had propelled Eddy inside and watched him climb the ladder, and then he had jerked on the scaffolding to make Eddy fall, and at last he had brought the sledgehammer down on Eddy's tender skull.

"What the hell are you doing here? Get off my property."

Homer looked around guiltily at Robert Gast, who was standing beside him in a raincoat and a child's rainhat. "Sorry," said Homer.

"Oh, it's you," said Gast, recognizing Annie's interfering uncle. "I will thank you to leave my premises."

Homer made a gesture of total inadequacy and inability to cope, and stumbled away. Then something appeared miraculously on top of the fence, teetered there for a moment, and fell to the ground. Mary had divined his need. It was the folding chair.

Chapter 51

❧

Judge Aufsesser, the father of Cissie Aufsesser, who had been blackmailed out of her camera by Charlene Gast, had not forgotten his daughter's case. He had been unsuccessful in persuading Mrs. Rutledge to believe in Charlene's perfidious behavior, and he had failed to convince the headmistress of Weston Country Day. But in the private-school system of Middlesex County there was a higher court, the Board of Independent Schools.

At their next meeting he explained his grievance. "The trouble is, I'm still not satisfied with my daughter's case. The child who oppressed her has not been made accountable. According to Cissie, she still tyrannizes the entire class. And her teacher backs her up at every turn."

The members of the Board were shocked. "You mean one ten-year-old child can dominate all the rest?" said Barbara Campoggio, whose son was a senior at Fenn School in Concord.

"Precisely," said the judge. "They're too young to know what's happening. They try out every kind of human social organization without realizing it—oligarchy, monarchy, dictatorship, sometimes carrying it to extreme lengths. Sometimes they even stumble on social equality."

"The question is, what are we going to do about it in this case?" said Dick Pringle, whose twin boys were sophomores at Concord Academy.

The solution was obvious. They voted to call their next meeting at the school and confront the child herself, along with her parents. Judge Aufsesser would of course be present.

"And we've got to do it soon," cautioned Barbara Campoggio. "Don't forget, the school year's almost over."

❧

"Charlene, dear," said Mrs. Rutledge excitedly. "You're wanted in the library." She beamed at Charlene and accompanied her into the hall. "It's the members of the Independent School Board, all three of them, along with Judge Aufsesser and your mother. It's obviously some great honor. Not just for you, dear. For the whole school."

Charlene's glasses flickered. She wasn't as sure as Mrs. Rutledge that this was going to be a great honor for the school. The presence of Judge Aufsesser sounded ominous.

When she came back, walking slowly into the classroom, she went straight to her seat without looking at Mrs. Rutledge. At once the teacher sent her a note—"Oh, Charlene, what did they say?"

Charlene did not reply.

By next morning she had worked out a plan of revenge, and she put it into practice at once. When Mrs. Rutledge called on her to read another chapter of *The Flying Family*, she said, "I'm feeling sort of tired, Mrs. Rutledge. Maybe Cissie could read instead."

The whole class turned to look at Cissie, who was flabbergasted. She wasn't a very good reader. She took the book and did her best, stumbling over words, while the other kids kept saying, "Louder!"

" 'Even though Bitsy was the baby of the family, she was soon flying as well as big sister Joan. "Come on, Bitsy," ' "—

The next word was too hard. " 'Exclaimed,' " said Mrs. Rutledge impatiently.

" '. . . exclaimed Joan, helping her climb to the highest branch of the tree. "We'll fly together. All right now, jump!" Bitsy and Joan jumped, and together they flew in circles around the house, side by side.

" ' "Oh, look, Bitsy," cried Joan. "See that fox down there? It's caught a baby—a baby—" ' "

"Rabbit! All right, Cissie, that's enough. We'll read some more tomorrow. Outdoors now, everybody! The bell's about to ring. Mrs. Kelly will be with you today on the playground."

Mary stood up from her desk at the back of the room and followed the fifth-grade girls outdoors. Standing beside the tall pole supporting the basketball net, she kept her eyes on Charlene Gast. What on earth was going on? Why was Charlene putting her arm around Cissie Aufsesser and whispering in her ear? Was she threatening her?

"What did you say?" murmured Cissie, unable to believe her ears.

"I said best friends," said Charlene. "I want us to be best friends, Cissie."

At once Cissie forgot all that had gone before. She was overjoyed. "Oh, yes, Charlene, yes, yes!"

Mary Kelly had been present in the library when Charlene was chastised by Judge Aufsesser and the Board of Independent Schools. She had been working at a desk between two sections of book stacks. She had at last beheld the great judge in person. She had heard everything that was said.

Now, on the playground, she watched as Charlene took Cissie's hand and whispered in her ear. She saw Cissie blush and smile and walk off with Charlene arm in arm.

How strange. How very strange!

❧

"My grandmother, what big teeth you have!"
"So that I can eat you up!"

Charles Perrault, "Little Red Riding Hood"

Chapter 52

❧

Homer's class was still meeting in the Concord prison. Even though daily life had become increasingly insane, he attended faithfully, once a week.

Jimmy and Ferris were gone. Ernest Beckwith was new. He was enraged at the length of his sentence for selling hashish. "That judge," said Ernest, "he didn't like me none."

It was obvious to Homer that Ernest was right. The judge had gloated over the opportunity to make him an example. He had brought down against him the full force of the mandatory minimum sentencing law. Ernest was in for twenty-one years, with no opportunity for parole. "Twenty-one years!" said Homer. "It's barbaric."

As for Hank, he was now so angry about the lack of recompense for services rendered, he could hardly speak.

"Wait a minute," said Homer, "I can't help you unless I know more about it. What were the services you rendered? What did you do that you were not paid for?"

Hank shifted his angry glance down to his shoes and muttered something under his breath.

"Well, what kind of work do you do, Hank? I mean, on the outside?"

"I'm an auto mechanic," snarled Hank. "I was like fifteen when I started in my uncle's garage. I got twenty-five years' experience."

Homer tipped his chair back lazily. "Well, were you repairing somebody's car? Was that it? The job you didn't get paid for?"

"Not repairing it," burst out Hank, "not repairing it, for shit's sake. The *opposite* of repairing it." His eyes moved left to Gordie and Barkley, right to Fergie and Ernest. "I mean, this guy appears

241

at my shop in this old heap and asks me to loosen the brakes, so it, like, wouldn't have any brakes at all, so I says what for, and he says none of your goddamn business, so I figure he's going to wreck it, claim it was an accident, get the insurance. But, shit, better not to ask what for, what the hell, so he drove it to my place and I did what he said, not much to it, he must be an ignoramus not to be able to do it himself, so then a tow truck come and took it away. He was supposed to pay me a goddamn thousand the next day, only I got picked up for dealing and they put me in here, lousy mandatory sentence, me and Ernest and a lotta other guys gonna spend half our lives incarcerated, only the guy never paid me, he was gonna pay in cash, only he didn't."

"That's crazy," said Homer. "You could get him in real trouble. Did you have an invoice, a bill or something with his name on it?"

"Hell no, he said verbal agreement, okay? I don't even know his name."

Homer thought about it. "So you want me to find him, is that it?"

"Right, like you're free of charge, right?"

Homer sighed. "That's right. What towing company was it?"

"Jeez, I don't know. Big wrecker."

"What did he look like, this guy?"

"Medium height, sweat suit, Bruins cap."

"My God, Hank, it could be anybody." Homer rubbed his chin. "What make was the car, what year?"

"Chevy Cutlass. Lousy old green four-door. Early eighties. Tires really bald. I told him, I said, nobody oughta drive that heap. Oughta be in a junkyard."

"Junkyard, there's an idea. I could find out if it turned up at Boozer Brown's place."

"Boozer Brown? Oh, yeah, I heard of Boozer Brown. Biggest junkyard in Massachusetts, right?"

❧

The good thing about Boozer, reflected Homer, driving out Route 9, was the personal interest he took in every old hulk that appeared on his lot. He was like an antiquarian bookseller, cherishing every ancient volume on his shelves. Maybe it was this loving attention that had made him so successful.

"My God, Boozer," said Homer, surveying the vast acreage of Boozer's territory, spreading in all directions, littered with wrecks, "you've expanded. When we first met, out there on Nantucket, you had just four or five old cars. And a couple years ago, when I was here, it wasn't anything like this. Look at you now. You must be visible from the moon, like the Great Wall of China. Congratulations."

Boozer smiled proudly. "Thash right. More people driving too fasht, crazhy kidzh, nutsh onna highway, I get what'sh left. You should jusht shee the way they pour in here, day after day. Blood! Shome of 'em, shoaked in blood. Shometimes an arm or a leg."

Homer was used to Boozer's apocalyptic pronouncements, but he flinched anyway. "Listen, Boozer, what I'm looking for this time is a green Chevy Cutlass, early eighties, four-door sedan."

Boozer's ruined face lighted up. "Oh, sure, I got a coupla thozhe. Wants shee? I put 'em shide by shide. Like I file my shtock in categoriezh, short of. You oughta shee my Lamborghini collection. Shix or sheven Lamborghinizh, shtupid driverzh think they oughta go like hell."

Sin and its punishment, thought Homer, as they walked companionably through Boozer Brown's emporium. Where else was it displayed so simply? There should be a sign over the entrance to Boozer's junkyard, "Quod Erat Demonstrandum." Theologians should bring their congregations here on Sunday morning, philosophers should trot their students up and down the aisles between shattered Lamborghinis and crushed Mitsubishis, opening a door now and then, holding up an arm or a leg.

"Here we are," said Boozer proudly, stopping beside a pair of Cutlasses. One was crumpled into a frightful crescent of twisted metal, the other was a sad-looking heap with a missing door. Homer reached in and tested the hand brake. It wobbled in his hand.

"Shperfectly okay," said Boozer. "Jusha lil problem with the brakes. Needzha new door. You want it? Fifty bucksh, she'zh yourzh."

"Oh, no thank you, Boozer. Tell me, how do these—uh—automobiles get here? Wreckers bring them? Company's got a contract or something?"

"Right." Boozer pulled an old-fashioned hip flask from his pocket, took a swig, and wiped his mouth on his sleeve. "Thish one, wrecker come from Waltham. Waltham Towing. I know the guy. He prolly collected it from shome garage, getzh a bunch of 'em, bringzh 'em all at onczh on a trailer. You know."

"Good, Boozer. That's great. I'll try Waltham Towing, see if I can track down who it belonged to." Homer glanced again at the car. "I don't suppose—"

"Regishtration? Take a look." Obligingly Boozer opened the car door, flipped open the glove compartment, pawed inside it, and brought out an envelope. "Thish izh your lucky day."

"Great." Homer reached for it, congratulating himself for so easily solving Hank's grievance. Whoever the bastard was, he'd have to pay up, and then—very possibly—he'd be in much worse trouble. Grinning, Homer slipped out the registration and read the name of the owner of the battered green Chevy Cutlass.

It was Robert Gast.

Chapter 53

❧

. . . I passed the night and awoke possessing not a piece of silver nor one of gold, and I said within myself, This is the work of the Devil!
The Thousand and One Nights

Cindy Foxweiler's swim cap was yellow, her pink feet lashed the water. Charlene threw all her strength into her strong arms and hurled her body forward, but she couldn't swim fast enough, she couldn't catch Cindy. At the edge of the pool Cindy's yellow cap bobbed up, glistening in the light, and Cindy's coach bent down to her, laughing, and Cindy tore off her goggles, her grin wide and triumphant, her teeth dazzling in her freckled face.

Charlene couldn't believe it. She heard the wild applause and looked up at the cheering people in the bleachers, then ducked her head under the water. In all the other lanes kids were climbing out, pulling off their goggles and caps. Charlene lay still.

In the end her coach had to jump in and pull her out. "Charlene," he said anxiously, wrapping a towel around her shoulders and holding her upright, "are you okay?"

Charlene said nothing. The water streaming down her face was only partly the chlorinated water of the pool. The rest was tears. She had lost the Junior Olympics.

❧

"I saw it," said Annie in triumph. "I saw that car plunge down the hill. Flimnap was out there in the vegetable garden, and he raced across and jumped in the car and tried to turn it sideways because it was heading for those big oak trees down there. Eddy would have been killed."

Homer and Mary were sitting with Annie in the shade of one of the giddy awnings that had been rigged up by Henry Coombs, a set of old bedspreads swaying on poles. The poles creaked, the bedspreads billowed out like sails, giving Annie's ruined house a festive air. Before them lay the mounded wreckage of her south windows and bookcases, her shattered bedroom and ruined bath. Some tasteful person had removed the toilet, or shoved it behind a bush.

Behind them as they sat under the awning, Annie's wall was still bright and perfect, although it was more endangered than a whooping crane or a shrinking population of whales. Her figures gazed out serenely from their fanciful gallery, as if their future were assured. Annie had washed the wall with soap and water. The colors sparkled, the painted columns shone.

Hunched over cups of coffee, they ignored the wall and talked about the car that Homer had found at Boozer Brown's.

"I thought it was strange," said Annie. "I hadn't seen that car since the day they came here to look at the house. Pretending to be so poor." Angrily she turned to Mary. "Such a sweet impoverished young family. I fell for it and knocked the rent way down. Then, when they moved in, there was no more old Chevy, just a couple of sporty new cars."

Mary nodded wisely. "But the Chevy turned up again when they wanted to get rid of Eddy, is that it?"

"That's right. There it was again. Flimnap saw it parked at the top of the hill, sort of poised on the edge with the driver's door open."

"I'll bet Eddy's weight was all it took to start it rolling," grumbled Homer. "They left the door open to entice him inside."

" 'Come into my parlor,' " said Annie angrily. "It's what they accuse me of doing, luring him into my house, leaving the door unlocked. Only it must have been Bob Gast who unlocked my door with his key, the one he copied at the hardware store! And listen, what about the time Eddy was almost run over on Route 2? They used to let him run loose all the time! And whenever he came to my house they never looked for him. As far as they knew, he might be lost in the woods. I suppose they hoped he'd end up on Route 2 again and be run over for real this time."

"And the sledgehammer," said Homer, his voice heavy with indignation. "Don't forget the sledgehammer. Gast bought a nice new sledgehammer at the hardware store. In case the kid didn't die when he fell off the scaffolding, the sledgehammer would finish him off."

Annie gasped. Mary shuddered. "Oh, for heaven's sake, Homer."

"And then," Homer went on cheerfully, "he washed off the sledgehammer so no little bits of bloody scalp would be stuck in a crack anywhere, and then he washed his hands and scrubbed his fingernails, *scrubba-dubba-dub.*" Homer demonstrated with an imaginary brush. "And then, when everything was all clean and tidy, he called the police, full of righteous indignation and fatherly grief."

"What about an autopsy?" demanded Annie. "Wouldn't an autopsy show what really happened?"

"A fractured skull, that's all, perfectly consistent with the impact of the kid's head on the tile floor. And of course it would be perfectly consistent with a sledgehammer blow too, only Gast must have been careful to strike in the same place."

"Oh, I hate him," groaned Mary.

Annie gripped Homer's arm. "It all adds up. The Chevy, the key, the sledgehammer. We've got him, Uncle Homer."

Homer shook his head gloomily. "No, we haven't."

"Oh, Homer," said Mary, "surely it's enough."

"No, it's not. Ron at the hardware store, he can't remember what tools Gast bought that day. The sledgehammer still has a price tag on it, but it might be three or four years old. Even if it's brand-new, there's no way of proving it was used to murder Eddy. And as for the keys, there's no law against copying somebody else's keys."

"But what about the failing brakes?" cried Annie. "Uncle Homer, he hired that guy in prison to make the brakes fail."

"You mean you'd take the word of a convicted felon over that of an upstanding citizen like Gast? There was no contract, no writing on a piece of paper. Gast can claim he never met the guy. He never paid him, there was no written agreement to do anything." Homer looked at Annie dolefully. "So you see, it's no good. It's just not good enough."

They stared at each other and fell silent. Then Mary looked at her watch and jumped up. "It's quarter to ten. I should be in school. Thank God, there are only a few more days."

There was a loud knocking at Annie's front door. "Hey, you guys, let me in!" It was Perry Chestnut, coming to take Homer's place. Homer got up and opened the door, then slipped past Perry and hurried across the driveway to his car. Tim Foley, the good-looking young photographer from the *Globe*, took his picture.

Behind Tim a dumpy middle-aged camerawoman let the opportunity go by. Bertha Rugg remembered what her boss had said, *Come back with a picture of Anna Swann,* and she intended to do just that.

✑

Dirk Sprocket's bill was in the mail. Bob Gast looked at it in horror. "But you're part of the firm," he said to Roberta. "I thought it was sort of like a family, you helped each other out."

"We do. That sum, it's nothing. It would normally be three times that." Then Roberta burst out at him, "You said we were doing so well. When your mother died you said—what was it you said?—we're sitting pretty, that's what you said."

Gast's toupee had slipped over his forehead. Wrathfully he

thrust it back. "Well, we're not. Not anymore. My God, with all those fucking wrecking companies and Charlene's goddamned private school and, look here, just look at this little reminder from her swimming coach! God*damnit,* Roberta, we can't afford an indoor swimming pool."

"How are you going to tell her that? The poor kid has just lost the Junior Olympics."

"Well, it's too bad. It's not my fault, is it? I've done my best, my goddamned best." Gast was nearly in tears. "She'll just have to take it. There isn't going to be any indoor pool."

At this there was a scream behind his back. It was Charlene, coming into the room. "Daddy! You said! You promised!"

He whirled around and faced her, his daughter, his enemy. "We can't do it, Charlene. There'll be no indoor swimming pool. It's impossible, it's absolutely impossible. Face facts. Have a little pity."

Charlene had no pity. She stared at him, another scream bursting in her throat as the vision faded, the blue-green water, the track lighting, the deck chairs, the tropical plants. Stiffly she turned and walked away, betrayed by her own father.

Chapter 54

❧

Who'll be chief mourner?
I, said the Dove,
I mourn for my love,
I'll be chief mourner.

Mother Goose rhyme

Sergeant Bill Kennebunk was on the phone again.

"Oh, hi, Bill," said Homer. "What's new?"

"That forensic botanist, he finally made his report."

"Oh, of course. I forgot about the forensic botanist. What did he say?"

"Those leaf fragments, some of them are *Ajuga canadensis*. It's a member of the mint family, a kind of low-growing ground cover."

"Well, okay. Small's coat was covered with burdock burrs and *Ajuga canadensis*. So what?"

"It's very interesting, that's what. *Ajuga canadensis* is very rare in Massachusetts. I happen to know that it grows in only one place in Norfolk County. Last year I wrote it up for the local paper."

"I see." Homer gripped the telephone eagerly. "So you know where that fleecy coat of Small's picked up all those leaves? Are you sure he wasn't a wildflower enthusiast, just like you?"

"I doubt it very much. So how'd you like to join me? It's one of the last remaining patches of woods around here. It's not in Southtown, it's next door in Northtown, on Route 109."

"How about this afternoon? My class in Cambridge is over at two."

"I'll meet you at three. There's a Mobil station on 109 about a mile beyond Westwood. It's right across from the woods. Three o'clock, okay?"

❧

The trees on the edge of the woods in Northtown were lopped to make room for tiers of telephone wires. Homer parked on the shoulder of the road behind Kennebunk's elderly Volvo, and together they walked through the mangled trees.

Deeper into the woods the trees had been left alone. Birches bent this way and that. There were yellow growing tips on the lacy branches of the hemlocks. Below the trees the undergrowth was thick with ferns. "Look," murmured Kennebunk, "princess pine."

They walked on, and Kennebunk pointed out the miniature creeping plant he called *Ajuga canadensis*. Homer bent down to look at its microscopic flowers. Then Sergeant Kennebunk beckoned, and they went farther into the woods, following no path, climbing over fallen tree trunks, wading through densely interlaced dead branches. At last Bill Kennebunk stopped and said softly, "Here we are," and Homer muttered, "Oh, my God."

If it had not been strewn with fresh flowers, they would have missed it. The grave was only a slight rise in the ground, littered with fallen twigs and a rotting stump that had been dragged over the ground to cover it.

"Who brought the flowers?" whispered Homer.

"I don't know, but I'll bet it wasn't Small."

"The lover?" said Homer. He watched as Sergeant Kennebunk reached down and gathered up a handful of wildflowers—yarrow and chicory, daisies and clover. "Look," he said, "they're fresh. They must have been picked very recently." He glanced at Homer, and together they stared around into the surrounding trees. "Come on," said Kennebunk. "Let's take a look."

They moved in a circle, exploring the nearby woods, finding only scatterings of dead wildflowers. Someone had been bringing them to the grave, gathering up the old flowers and tossing them away.

At last they gave up and walked back to the road, where Kennebunk reached into the back of his car and brought out a couple of shovels. Together they returned to the grave and cleared it of fallen branches and the rotten stump. Meticulously, for no reason he could think of, Homer picked up all the flowers and set them aside. Then, solemnly, resolutely, they began to dig.

It wasn't hard. The original burial must have been much more difficult—Homer pictured Frederick Small sweating, cursing at the root-packed dirt. Before long they had shoveled out a heap of sandy soil, leaving a steep-sided hole bristling with the torn ends of roots. Only two feet down they put aside their shovels and Homer said, "Oh, Christ."

In the dry cavity, spreading out from the mound of dirt still covering the body, was an aureole of golden hair.

"That goddamned bastard," said Kennebunk. He looked up at Homer. "You know, McNutt isn't going to like this. He'll think of some excuse to hush it up."

"Why don't you put it in the paper first?" suggested Homer brightly. "I mean, before you tell him?"

"He won't like that either, but what the hell?"

❧

Bob Gast too said, *What the hell?* Bob had a new number for Fred Small, but he was so blinded with rage, he misdialed it again and again. When he got through at last, Small merely whispered his hello.

Bob roared at him. "What the hell's going on? What the hell, what the hell?"

❧

Mary Kelly did not swear when Homer told her what he and Sergeant Kennebunk had found in the Northtown woods, she wept. When she stopped weeping, she said, "Oh, Homer, what happens now? What will they do with her now?"

"Well, there'll have to be an autopsy," said Homer uncomfortably, wincing at the memory of the pathetic remains he had seen in Pearl's grave. "Fortunately, we found her in Northtown, not Southtown, so Kennebunk doesn't have to deal with Chief McNutt. The chief officer in Northtown was reasonable enough. He's starting a serious search for Small, spreading a wide net, bringing in people from all over. He seems to know what he's doing."

"Well, I hope to God they find the bastard."

Chapter 55

❧

The whole castle was surrounded by a thicket of thorns that grew ever higher. No longer could anything be seen at all.

The Brothers Grimm, "Little Brier Rose"

Bertha Rugg was a small homely woman who had been taking pictures all her life. She was an experienced and clever photographer, the only survivor of her generation on the staff of the *Boston Globe*. Gone were the old Linotypists, skilled operators of the deafening machines that had turned reservoirs of molten lead into slugs of type. Gone too were the compositors who had clamped the slugs into chases, who could read them backward and upside down. Everything was done with computers nowadays. All over the building there was a soft perpetual clickety-click, as kids barely out of school turned copy into print.

Bertha was painfully conscious of her incompatibility with the current staff of the *Globe*. She had nothing in common with the burly guys and classy girls who were her picture-taking colleagues. She wasn't *with-it,* if that was the right expression. She didn't understand their jokes. She didn't speak their language.

But Bertha knew how to do one thing very well. She knew how to get a picture, and by God she was going to get one now.

There was something else she knew that the young ones didn't, and that was how to get up early. On the day after Homer Kelly and Sergeant Bill Kennebunk unearthed the body of Pearl Small in the woods in Northtown, it was only eight o'clock in the morning when Bertha pulled her car to the side of Baker Bridge Road and took out her binoculars.

From here she could see only the battered roof of the house. The rest was hidden by a tangle of shrubs and a thick stand of trees with bushy new leaves. It was a green blur, a dense jungle, directly in the way.

Twisting the knob of her binoculars, she brought the trees into focus. Very slowly she swept her gaze across them, examining every branch and twig, raising her sights every now and then to check the lineup of a particular tree with the roof of the house behind it. Then she took out her pocket diary and drew precisely what she saw in one place, a little to the left of the tall aspen that was next to the short aspen that was next to the oak tree. When she was done, she reached into the back seat for her long-handled clippers, slung her camera over her shoulder, and set off across the cornfield in a straight line.

The field was like a battleground, with deep trenches between the emerging rows of corn. Her shoes sank in. She could feel small pops along her heavy calves as her pantyhose burst into runs.

Two hours later, she returned to her car, bitten by mosquitoes, stung by a hornet, scratched by thorns and brambles. Her hair stood on end, her arms were sunburned, her face was dirty. Tim Foley shot past her on the road and gave her a surprised look. It was ten o'clock in the morning.

Bertha smiled. The early bird catches the worm.

✺

Once again Harvey Broadstairs looked up at the seven young photographers crowded around his desk. This time he was smiling. He shuffled through the sheaf of pictures—Minnie Peck in her studio, Charlene Gast with a swimming-pool brochure, Homer Kelly coming out the front door, Mary Kelly with a bowl of salad, Henry Coombs with a cake—and picked up a big glossy photograph of Anna Swann standing in front of the dark cavern of her ruined house, her face brightly lit by the sun. She was smiling directly at the camera. Beside her a man stood upside down, his head nearly touching the ground, his feet in the air.

"Hey, this is great," said Broadstairs. "Who took this one?"

The seven young photographers looked blankly at each other. Then they stepped aside to reveal a small dumpy shape at the back of the room. "It's mine," said Bertha Rugg.

"Well, good for you, Bertha," said Broadstairs.

"Who the hell is the guy?" said Tim Foley. They all bowed over the picture, making room this time for Bertha Rugg.

"As a matter of fact," said Broadstairs, rubbing his chin, "I just happen to know who it is, but I promised not to say."

๑๛

Next morning the picture appeared on page one, and Bertha was paid at page-one rates. But next morning was too late for Bertha Rugg. That very afternoon she faxed it directly to CBS News in New York, and there it was on the evening news. At last the whole country knew what Annie Swann looked like.

Flimnap, who might have been cut out of the picture if he had been standing on his feet, was included as an oddity.

Chapter 56

❧

Like one, that on a lonesome road
Doth walk in fear and dread . . .
Because he knows, a frightful fiend
Doth close behind him tread.
    Samuel Taylor Coleridge,
    "The Rime of the Ancient Mariner"

Joe had abandoned his new book months ago. But lately he had started to work on it again. He sat now in the cab of his truck with his sketchbook in his lap and sharpened a pencil to a stiletto point with a tiny razor-edged grinder. As usual, his nimble fingers were in perfect control. His large images filled the space, nudging the edges of the page.

The story was common as dirt, the old folk tale of Hansel and Gretel. Joe's Hansel was a generic moppet with a Dutch haircut, but Gretel was a real person, a tall stocky child with big hands and feet—Annie Swann to the life. The wicked witch was a sly portrait of Roberta Gast. She was urging Annie into the oven—*Just creep in and see if it is hot.* Clever Annie was holding back, begging for a demonstration—*I don't know how. Show me!*

The drawing was done, ready to be rendered in color. Joe looked at it critically, and touched the face of Gretel. Then he closed the sketchbook and laid it gently on the shelf under the rear window. Gripping the handle of the door, he inspected the surrounding woods.

The trees stood silent, the undergrowth was empty. Satisfied, Joe got out, locked the pickup doors, and ambled down the hill, turning now and then to glance at the road behind him.

As always, he had to take care. All it would take was a single shot.

❧

The television set shone brightly in Annie Swann's dark fortress. Annie, Flimnap and Homer Kelly played gin rummy at the rickety card table. Homer boldly picked up fistfuls of extra cards and couldn't get rid of them, Annie was too cautious, Flimnap always won. Their heads turned as the voice of the late-night newsman pronounced the name of Anna Swann.

"My God!" said Annie. There she was, as big as life. The camera zoomed in on her face, then moved sideways to show Flimnap upside down. It was the picture taken by Bertha Rugg from the cornfield, after wrenching off with her clippers the branches of a dozen scrub oak trees and slashing her way through a forest of maple saplings.

"Oh, Christ," said Flimnap, jumping to his feet.

"There you are, the two of you," said Homer gleefully, "on network television."

The newsman's interest shifted to a scandal involving a senator's wife. Flimnap knocked over his chair, took Annie in his arms and kissed her, then let her go, started for the door, came back to kiss her with more passion, and vanished.

"Good Lord," said Homer, "what was that all about?"

Annie was speechless.

❧

It did not occur to Joe that the late news might be a repetition of a broadcast five hours earlier. He walked up the hill to his truck. There was plenty of time to clear out.

He was wrong. Millions of television viewers had already seen the photograph taken by Bertha Rugg. One took a special interest in the six o'clock appearance of Anna Swann and her upside-down friend. In his rented room on a back street in the city of Worcester, Frederick Small stared at Joseph Noakes, thunderstruck. Leaping to his feet, he shouted in triumph.

‿

It was Homer's turn to spend the night in the tent at Fortress Annie. After a long day of grading the final papers of the forty-nine undergraduates in his Thoreau class, he had stopped on the way home to buy buckets of Chinese food; he had brought them home to Annie's and heated them up in the microwave, and then the three of them had played gin rummy all evening. At last, after gaping at the television image of Flimnap standing on his hands beside Annie, Homer crawled into the tent, emotionally exhausted, and fell asleep at once.

At the sudden noise, he jerked awake and sat up. It had sounded like a gunshot, a loud blast followed by sharp crackling echoes. Did the hunting season begin in June? Homer didn't know. Should he get up and look around?

He lay down to think it over.

Annie too heard the shot. With her heart in her mouth she scrambled out of her sleeping bag, went to the door and looked out. For a moment she could hear a car moving away along Concord Road, and then there was only the soft sighing of the trees.

Had Flimnap been shot by some murdering bastard, up there in the woods where he parked his pickup? Was he mortally hurt, was he bleeding to death? Annie grabbed her coat, snatched up her flashlight, and began running up the hill. Flimnap's ravenous kisses had aroused a trembling fervor. Following the spot of light, stumbling on the stony driveway, she tripped and fell, then scrambled up to run again, and tripped again, and staggered to her feet.

Halfway up the hill she found a track leading off to the left through a low thicket of fern and blueberry. Annie followed it for a hundred yards as it wound its way among pines and hemlocks, until suddenly—there it was—Flimnap's pickup, a bulky shape looming up in the dark.

The wooden structure that had once formed the back of the truck was gone, Flimnap's gypsy caravan. He had rebuilt it inside Annie's ruined house as a bulwark against the collapse of the roof. Now the back of the pickup was open to the sky. Annie's flashlight explored the empty sleeping bag, the boxes of gear, the duffel bag.

Then, fearing what she might see, she aimed it through the window of the cab, but the wobbling cone of light revealed only the shiny vinyl of the seat.

"Hey," said Homer Kelly, groping his way into the woods, following the glimmer, "is that you, Annie?"

Feeling for him clumsily in the dark, Annie clutched his arm and said in a tense whisper, "That noise, Uncle Homer! What was that terrible noise?"

He patted her back and put his arm around her. "I don't know," he said uneasily. "Probably just a backfire, out there on Concord Road."

But he was lying. They both knew he was lying.

Chapter 57

❧

The road to the forest led him to the gallows.
The Brothers Grimm, "The Two Travelers"

"Get in my car." Small gestured with his handgun. "The other side. You're driving."

Small's cartridge had nearly missed its target, but not quite. It left a bloody crease along one side of Joe's head. He felt no pain. Raging at himself for the careless stupidity that had allowed him to take his time, he climbed in behind the wheel of Small's big van.

There was no arguing with an AK-47 backed up by a Beretta with fifteen rounds nestled in its little magazine.

In the van the rifle was an awkward size. Small laid it in his lap and sat sideways with his left elbow on the back of the seat. He held the Beretta to Joe's head and said, "Okay, you bastard, head for Southtown."

❧

In the dawnlight the ninety-nine acres of Songsparrow Estates was a bald tract of graded dirt. Joe cursed silently as the van plunged along the Pig Road. The feeding platforms had been extracted like bad teeth, and every one of Pearl's trees had been bulldozed and uprooted, every one of her infant hemlocks and birches, her red cedars and pasture junipers, her bushy little white pines.

The road came to an end at the chain-link fence. Beyond the fence the tops of the rusty scalping towers were bright orange in the morning sun. Joe stopped the car and turned off the engine, thinking swiftly, trying to guess what would happen next.

Small had been talking incessantly. His voice was soft and cheerful and his rabbit eyes were lustrous, as he blamed Joe and Pearl for everything that had happened since the beginning of time. Joe had long since stopped listening. Now Small said, "Get out!" His cheerfulness had vanished. He lowered himself carefully from the van, keeping his eyes on Joe and lifting the rifle to the roof of the car.

Joe slid out from behind the wheel, noting that it was to be the rifle from now on. The Beretta had disappeared. From somewhere Small produced a key to the padlock on the gate of the fence, swung it open, and urged Joe through.

The gravel pit opened below them. At the edge of the cliff a set of steps led to a ramp that rose all the way to the top of the tower. "Up," said Small, gesturing with the rifle. "Go ahead, go on up."

Joe climbed the steps slowly, guessing at once the nature of Frederick Small's grand overarching plan. Since the discovery of a bullet-ridden body might lead to awkward questions, Joe's death was to be a freakish misadventure. Small would simply shove him off the top of the tower. Sooner or later people would find his flattened carcass, and then they would tut-tut and call it an accident. After all, any fool who neglected the "No Trespassing" sign and joked around at the top of a dangerous tower deserved whatever he got.

Joe's fear subsided. He grasped the railings firmly, his deft hands flexing and relaxing, his feet nimble on the ramp, which quivered and bounced under his weight.

Small could not keep up. He was out of breath. He grunted at Joe to stop. Obligingly Joe stopped climbing and looked back at him serenely. At last Small nodded, frowning, and they went on climbing.

At the top of the third ramp they stepped off onto a metal

platform. "Wait," gasped Small, struggling to recover his breath.

Joe waited, glancing around at the descending conveyor belts, the sorting screens, the rock crushers, the tilted bin with its gigantic screws, the hoppers on their heavy metal legs. The floor of the quarry was heaped with conical mounds of sand.

Small was breathing normally now, aiming the rifle steadily, staring at Joe. Then, for an instant, his eyes flickered away. The fingers of his left hand moved over a panel and found a switch.

At once the long belt-driven conveyors began to shiver and hum. Some hurried up, others hastened down. They vibrated and shook, climbing and descending steeply. In the slanted bin below the platform the gigantic screws turned slowly, over-lapping, meshing smoothly together.

"Okay, now, just stand right over there." Small did not look at Joe. Nervously he pointed with the AK-47 at the edge of the platform, high above the uppermost descending belt of the system of interlocking conveyors that had for so many years sent millions of tons of rock rattling and thundering down from one belt to another, dropping them at last into the hoppers, and then into an endless procession of trucks to be carried away, far away, supplying armies of highway engineers with the raw material for a thousand miles of highway.

Smiling, Joe looked down, hardly seeing the inexorable descent of the conveyors, thinking instead of the old story by the Brothers Grimm, thinking of Gretel, clever Gretel, who had refused so craftily to crawl into the fiery oven of the wicked witch. Small's intention was so crude! *Just creep in and see if it is hot!*

"I don't get it," Joe said stupidly. "What do you mean?" *I don't know how. Show me!*

Small glowered at him, and hissed, "Asshole." Fussily, like a grumpy governess, he tramped across the platform and stamped his foot. "Right over here, you fathead. Stand on this spot right here."

But Frederick Small had never turned a dozen handsprings

one after another, he had never balanced upside down on six superimposed chairs, he had never found an egg in anyone's ear. Now when Joe threw out his arm it was exactly like the tossing of his wooden top. And like the turning top unwinding from its string, Small was whirled downward through the air, landing face down on the moving belt of the conveyor. Screaming, clinging to his rifle, he clawed with his free hand at the railing, but the belt carried him down like a load of gravel. Falling, plummeting, pawing at the railing, he jerked convulsively on the trigger of the gun and fired off a wild rattle of shots. One streaked past Joe's head and slammed into the panel of switches, which exploded in a burst of fireworks and set off a series of insane commands. Joe dodged sideways as an overhead bin discharged its load, and a slurry mix of water and rock began flowing down the chute. In a couple of seconds it caught up with Small and flowed over and around him, blinding him, battering his body, dumping him at last into the hopper below the moving conveyor, burying him under one and a half tons of three-quarter-inch gravel.

Joe sat down on the metal grille of the platform and put his head between his knees, trying to control the churning of his stomach and an overpowering impulse to weep. Then he stopped trying and let the sobs come. When the spasm passed, he stood up shakily and wiped his face with his sleeve. The wound along the side of his head had at last begun to throb. Wincing, Joe pulled a bandanna kerchief out of his pocket, twisted it into a narrow band and tied it around his head, Indian-fashion. Then he did several things very carefully, thinking them out slowly, one at a time.

❦

That afternoon, after school, a couple of thirteen-year-old boys from the Meadowlark housing development approached the chain-link fence. Usually they climbed over it, sticking the toes of their sneakers into the diamond-shaped spaces between the links, grasping with their fists the sharp twisted wires at the top. But this time the gate was wide open, and they walked right in.

As usual they had been attracted by the sign that said "No Trespassing," and by the weird towers with their long slanting ramps. It wasn't the first time they had trespassed on the gravel pit. It was a great place for smoking joints and telling dirty stories.

At once they saw the legs sticking up out of the heaped-up gravel in one of the hoppers, and they ran down the steep slope, skidding and sliding, to take a closer look. Clasping one of the hopper's metal supports with their arms and wrapping their legs around it, they shinnied up and clambered over the metal wall. Then, moving cautiously over the surface of the gravel, they reached the broken and asphyxiated body of Frederick Small, hauled it out, heaved it over the side, and let it fall to the ground. Then they climbed down after it, examined it with horrified delight, and scrambled up the steep slope to telephone the cops.

As they ran through the gate of the chain-link fence, a crow flapped down from a tree, settled on Frederick Small's dead face, and began pecking at his wide shining eyes.

❧

Then Gretel gave her a push, so that she fell right in. . . . Oh! how horribly she howled; but Gretel ran away, and left the ungodly witch to burn to ashes.

The Brothers Grimm, "Hansel and Gretel"

Chapter 58

❧

All the little boys and girls . . .
Tripping and skipping, ran merrily after
The wonderful music with shouting and laughter.
        Robert Browning, "The Pied Piper of Hamelin"

It was the last day of school.

"Charlene, dear," said Mrs. Rutledge, whispering to her in the corridor, "I'm so sorry about the Junior Olympics."

Charlene's face was stony. She stared at the coathooks on the wall.

Mrs. Rutledge was all sympathy and understanding. "It was that girl Cindy Foxweiler, she won again, didn't she?"

Charlene turned to Mrs. Rutledge and burst out, "It wasn't *my* fault! It's my father! It's his fault I lost!"

"There now, dear, there now." Mrs. Rutledge put her arm around Charlene and turned her toward the classroom door. "I'm sure you'll win next time. Now, come on, dear, they're all waiting. It's time for our reading."

The story was the last chapter of *The Flying Family*. Mary Kelly sighed, and sat down, squeezing herself into one of the small chairs in the last row. Why had the woman chosen this dreary book?

"Charlene," said Mrs. Rutledge, "will you do the honors?"

Charlene's customary poise returned. "Is it okay if I share it with Cissie?"

Once again Mrs. Rutledge was surprised at Charlene's odd choice of a friend. "Well, of course, Charlene."

Cissie was pink with joy.

Charlene read the first part of the chapter, then handed the book to Cissie, to give her the satisfaction of reading the last page. Blushing, Cissie took over. This time she was a better reader than she had ever been before.

"Let's have one last flight before we leave this special place," exclaimed Dad.

"Oh, yes," shouted Joan and Jim.

"Me too," cried Bitsy.

"Yes, of course," chuckled Mother. "You, too, little one."

"For the last time they walked into the magic forest and climbed the enchanted tree. Then they flew to their hearts' content, up in the sky, over the clouds, soaring like birds, looking down on the tops of the trees in the magic forest. At last it was time to go home.

"Can we come again next summer?" pleaded Joan.

"Oh, please, Dad," begged Jim.

"Me too?" squeaked Bitsy.

"Of course we can," promised Mother and Dad. "Next summer and every summer, forever and ever."

Smiling broadly, Cissie closed the book and said, "The end."

Mrs. Rutledge was delighted. "Very good, Cissie! Very good, Charlene! Class, shall we give them a hand?" Everyone clapped.

It was time for morning break. Beaming, Charlene and Cissie led the way to the playground. Charlene had her arm around Cissie. Timidly Cissie put hers around Charlene. She was glowing with happiness.

Mary Kelly was responsible for playground duty. But as she started outdoors, Mrs. Rutledge asked her to wait.

"Oh, Mary, I've got to show you. Some of the children have written such darling letters of appreciation. Look, you've got to read Charlene's. And here, Beverly Eckstein wrote one to you."

❦

Joseph Noakes left the van parked at the chain-link fence and walked away, leaving behind him the body of Frederick Small, who had suffered a tragic accident at his own sand-and-gravel company, who had fallen from a conveyor belt into a collecting bin, where he had been crushed and smothered by a ton and a half of three-quarter-inch stone.

It was a long walk back. Avoiding the highway, Joe cut through the intervening towns, finding shortcuts around discount stores in Needham, threading his way through suburban housing tracts in Wellesley, making his way at last to the Boston Post Road.

Weston Country Day School was on the Post Road. Noakes noticed the school sign with its carved letters and gold leaf as he walked by, swinging along tirelessly, heading for Annie, heading for home. He saw the trim buildings, the classrooms and the big new gym-and-theater complex for which the alumnae had been raising a lot of money. And he saw the group of children heading into the woods.

To his surprise he recognized the child at the head of the procession. It was young Charlene Gast. She was clutching another child to her side, urging her along, holding her tightly around the waist. Behind them the other children walked quickly, their faces grave. There was no teacher in sight.

Something odd was happening. Noakes did not slow his steps, he merely swerved and headed into the woods.

❦

When Mary ran out on the playground, she was surprised to find it empty. Where was everybody? There were no children swinging on the swings, no kids climbing the jungle gym. No one was tossing a ball at the basket. Where could they be?

Then she heard a sound, a distant murmuring, a faint chattering like a flock of birds. It came from the woods.

Slowly she walked toward the noise, staring into the sunlit spaces between the trees. The chattering stopped. Mary headed for the beech grove, which was everyone's favorite place. Here the leaves were thicker, the patches of sunlight fewer. Still she saw no children. Had she been mistaken? Then she heard a voice, high and clear, off to one side. And she found a path, barely visible in the undergrowth, carpeted with pale leaves. Mary moved forward quietly, her feet making no sound, and at last she saw the eighteen girls in Mrs. Rutledge's fifth-grade class.

They were not on the ground, they were high overhead, crowded on the branches of the beech trees. They looked like a gathering of sparrows, all facing one way.

Mary stood still. The voice she had heard was Charlene Gast's. Charlene and Cissie Aufsesser had climbed higher than all the rest. They stood on one of the topmost branches of the biggest tree in the grove. Charlene had one arm around Cissie. With the other she clung to the trunk of the tree. Cissie had nothing to hold on to, but the look on her face was exalted.

"We just have to believe," said Charlene. "You heard the way they did it in the book. They conquered their fear, and then they just slid off the magic tree and flew! They flew and flew!"

"No," said Mary, her voice catching in her throat. "No, Cissie, no."

No one was listening. It was as though she had not spoken.

"Ready, Cissie?" urged Charlene. "We'll jump together. Ready?"

"Oh, yes," squeaked Cissie, in a transport of happiness. "I'm ready, Charlene."

"No," croaked Mary, "stop, stop!"

But it was like a spell. Cissie bent her knees, held her arms in front of her and looked ecstatically at Charlene. Dutifully Charlene bent her knees too and held out one arm, hanging on with the other to the tree. The others gazed up at them, waiting for the miracle. They were all under Charlene's spell, and nothing could break it.

Except another spell. Suddenly there was a piercing whistle, and Flimnap O'Dougherty was there, turning cartwheel after cartwheel. Landing on his feet, he plucked colored balls out of his pocket and tossed them in the air. They were red and blue, silver and gold. Up they rose, higher and higher. Flimnap laughed. Out of his pocket came a cap, and now it was six balls and a cap. Then six balls, a cap, and a billfold. Then six balls, a cap, a billfold, and a pocketknife.

The children in the trees were laughing too. Mary tore her eyes away from Flimnap and gazed up fearfully at Cissie. The child's rapture had vanished. She was frightened. Very carefully she sat down on the branch and edged away from Charlene, who was screaming, "I'll tell, I'll tell!"

But the tables were turned, and in the pandemonium of laughter and clapping Charlene couldn't make herself heard. She came down from the tree, slithering too fast, scratching her face, her arms and legs, catching twigs in her hair, tearing holes in her shirt, shrieking, "I'll tell, I'll tell!"

Flimnap looked at her mildly as she tumbled to the ground. Then he grasped the lowest branch of the tree and began to climb. In a moment he was high in the leafy crown, reaching out to Cissie. "I've got you now," he said softly. "Just hold on around my neck," and soon the two of them were safely on the ground, and Cissie was crying, surrounded by all the other kids in the class. Many of them were crying too.

Charlene Gast wasn't crying. Charlene was telling. She told and told—getting back at Cindy Foxweiler, who had beaten her in the backstroke by only one second, and at Cissie Aufsesser, whose father had looked down at her from a great height and scolded and shamed her, and at all the girls in Mrs. Rutledge's fifth-grade class who had forgotten that Charlene Gast was the prettiest and smartest girl in the whole school, everybody's favorite, the brightest star at Weston Country Day—*Charlene Gast,* who would have been the youngest Junior Olympic swimmer in the whole entire world, if it hadn't been for her father.

It all spilled out of Charlene, the precious stories she had hugged to herself for so long, the secrets about Alice Mooney and the stolen math paper, and Cissie Aufsesser with Mrs. Rutledge's pocketbook, and Beverly Eckstein's dirty magazine. And there were other secrets, terrible secrets. *Do you know what Carrie Maxwell did? And Becca Smith?*

It was an orgy of revengeful telling. "Oh, stop it, Charlene," said Mary Kelly. "No one's listening."

Charlene stopped. And then she did something very strange. She took something out of her pocket and held it out like a gift.

"What's this?" said Mary, taking it.

"You'll see," said Charlene, looking at her darkly. Then Charlene turned and trailed after her classmates, as they followed Flimnap back to the playground.

He was tootling on a penny whistle, leading the way like the Pied Piper. The fifth-grade girls trotted after him like the children of Hamelin town.

Chapter 59

. . . When he came to the hedge of thorns it had turned into flowers, which drew apart and let him through . . .

The Brothers Grimm, "Little Brier Rose"

"**B**ut where is he?" said Annie.

"Oh, you know Flimnap," said Mary. "I offered to drive him home, but he said he wanted to walk." Mary looked at Annie's anxious face and took her arm. "Come on, Annie dear, why don't you spend the night at our house? Homer will stay here and stand guard."

"I will?" said Homer. "Oh, right, okay, I'll stay." He smiled at his niece with pitying affection. "I'll mind the store while you go home with Mary."

Annie glanced up at her wall, which was shadowy and dark under the clotted shreds of the remaining ceiling. "No, no, I can't leave. All those media people will be back in the morning, waiting around for the wrecking machine. I've got to stay. I'll be all right. Good night, Aunt Mary, good night, Uncle Homer."

Alone, she sat gloomily beside the mound of broken clapboards and fractured windows and chunks of plaster. Bits of glass glinted in the wreckage like splinters of sky. Fireflies glittered over the field. Bats darted overhead, and a throng of mosquitoes floated around Annie, whining, landing delicately on her arms. She told herself to take refuge in Flimnap's shelter, because Aunt Mary had nailed up a mosquito net around the door, an old curtain from the farmhouse on Barrett's Mill Road. Instead, Annie tore the curtain off its nails.

It was a hot summer night. She undressed in the open air, lay

down on top of her sleeping bag, and pulled the curtain over her naked self from head to toe. Through the torn gauze she could see the pink brightness of Boston to the east, and one or two stars high in the blue-black sky. There was no moon.

Then a light appeared, and flared up in the darkness in front of her wall, illuminating the Owl and the Pussy-cat and the wooden leg of Long John Silver.

It was a camping lantern with a glowing mantle. A dim face bent over it. Long fingers adjusted the knob at the side. The light increased. A stepladder appeared out of nowhere. The fingers lifted the lantern and set it on the top step. Then face and hands vanished. There was only Flimnap's dark silhouette between Annie and the lamp. He was climbing the ladder and setting a box down on the folding shelf.

Annie watched as he passed his hand over the bare place on the wall where he had painted out one mysterious face after another. Now, with a piece of chalk, he began to draw. His strokes were solid and sure.

So it had been Flimnap, all along. Of course it was Flimnap. He could draw after all. He could draw very well.

Annie sat up, wrapping the curtain around her, and watched as he laid in the structure of the small round skull, then added the slightly tilted eyes, the flat snub nose, the too-large mouth, the too-small ears.

By the time he began painting over his chalk lines, she guessed whose hand was holding the brush. But she waited in silence as Eddy's head became three-dimensional and round, his cheeks plump, his body a chunky cylinder in overalls. His stubby fingers were miracles of light and shade.

At last, toward morning, Flimnap lowered his brush and stepped slowly down from the ladder.

The missing piece of the puzzle had now been found. Every part of Flimnap was at last hooked firmly into every other part. "Joseph Noakes," murmured Annie. "I should have guessed."

He came and stood over her and touched the gauzy veil covering her face. Annie drew the curtain aside. Noakes fell to his knees beside her, whispering, "Annie, oh, Annie."

She wrapped her arms round him and pressed herself against him and murmured in his ear, "Too bad, Joseph Noakes. Three plates, is that all? I'd set my heart on a four-plate man."

Chapter 60

❧

It does not matter in the least having been born in a duckyard, if only you come out of a swan's egg!
                      Hans Christian Andersen, "The Ugly Duckling"

Next morning, as she was getting dressed, Mary remembered something. She pawed in the pocket of the jacket she had been wearing the day before. "Look, Homer, see what Charlene gave me."

"*Charlene* gave you something?" Homer couldn't believe it. "After what she did? After she almost killed that little girl?"

Mary held it up. "It's a roll of film."

"Uh-oh," said Homer. "Watch out. It'll be embarrassing. Catching us in the latrine."

But he took the film and held it in both hands like a jewel. "I'll take it to that place where they make prints in a hurry. In fact, I'll take it there right now. I am extraordinarily interested in this roll of film."

Three hours later, standing at the counter in the photo-finishing shop, he leafed quickly through the twelve pictures that had been taken by Charlene Gast. Eight were images of her frilly dolls.

The ninth was an out-of-focus image of her father, half obscured by a cloud of leaves, inserting a key in the French door on the south side of Annie's house.

The tenth had been taken through a window, and most of it was blurred by the edge of the window frame. But there he was, Robert Gast, right there on the other side of the glass, inside Annie's house. He had his hands on the scaffolding in front of her painted wall. His young son Eddy stood above him on the highest platform, still very much alive.

The eleventh was a wild picture of the ceiling, obviously a mistake.

The twelfth was a perfect shot. The lens in the camera that Charlene had conned out of Cissie Aufsesser was not much better than a chunk of bottle glass, but the automatic mechanisms had worked. The electric eye had measured the amount of light, the shutter had opened for the right fraction of a second, and the focusing apparatus had adjusted itself perfectly, creating a sharp image of Eddy Gast lying on the floor while his father towered over him with a sledgehammer.

Homer looked at the twelfth print long and hard, then put it back in the envelope with the rest. He glanced up at the kid behind the counter, who was making change for another customer. "Do you people ever look at your prints? I suppose all sorts of shocking things turn up, right?"

"Shocking things?" The kid snickered. "You mean little tots in the bathtub? Dogs and cats? The mother of the bride? Those poor guys in the darkroom, their life is boring enough without looking at every newborn baby in the Commonwealth of Massachusetts."

"Oh, right," said Homer, laughing, slipping into his pocket the picture that would send Robert Gast to prison for the rest of his life.

The wrecked car had not been enough. The copied key had not been enough. The sledgehammer on the workbench had not been enough. This was enough.

Charlene had said, "I'll tell," and she had told.

Part Four

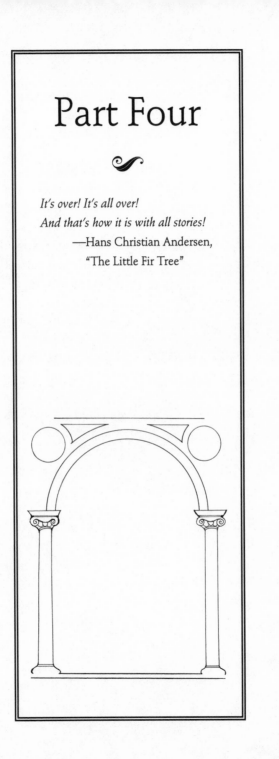

It's over! It's all over!
And that's how it is with all stories!
    —Hans Christian Andersen,
     "The Little Fir Tree"

Chapter 61

❧

"A secret is with me as is a house with a lock, whose key is lost, and whose door is sealed."   The Thousand and One Nights

The siege was over. The pressure from *Globe* editor Harvey Broadstairs and the rest of the media swelled for a while, then sagged. For a few days it scandalized the nation to learn that Annie's landlord had been arrested for the murder of his little son, but then other villainies caught the national attention and interest faded.

But not before Jerry Neville made a phone call.

"Homer? This is Jerry. I read about it in the paper. Tell Annie her champagne is waiting."

"You mean it's all okay now? She'll get her house back?"

"Of course she'll get her house back. I'm asking for a revocation of judgment, the cancellation of that goddamned out-of-court settlement."

"He'll have to pay, won't he, Jerry? I mean, even from prison, he'll have to pay to put her house back the way it was before he started tearing it down?"

"The trouble is, he's a turnip."

"A turnip? Oh, I see. You mean—?"

"The proverbial vegetable without any cardiovascular system to squeeze blood from. Don't get your hopes up. Gast's partnership with Frederick Small didn't do him any good."

"Frederick Small? You mean Pearl's husband? The wife-murderer? The one who turned up dead in his own gravel works? Gast was in partnership with Small?"

"Songsparrow Estates in Southtown, Gast was the developer.

He got a huge bank loan and spent a couple million on the place before he learned Small didn't own it, his wife owned it, and she was dead, and Small had forged her signature. Which left Robert Gast in desperate financial circumstances, to say the least."

"My God, Jerry, how did you find out all this stuff?"

"I learned to read in second grade. It's in today's *Globe*. Interview with a police sergeant in Southtown."

"Bill Kennebunk," exclaimed Homer, delighted. "Bless his heart. But, Jerry, you said Bob Gast is bankrupt. That means he can't pay Annie any damages?"

"I'm afraid that's right. She's out of luck."

"Oh, God, poor Annie." Homer's high spirits turned to gloom. "Listen, Jerry, do you think some people are disaster-prone? You know, they invite bizarre misfortune? They trip over the pot of gold at the end of the rainbow and break their leg?"

"Well, I suppose some people are like that. Who do you mean?"

"Annie, my niece Annie. She's that kind of girl. Hang in there, Jerry. Don't fall off a cliff. Sooner or later she'll need you again."

No sooner had Homer put down the phone than it jangled a second time. Another familiar voice boomed in his ear. "Homer?"

"Oh, hey, Bill, is that you? I've just been hearing about the far-famed exploits of Sergeant William Kennebunk."

Kennebunk cleared his throat with mock self-importance. "That's *Chief* Kennebunk, if you don't mind."

Homer gasped with pleasure. "No kidding! Well, congratulations, Chief. My God, whatever happened to McNutt?"

"Turned out he had an unfortunate connection with Frederick Small. They were in that real-estate scam together. McNutt knew Pearl was dead all along. And he knew it was Small who was in that Albany hotel with a blond hooker. He knew Small sent that postcard to himself."

"Jesus, Bill, how did you find that out?"

"No problem. After those kids discovered Small's body at the gravel pit, the pathologist let me look through his clothes, and I found a slip of paper with the name of a storage warehouse in Northtown and a bunch of numbers. It looked to me like a combination, and sure enough, that's what it was, the combination to the lockup where he stored his stuff—you know, when he moved out of his house before it was torn down. So I went over there with a search warrant, and the combination worked, and of course Small's rented compartment was full of chairs piled on tables and bedsprings jammed against the wall. And there was a very interesting-looking desk in one corner. In one of the drawers I found a couple of letters. Delightful letters, nicely incriminating the two of them, Small and his buddy McNutt."

"How charming! My God, how could Small have been so careless as to leave letters lying around?"

"Oh, Homer, there aren't any really crafty felons out there. The smarter they think they are, the dumber they behave."

"Except—don't forget, Chief—the really clever ones are never discovered. They may indeed exist, but we don't know whether they do or not. It's a logical enigma. It's like a blind spot in the center of the retina—the more you look, the more you don't see."

"Well, sometimes, Homer, I suspect the smartest ones aren't wily and clever at all. They don't think about anything, they just bash you on the head and take the swag and keep their mouths shut."

❧

Joseph Noakes was one of those who keep their mouths shut. He did not tell Homer Kelly about the fatal morning in Pearl's house when he burst into her bedroom in Southtown to find her husband standing over her body. Most unsaid of all, most carefully filed away in the deepest, most grieving place in Joe's memory, was Pearl's attempt to protect herself, to kill her husband with the handgun Joe had given her. Instead—Joe would never forgive himself for not guessing what would happen—Small in his overpowering strength had snatched it away and used it against her.

Joe Noakes did not tell Homer Kelly either of these things. His reticence was a perfect example of Homer's theory about the blind spot in the center of the retina. There was Joe in person, entirely visible, busying himself around Annie's place, making himself useful, helping her move into the old part of the house, moving in with her, marrying her maybe—who could tell what those crazy kids would do? Anyway, there he was in the flesh, and yet somehow he was partly invisible. He was a blind spot in the exact center of Homer's eye.

But Joe did tell Homer about Robert Gast.

"You knew about him, is that right?" said Homer. "You knew he was working for Small? You knew he was helping to turn Pearl's land into house lots? That's why you came to Annie's place, because Gast was living there?"

"No, no," said Noakes, laughing. "I came to Annie's place because of Annie."

"Because of *Annie!*"

"Well, of course because of Annie. I knew her work, I heard her give a talk, I worshiped at her shrine already. Of course it was because of Annie. Gast didn't move in until later, and then I didn't know he had anything to do with Small until I happened to be in his study one day when he was out, and I—"

"Never mind," said Homer, holding up his hands. "I don't want to know."

Later on, Homer explained it to Mary. "I should have guessed about Flimnap. I knew his name rang a bell. Flimnap's the treasurer of Lilliput. He counts the sprugs."

"Sprugs? Oh, I remember now." Mary laughed. "Lilliputian money."

"Poor old Annie, what's she going to do for sprugs from now on? Her books are out of print and Jerry says the Gasts are bankrupt. They can't pay her back. What's going to happen to her wall?"

"Well, she can make more books. So can Joe. They'll be okay."

Homer looked doubtful. "Do you trust him? I worry that he's some kind of will-o'-the-wisp. Think about it! He's been lying to her the whole time."

Mary looked at Homer dreamily. "Not lying. Making up stories. He's a storyteller. So is she." Mary waxed sentimental. "That ex-husband of hers, Grainger Swann, and the other two, Burgess and Jack, you know what they were?"

"No, what?"

"Wind-up birds, that's all. Wind-up birds like the one in that wonderful story by Hans Christian Andersen."

Homer threw up his hands. "Story? What story?"

"Oh, you know, Homer, the one about the nightingale. The wind-up mechanical bird and the nightingale in the forest, singing its heart out." Mary beamed at Homer. "That's Joseph Noakes. He's the real nightingale, the one with the song that saves the emperor's life. He'll save Annie's. You'll see."

"Well, I don't know," said Homer grimly. "Don't say I didn't warn you."

Chapter 62

"**W**hy, Joe?" whispered Annie. "Why did you keep me in the dark? Why did you paint those faces on my wall?"

They were lying on the bed in Annie's old room at the southeast corner of the house, the original old house, the one she had rented to Robert and Roberta Gast. Instead of answering her question, Joe began talking softly about his childhood, about what it had been like to grow up with his sister Pearl.

"We weren't like other kids. We never played outdoors. We stayed inside, making things with hammers and nails and paste and beautiful white paper." Joe gazed at the ceiling, remembering. "I had a paintbox. I used to dip my brush in the glass and watch the water turn cloudy with cobalt blue or crimson lake."

"Or cadmium yellow," said Annie eagerly, because she had been like that too. "But, Joe—"

He held up his hand. "Wait." Turning, he kissed her ear, and then after a moment he began again. "We built a puppet theater. We made the puppets and the sets and acted out the stories on our small stage—The Ugly Duckling, The Bremen Town Musicians, The Three Little Pigs, Beauty and the Beast. I suppose you could say we were obsessed, but we didn't think about it at all. We were lost in it. We were just two pairs of hands cutting and pasting and painting. We went to school, but school meant nothing. Our real life was at home. It was more important than breathing, more important than food or sleep. Well, of course our parents didn't like it. Our mother was a sensible woman with both feet on the ground."

Annie wanted to ask if the bond between sister and brother had perhaps become too close. She had heard of sibling attachments that had turned abnormal, incestuous, *weird*. Cautiously she said, "But then you both grew up. What happened then?"

"Oh, for me it was all right. I kept right on with the paintbox and the beautiful white paper. I turned the stories into books."

"But what about Pearl?"

Joe's face darkened. Bitterly he said, "She married Frederick Small."

"Of course," said Annie sadly. She had heard Pearl's terrible history from Aunt Mary and Uncle Homer. Now she stroked Joe's face and said no more. The poor guy was grieving for his sister.

But then Joe's voice softened, and he drew Annie closer. "When I saw what you were doing on your wall, it was like going back in time. It was our own lost world all over again, and right away I knew I had to paint her there. It was a sort of memorial, I suppose, as though I could send her back where she belonged."

Annie was dumbfounded. "And to think that I—" She stopped, because her own selfish feelings didn't matter, not now, not beside the tragic loss of Joe's beloved sister. Her old disappointment wasn't important, her bafflement when Joe had not seemed to notice what she was doing, as though her wall meant nothing to him at all. Then Annie forgot her wounded vanity and asked another question. "And the horrible faces, what about those terrible faces?"

Joe's arm around her stiffened, and he gripped her shoulder. "Your wall was wrong, you see, Annie, it was all wrong. I could see at once that it was too pleasant, too gentle. A lot of the old stories are bitter and bloody. Your cheerful images show only half the truth. The rest is all hanged men and dismembered children, and women hacked to pieces in cold blood."

Bluebeard, thought Annie. The awful faces had been portraits of the Bluebeard who had killed Joe's sister Pearl. The savage part of the truth had found a place on her wall after all. "But darling Joe, why didn't you tell me? Why did you pretend you had nothing to do with them?"

Joe threw his legs over the side of the bed and began walking up and down, talking convulsively, hardly stopping for breath. Annie sat up in bed, astonished.

"I was afraid. I knew he was out there somewhere, looking for me. I had a waking nightmare—one day I'd come around the corner of the house and there'd be a blast from the bushes, and that would be the end. I didn't dare tell you. I didn't dare tell anyone. If you were to discover who I was, it would soon be common knowledge, and then he'd find me. I was like an escaped convict with the dogs barking at my heels. I was afraid of him, and yet at the same time I was haunted by him. Somehow I had to get him before he got me. I didn't know how it would happen, I only knew it had to happen. Oh, Annie, I was too eaten up with loathing and fear to tell you. I couldn't tell you and I couldn't love you." Joe sat down again on the bed and leaned over. "But I can love you now, if you'll let me," and Annie let him.

Chapter 63

❧

The wall was finished. Noakes had filled in the last piece of bare plaster with the face of Eddy Gast. So it was all done, Annie's condensed history of the human race from the delirious perspective of Edward Lear and Mother Goose.

Still, perhaps some of the details could be improved. Annie walked back and forth in front of the wall and decided to tone down the giddy orange of the pumpkin coach and ginger up the Secret Garden with scarlet flowers. Hans Christian Andersen looked down at her mildly, Aesop stooped to watch the dozing hare, the emperor paraded in his underwear, Mother Goose took flight, and Scheherazade told one more of her interlocking tales, warding off death for yet another night.

The stories of the last year of Annie's life were interlocking too. They were a set of nested tales growing out of one another, beginning with the appearance of Flimnap like a prince in disguise, and ending with the dragon-like machines that had nearly gobbled up her storytelling wall. Real life was as fantastic as Wonderland, and Joe was right, it was just as dangerous. The Red Queen never stopped shouting *"Off with her head!"* and the wolf kept right on munching the bones of Little Red Riding Hood. All over the world the carcasses of Bluebeard's wives piled up in forbidden rooms. And the Mad Tea Party happened every day, everywhere, in a bewildering slop of tea and nonsense and spilled milk and the crash of breaking china.

Of course not all of the stories were disasters. A few had happy endings, if you could call them that. Goose girls were transformed into princesses and youngest sons triumphed. But the other dramatis personae—miscellaneous ogres, witches, elder brothers, and wicked kings—were beheaded or burned at the stake or drowned in the river in a sack.

In the case of the unlucky Gast family, it was the ax, the stake, and the sack.

Robert Gast was tried for murder, convicted and incarcerated in Walpole State Penitentiary. His wife was convicted of conspiracy and confined to the women's prison in Framingham. Their daughter Charlene was placed in a foster home, but then Judge Aufsesser got on her case and had her removed to a school for juvenile offenders.

Mary Kelly happened to be at Annie's when the last of the Gasts' possessions left the house. She watched the camelback sofa go into the moving van along with the elegant side chairs. The dangling bobbles of the chandelier caught the sunlight for an instant before blinking out in the dark interior of the van. The last thing to be removed from the house was the splendid mirror that had so often stared back at the anxious face of Roberta Gast. It went out of the house on the head of one of the moving men, reflecting only the pure unsullied sky.

࿇

The fisherman launched his boat at the height of the tempest. Bolts of lightning clove the air, shattering the prow of his little craft, splitting the very oars he clutched in his hands. In terror he cried, "Lord Fish, Lord Fish! What shall I do? My wife wants to rule the heavens!"

Solemnly the great fish spoke to the fisherman in the crash of the thunder, in the echo rumbling in the surrounding hills, in the wind lashing the dark trees, in the harsh screams of the ravens in the sky—"Go home, my friend. Everything shall now be once more as it was in the beginning."

Sadly the fisherman rowed his wrecked boat to the shore and limped back to his wife. He found her in their miserable hovel, weeping.

T h e   W a l l

❧

Two Whites look down from the roundels—on the left, E. B. White, author of *Stuart Little* and *Charlotte's Web*; on the right, T. H. White, who wrote *The Sword in the Stone*. In the scene below, the boy Wart, who will one day be King Arthur, flourishes the famous sword.

On the left, the Homeric bard stands with upraised arms, reciting Homer's epic poem *The Odyssey*. On the Mediterranean horizon sails the ship of Odysseus (copied from a Greek vase painting).

In the circle Scheherazade tells one of her thousand and one tales to the sultan, leaving the story unfinished so that he will spare her life for another day.

Aesop, the teller of animal fables, looks down at the sleeping hare, which has just been overtaken by the tortoise in their famous race.

THE SECOND SPAN

At left, Beatrix Potter appears in her old age as an active countrywoman.

On the right, Hans Christian Andersen releases the living nightingale with one hand and holds the wind-up bird in the other, from his story "The Emperor's Nightingale." Above his head is a scene from his "Story of a Mother," Death carrying away a little child. In the circle a boy proclaims what no one else has dared to say, that the Emperor's new clothes do not exist.

On the sea horizon a fisherman hooks an enchanted fish, from the tale of "The Fisherman and His Wife," by the Brothers Grimm.

The strange creatures with paper faces are the Ugly-Wuglies, from *The Enchanted Castle*, by E. Nesbit. The children in her story have made them from walking sticks and hats and coats, and are dismayed when they come alive. Edith Nesbit herself appears in the roundel above.

THE THIRD SPAN

Mark Twain holds forth at left, telling the story of Tom Sawyer, who appears in the central circle, lost in the cave with Becky Thatcher. The Mediterranean has become the Mississippi. Huckleberry Finn and Jim, the runaway slave, drift down the river on their raft.

Mother Goose flies above.

The Brothers Grimm, Wilhelm and Jacob, appear at right. Above them are Hansel and Gretel and the wicked witch. Crouching at the bottom, the wolf gobbles up Little Red Riding Hood.

In the roundel at upper right is Arthur Ransome, author of a series of books about the sailing adventures of two families of children.

THE FOURTH SPAN

Lewis Carroll reads to young Alice Liddell the tale he has made up for her and her sisters, *Alice's Adventures in Wonderland*.

Laura Ingalls Wilder examines the brand-new town of DeSmet in Dakota Territory, from one of her stories about her pioneer childhood, *By the Shores of Silver Lake*.

The boy in the wheelchair is Colin, who is restored to health in Frances Hodgson Burnett's *The Secret Garden*. She appears above.

The left part of the water horizon is now an English river, in Kenneth Grahame's *Wind in the Willows*. Rat and Mole set off on a boating picnic.

On the right the river has become Lake Windemere, in one of Arthur Ransome's idyllic stories. The little boats belong to the *Swallows and Amazons*.

THE FIFTH SPAN

Robert Louis Stevenson stands at left, his hand on the shoulder of swashbuckling pirate Long John Silver, who steals the show in *Treasure Island*.

Beside him, Cinderella goes to the ball in her pumpkin coach.

On the right, leaning against the column, nonsense poet Edward Lear holds in his arms his cat, Foss. At left above, his Owl and Pussy-cat go to sea in their beautiful pea-green boat.

Opposite them is "Toomai of the Elephants," from the story by Rudyard Kipling in *The Jungle Book*. Kipling himself appears above.

The empty circle in the middle is the space where the face on the wall appears again and yet again.